The
BOOK
of
CELTIC MYTHS

The
BOOK
of
CELTIC
MYTHS

From the Mystic Might of
the Celtic Warriors to the
Magic of the Fey Folk,
*the Storied History and
Folklore of Ireland, Scotland,
Brittany, and Wales*

JENNIFER EMICK

Adams Media
New York   London   Toronto   Sydney   New Delhi

Adams Media
An Imprint of Simon & Schuster, Inc.
100 Technology Center Drive
Stoughton, MA 02072

For information about special discounts for bulk purchases, please contact Simon & Schuster Special Sales at 1-866-506-1949 or business@simonandschuster.com.

The Simon & Schuster Speakers Bureau can bring authors to your live event. For more information or to book an event contact the Simon & Schuster Speakers Bureau at 1-866-248-3049 or visit our website at www.simonspeakers.com.

Manufactured in the United States of America

7 2023

Library of Congress Cataloging-in-Publication Data has been applied for.

ISBN 978-1-5072-0087-2
ISBN 978-1-5072-0088-9 (ebook)

Contents

Introduction: Who Were the Celts?. 9

CHAPTER ONE
Celtic Mythology and the Book of Invasions. 13

CHAPTER TWO
The Ulster Cycle and the Fenian Cycle 21

CHAPTER THREE
The Mother Goddesses 29

CHAPTER FOUR
The Gods of the Celts 41

CHAPTER FIVE
The Mabinogion 55

CHAPTER SIX
The Tuatha Dé Danann..........................65

CHAPTER SEVEN
The Druids 81

CHAPTER EIGHT
Celtic Storytellers 97

CHAPTER NINE
The Heroes 113

CHAPTER TEN
Fairies and Fey Folk..........................125

CHAPTER ELEVEN
The Otherworld 139

CHAPTER TWELVE
The Tree of Life............................151

CHAPTER THIRTEEN
Sacred Beasts..............................167

CHAPTER FOURTEEN
Sacred Places..............................181

CHAPTER FIFTEEN
King Arthur and the Celts. .199

CHAPTER SIXTEEN
The Turn of the Year 215

CHAPTER SEVENTEEN
Celtic Christianity. 231

Index. 249

INTRODUCTION:
WHO WERE THE CELTS?

"The Celt, and his cromlechs, and his pillar-stones, these will not change much—indeed, it is doubtful if anybody at all changes at any time. In spite of hosts of deniers, and asserters, and wise-men, and professors, the majority still are averse to sitting down to dine thirteen at table, or being helped to salt, or walking under a ladder, or seeing a single magpie flirting his chequered tail."

—WILLIAM BUTLER YEATS

Warriors, poets, scholars, and visionaries—from the depths of time the ancient Celts fascinate us. Their rich heritage lives on today through the millions of people who can claim Celtic ancestry. Celts and their traditions are among the foundation stones of our culture.

But who were they? In the following pages, we will explore the wonder and wisdom of this mysterious people.

The people we call the Celts arose about 7,000 years ago in the Caucasus Mountains, bordering the Black Sea. Rapidly they moved west, settling in what are now France, Germany, Spain, and Italy. Finally, they crossed the North Sea, settling in Britain and Ireland.

The Celts had no defining physical characteristics. What we mean today by the term "Celt" is people who spoke a certain family of languages. These include Scots Gaelic, Irish, Manx, Cornish, Welsh, and Breton. Sadly, most of the Celtic languages are extinct, although a few such as Welsh have undergone a revival.

As the Celts moved west, they found ancient monuments built by those who worked the land before them—circles of standing stones, pointing like lonely fingers at the sky. Often isolated stones displayed carved designs featuring loops and whorls. The Celts wove these places into their myths. The stones marked entrances to another world, they said. There dwelt the Tuatha Dé Danann, a strange folk of great magical craft and power.

The most notable characteristic of the early Celts was their extraordinary artistic ability. Highly skilled metalworkers, they introduced all of Europe to the art of iron forging, and with it brought advances in agriculture and warfare. From the forges of the Celtic smiths came both farm implements and fearsome weapons, from swords and spears to great wheels for wagons and war-chariots. These objects were common in the great Celtic civilization that arose in Northern Italy about 300 B.C.E.: the La Tène culture. It was these people who refined the artistic style we now associate with the Celts: undulating lines, spirals, and the first appearance of what we all instinctively recognize today as the Celtic knot, sinuous patterns of interlaced loops and curves. The La Tène people flourished until they ran up against the rising power in Europe: Rome.

The beginning of the conquest of European Celts by the Romans was described by Julius Caesar, by whom it was called the Gallic Wars. These wars, continuing long after Caesar's assassination in 44 B.C.E., were fought during the latter part of the first century B.C.E. and for 150 years afterward. By the end, the Celts had been conquered, but their culture continued. Celts had passed across the North Sea to the British Isles. There they established themselves in the south and the north, and to the west in Ireland.

CELTIC SOCIETY

Early Celtic society was divided into tribal groups called *tuatha*. A tuath (singular) was like a kingdom in miniature, a family group that usually claimed descent from a common ancestor.

Each tuath was headed by a king (or sometimes a queen) who usually claimed descent from one or more tribal ancestral deities. In times of peace, the king was both ruler and an administrator of justice; in times of conflict, he was a warlord. The king was vested in his office through his symbolic marriage with the land, which was personified as a goddess. This rite of investiture ensured the fertility of the land and is echoed endlessly in mythological tales.

Under the king were the nobles or *flaitha,* warriors, artisans, lawyers, poets, and other skilled citizens. Under the noble class were the freemen who kept the flocks, tilled the soil, and paid rent to the nobles.

One respect in which the Celts were different from their neighbors is noteworthy: Women occupied an important place in society. Many of the most significant deities of the Celtic pantheons were female, ranging from powerful, nurturing earth mothers to fierce goddesses of war.

The women of Celtic mythology are likewise portrayed as brave, resourceful, even crafty. These heroines did what they wanted, when they wanted, even when it meant disaster.

Celtic wives often accompanied their husbands to battle and were not always content to keep to the sidelines; there are numerous accounts of Celtic warrior women and their achievements in battle. Some of these warrior women were so notable in their achievements that they became teachers of the art of war, owners of their own martial academies. Many became legendary.

THE OTHERWORLD

The body of Celtic mythology gives much evidence of Celtic beliefs in reincarnation and life after death. These stories spoke of the Otherworld, for although its entrances are usually under the earth, it is believed to exist commingled with the world of men and can even be reached by sea. At certain times of the year, and in certain geographical locations, the veils or mists that conceal one world from the next could be breached, and both men and spirits could travel between them.

One such place found in the Welsh Otherworld was Annwn, the Isle of Apples, which came to be known later as Avalon and figures heavily in Arthurian legend, as we'll explore in a later chapter. Although Arthur is portrayed as a Christian king, it is to Avalon where he is taken to die after being mortally wounded by his nephew Mordred. Today, Avalon is often associated with the great tor that soars above the town of Glastonbury in southern England.

There is also much evidence that Celts believed in reincarnation. Mythological stories abound with episodes of rebirth and reincarnation, especially in relation to water. A repeating feature of battle stories is the cauldron or spring of rebirth, by which slain warriors return to life.

The Celts were, as we can see, a deeply spiritual and artistic people. Gods, magic, and wisdom made up an intimate part of their lives. In the following pages, we'll explore together the legends their bards sang as the people gathered around the fire and a pale moon shone down upon silent standing stones.

CHAPTER ONE

Celtic Mythology and the Book of Invasions

The ancient Celts had a noted abhorrence of written records. They kept no scriptures, history, or genealogy and preferred to preserve their religious teachings through the sacred oral traditions of the druids. Unfortunately, the majority of this ancient wisdom was lost forever with the coming of Christianity to the Celtic Isles. Druidry gave way to the persuasive proselytizing of westward-sweeping Christians, and with none to take on the bardic task, the old ways gradually fell away. Ironically, the task of recording the remnants of Celtic mythology fell to the Christian monasteries, and the remnant of Celtic wisdom was preserved by those who destroyed it.

SOURCES OF CELTIC MYTHOLOGY

In the time of the druids, the ancient oral myths and stories were maintained in strict secrecy. As the druidic tradition faded, these stories spread among the wider population. The Irish Church undertook to preserve Celtic mythology in the seventh century, when its monasteries began to set pagan tales to paper. These scribes of the Church rewrote the ancient gods as human beings, heroes, and magicians whose tales they regarded as the history of the Celts. As well, the monks often added Christian elements to the stories, often distorting them almost beyond recognition.

Because these tales are presented as histories, they neglect any intentional exploration of Celtic theological ideas, resulting in a paucity of stories of the creation of earth or mankind. The myth cycles do, however, give a very good idea of ancient Celtic customs and lifestyles, and they reveal much about the character of the ancient gods and goddesses.

The greatest wealth of Celtic mythology is contained in three major collections of texts known as the Mythological Cycle, the Ulster Cycle, and the Fenian or Fionn Cycle. A looser, less-regarded collection is known as the Historical or Kings Cycle, a record of the lives and adventures of the legendary kings of Ireland. Another popular source of mythological tales is *The Mabinogion*, a series of Welsh mythological tales with early Arthurian elements.

THE DAGDA AND BRIGHID

According to one version of the Celtic origin myth not contained in the Book of Invasions, in the beginning, there was a great void. Although the Earth existed, it was in chaos, bubbling and boiling in confusion.

Into this, there poured from the skies streams of water that cooled the volcanoes and watered the deserts. They gave rise to life.

From the newly formed soil sprang a great tree, a sacred oak named Bíle. The divine water, called Danu, nourished and fed it until it produced two great acorns. From the first acorn came a god, the Dagda, who was male and known as "the Good God." From the second came a goddess, Brighid, "the Exalted One."

The two settled by a great stream of water. Since it had its origins in Danu, they named it Danuvius, a name that is preserved to the present day as the Danube River, which flows through the European continent. The Dagda and Brighid built four great cities: Falias, Gorias, Finias, and Murias.

The descendants of the Dagda and Brighid inhabited these cities. Those who paid special worship to Brighid and to the knowledge she imparted learned of crafts, of healing, and of poetry. The early Celtic word for "knowledge" was *vid*, and the word for "oak" was *dru*. Thus in time these people became the druids—that is, the people possessing knowledge from the Sacred Oak.

THE CHILDREN OF THE GODS

The two foremost children of the Dagda and Brighid were Nuada and Oghma. Nuada was the favorite son of the Dagda, while Oghma was loved better by his mother. He was known as Oghma of the Sunny Countenance and invented writing, in a calligraphy that was called ogham.

At last the Dagda and Brighid gathered their children and told them they were destined to populate the Earth.

The children of the Dagda and Brighid left their cities and traveled to the Island of Destiny, where they waited for their destiny to be fulfilled. Three of the children, beautiful sisters, were named Banba, Fótla, and Éire, and each one hoped the Island of Destiny would be named for her. Thus the Celts came to Ireland.

DIFFERING VERSIONS

In other versions of the myth of the Dagda and Brighid, she is his daughter, not his mate. Nuada is sometimes described as the Dagda's predecessor as high king of the Tuatha Dé Danann and Oghma as the Dagda's half brother.

THE BOOK OF INVASIONS

The chief work of the Mythological Cycle, known as the Book of Invasions, ignores Celtic mythological tales of the world's origin. It was compiled in the twelfth century by monks of the Irish Church and purports to be a chronological history of successive waves of invading tribes said to have occupied ancient Ireland. However, most of the stories it contains are bowdlerized versions of ancient tales of Celtic gods and goddesses.

THE SON OF NOAH

The Book of Invasions begins with the biblical account of the great flood. Unlike the canonical story of the flood, however, the twelfth-century monks' version had a twist. A Celtic son of Noah, Bith (meaning "life"), is excluded from his father's ark and therefore constructs his own ships. Bith and his ships sail into the unknown, and all but his own vessel are lost. Bith's solitary ship with its passengers wanders lost for many months, finally arriving in Ireland, where the occupants await the deluge. The floods eventually arrive and wipe out all but a single man called Finntan, who survives for many thousands of years by shape-shifting into the forms of various animals.

It was Finntan, claimed the monks, who returned after so many years with the countenance of an ancient druid and prophesied to the Gaels the coming of St. Patrick, whom he describes as a "druid of an unknown faith." Patrick, according to this prophecy, would cleanse Finntan of his sins and allow him to cease his endless wanderings.

THE FIVE PARTS OF IRELAND

Finntan is also credited with the traditional division of Ireland into five parts: Ulster, Leinster, Connacht, and Munster all ringed about Meath, the location of the Hill of Tara, the legendary seat of Irish kings.

After the time of Bith, the islands remained devoid of human life until the coming of Partholon, another descendant of Noah, who sets foot on Irish shores with Ireland's next wave of colonists. Partholon is more successful at colonization than Bith; he goes about the business of settlement, building houses, planting crops, and battling monstrous, mutated invaders called Fomorians.

THE FOMORIANS

The Fomorians, according to the book, were demonic beings and were the original inhabitants of Ireland. They fought against Partholon and his descendants, using supernatural means as well as martial might.

TUAN THE SHAPE-SHIFTER

It is not the Fomorians who doom Partholon's settlers, but a fatal disease. All but one man, a nephew of Partholon named Tuan, are destroyed. In an odd echo of Finntan's story, this lone survivor again must make his way through successive shape-shifting. Tuan becomes a stag that leads herds of deer; a boar that roots in the woods; and an eagle that takes to the skies. At last he becomes a salmon, and swims in the sacred pools until humans returned to Ireland.

The salmon Tuan is caught and eaten by an Irish queen, who in turn becomes his mother. The newly reborn Tuan is born with all of his wisdom intact and recounts to his mother's people the history of Ireland, continuing the tale where it left off: with Partholon's successors Nemed and his people, who are driven out of Ireland by the Fomorians and who return as the noble Tuatha Dé Danann and the wicked and clumsy Fir Bolg.

THE FIR BOLG

The Fir Bolg ("bag men") were also invaders of Ireland whom the Tuatha Dé Danann defeated at the battle of Magh Tuireadh. They retreated to the Aran Islands off the west coast of Ireland, where they are said to have built a great fort called Dun Aonghusa.

Nemed is said to be a Scythian Greek, who comes to Ireland with his four sons. Nemed and his followers are enslaved and oppressed by the Fomorians, who finally drive them away. Some move to the far shores to be left in peace and become the ancestors of the Fir Bolg. The remainder travel to the west, where they are schooled in the magical arts. The descendants of Nemed return many years later as the Tuatha Dé Danann to drive the Fomorians away and retake Ireland.

THE TUATHA DÉ DANANN

The Fir Bolg tribes are also vanquished by the Tuatha Dé Danann, the "People of the Goddess Danu," who are but the gods of the pagan Celts in disguise. The stories of the Tuatha Dé Danann provide the best record of Celtic mythological tales—the gods are stripped of their divinity but retain most of their magical powers and abilities. The gods of the Irish are recounted in the Book of Invasions as yet another conquering tribe, albeit one with fantastic occult powers. The Dé Danann hero Lugh finally defeats the Fomorians by driving them into the sea.

TRAVELERS TO THE WEST

The works of fantasy fiction author J.R.R. Tolkien are heavily based in ancient Norse and Irish mythological tales. Some critics have argued that the inspiration for the races of elves who "sail into the West" in Tolkien's ring trilogy is the story of the Tuatha Dé Danann, who recede into the underworld at the coming of the Gaels.

However, Tolkien himself professed a general dislike for most Celtic things, preferring the stories of Scandinavian civilizations, from which he drew many of the names for his characters and creatures.

THE COMING OF THE MILESIANS

The Tuatha Dé Danann continue to rule Ireland in peace until the arrival of the last invaders, the Gaulish Milesians. The Milesians are named for their chieftain, Míl. The Milesians sail to Ireland on the advice of druid seers, and among their party is Míl's son, the legendary bard Amergin. The Milesians are not welcomed by the Dé Dananns, and a series of fierce battles ensues, in which the kings of both tribes are killed.

Eventually, the warring parties reach a compromise. The Milesians will rule the upper, daylight world, and the People of Danu will take the Otherworld and pass into legend. Ever after, they are known as the Sídhe, the people of the fairy mounds.

CHAPTER TWO

The Ulster Cycle and the Fenian Cycle

The Ulster Cycle was told in two places: the eleventh-century Book of the Dun Cow and the fourteenth-century Yellow Book of Lecan. The Ulster Cycle chronicles the adventures of a succession of great heroes, most notably Cuchulainn, a warrior of tremendous stature and ferocity. The cycle begins with the tale of Fergus, an impossibly gigantic king of Ulster. Fergus wishes to marry Nessa, his brother's widow, who will only consent if Fergus will make her young son king. Fergus, all too glad to be rid of the responsibility, readily agrees, and seven-year-old Connor becomes king of Ulster.

Despite King Connor's youth, all went well under his reign until one terrible incident. A wealthy cattleman by the name of Cruinniuc boasted that his wife Macha, a swift runner, could outrace the king's chariots. Despite her protests, the king forced the heavily pregnant Macha to compete. She won the race, but the exertion proved too much. After giving birth to twin babies, she expired at the finish line, cursing the insensitive men of Ulster to suffer a woman's labor pains whenever the kingdom was under threat. Macha's curse carried down nine generations of Ulster men, until the birth of the semi-divine hero Cuchulainn.

MACHA AND THE MORRIGÁN

Macha, one of the older Celtic goddesses, was often portrayed as a horse. She is sometimes seen as an attribute of the Morrigán, a triplicate goddess of fertility, war, and death. It was to Macha that the heads of the battle-dead belonged. The Morrigán, on the other hand, is sometimes referred to as the Queen of Battles and is often accompanied by her sisters, Badh the Crow, Nemain the Venomous, and Fea the Hateful.

CUCHULAINN THE GREAT

Cuchulainn's name means "The Hound of Culann." Mightiest of all Celtic heroes, he was the son of the god Lugh, and his mother was Dechtire (also known as Deichtine), sister of King Conchobar mac Nessa, ruler of Ulster. Two horses were born at the same moment as he, so he took them as his own—the Grey of Macha and the Black of Saingliu.

Like many other mythic heroes, Cuchulainn's deeds began when he was a boy. When he arrived late at a banquet given in the house of Culann, a great craftsman and smith, he was confronted by the smith's hound, which growled and snarled at him. Threatened by the ferocious dog, the boy stuffed a ball down the beast's throat, and as it choked, he smashed it against a wall, killing it. Culann mourned his loyal animal, and the boy, regretting his deed, said that he himself would perform the duties of the hound. Thus he gained his name, the Hound of Culann.

Like most great heroes, Cuchulainn is armed with magical weapons; these include his spear, which inflicts only fatal wounds, and a visor given him by the sea god, Manannan mac Lir. In battle a fury comes over him so that he seems transformed into a monster, filled with rage and bent on destroying his foes.

THE CATTLE RAID OF COOLEY

The central tale of the Ulster Cycle is known as the Cattle Raid of Cooley (the Táin bó Cuailnge), which tells the tales of two magical bulls. These are Donn Cuailnge, the brown bull of Cooley, and Finnbennach, the white-horned bull of Ai. The white-horned bull belongs to the wealthy, powerful, and exceedingly avaricious Queen Medb (Maeve), whose enormous greed cannot be satisfied. Medb wishes to humiliate her ineffectual husband, Ailill, and desires to add the brown bull to her already prodigious wealth. Upon hearing of the mysterious affliction of the Ulster men, she set off with her armies to seize the great bull.

THE BULLS OF COOLEY

The brown and white bulls of the Cooley saga are no ordinary bulls, of course, but the result of a magical battle between two enchanted shape-changers, a pair of foolish magicians whose end came in a most fitting way.

Medb's armies are not aware of the existence of Cuchulainn, however, and soon meet with furious resistance. Clever Cuchulainn invokes the ancient right of single combat and staves off Medb's army for months, slaying every champion the queen sends to meet him.

Cuchulainn's distractions are successful, and the men of Ulster, recovered from their labor pains, are able to easily defeat Medb's depleted forces.

But Queen Medb is clever. She succeeds in stealing the bull anyway, while the men are distracted by the battles. In the end, all the fighting is to no avail. The two bulls, having picked up an old disagreement, soon commence battling between themselves over which is superior. The battle between the bulls rages all night and ranges the breadth of Ireland, until at last the white-horned bull Finnbennach lies dead. The brown bull, now bored, breaks free and returns to his home in Ulster, where he too expires from his exertions.

Medb, of course, is not finished with Cuchulainn, and seeks her revenge on him through more trickery. Cuchulainn, like most Celtic heroes, is under a *geas*, a magical proscription which becomes a curse if broken. Cuchulainn's geas is that he must accept any meal offered him but he must never eat dog's meat. When the geas is discovered, Medb's simple solution is to offer the hero a meal of dog's meat. Spiritually broken, Cuchulainn is easily defeated, felled by the spear of Lugaid, said to have been forged by Vulcan.

FIONN AND THE FIANNA

The Fenian Cycle concerns the hero Fionn mac Cumhaill (Finn MacCool) and his followers, the Fianna. Fionn is believed to be a form of the ubiquitous Celtic antlered god Cernunnos, a forest deity who eventually acquired human characteristics over time. Most of the naming conventions used in stories of Fionn, from his youthful alias to the name of his wife, are related to deer.

As Fionn's legend begins, he is Demne ("deer"), a young man apprenticed to a druid poet, Finnegas. Fionn's heroic career begins when he is entrusted by the druid to cook a magical salmon. Fionn is sternly warned not to eat even a morsel, as the fish's magic is reserved for Finnegas—but while the young man is minding the fire, a heat blister rises on the side of the fish. Fionn unthinkingly pops the hot blister with his thumb. When he sucks on the burnt finger, the salmon's wisdom is transferred to him, and Fionn receives the power of prophecy.

FIONN'S TALE IN OTHER MYTHOLOGIES

The story of Fionn has a parallel in Welsh mythology. This time, it is Gwion who tends to the goddess Cerridwen's cauldron of knowledge. When he accidentally receives the gift of prophecy, the goddess is angered. Gwion transforms himself into a grain of wheat, and Cerridwen becomes a hen and devours him. When she becomes a woman again, she finds herself pregnant with him, and soon gives birth. Cerridwen binds the infant into a sack and throws him into a river. He is discovered by a king, who calls him Taliesin, "shining brow."

THE FIANNA

After many adventures, Fionn finds himself back in Tara, at the court of the Irish High King, Cormac mac Art, near the time of Samhain. Instead of the holiday preparations he expects, Fionn finds the kingdom in an uproar of panic. During Fionn's absence, Cormac's kingdom has been plagued by a rogue specter, a wandering fairy of the Tuatha Dé

Danann. This is Aillen mac Midna, a musician who appears every year at Samhain. Aillen always approaches as a musician—at first by invoking the king's hospitality, but later by charming his way through the doors. He then plays a melody of enchantment, putting all of the court to sleep, after which he roams the countryside all night, breathing fire and laying waste to the kingdom.

Fionn offers his services to King Cormac, offering to guard the land against their supernatural enemy in return for a request granted. Like Cuchulainn, Fionn is possessed of a magical spear created in the Otherworld. At the fairy's approach, Fionn uses the spear to prod himself awake, avoiding the sleep-spell. When Aillen opens his mouth to loose his flames, Fionn lets fly his infallible spear and dispatches the murderous fairy with a blow to the back. His quest fulfilled, Fionn returns to King Cormac for his boon: He requests the leadership of the Fianna, a force of 20,000 men.

The Fianna are an elite force of warriors, highly skilled in poetry as well as in the arts of war. The members of this small army are skilled bards as well as accomplished fighters. Additionally, the warriors are subjected to extraordinary tests of strength and skill—a man wishing to join the Fianna must be able to leap over a stave of his own height, dive under one the height of his knee, and pluck a thorn from his foot—all while running paces. Another test involves burying the candidate up to his waist in sand, where he must defend himself from spear-wielding warriors using only a staff and a wooden shield.

THE RED DEER

Fionn and his warriors have many adventures and win many battles. When Fionn is not with the Fianna, however, he prefers the company of his magical hounds, Bran and Sceolan. His hounds, like himself, are the product of magical marriage, their mother being a fairy woman.

One of Fionn's most famous adventures occurs during a hunting expedition with Bran and Sceolan, during which he encounters a beautiful red fawn. As much as Fionn desires this deer, however, his enchanted hounds balk and refuse to attack it. He watches, amazed, as his hounds joyfully cavort about the meadow with his would-be prey.

A disappointed Fionn finally gives up and heads for home, but the deer follows. As the hunting party enters the gate of Fionn's estate, the red deer suddenly transforms into a beautiful woman. The woman is Sadhbh ("doe"), who has labored under a curse for refusing the advances of a love-struck druid. Because Fionn's hounds recognized her predicament, the curse is lifted. Fionn and Sadhbh fall in love and marry, and Sadhbh soon becomes pregnant.

Unfortunately, because Sadhbh is innocent and trusting, she is lured away once more by the wicked enchanter and forced to return to the forest with him. Fionn searches endlessly for his missing bride, but he is never able to recover her from the wily druid. One day, seven years after Sadhbh's disappearance, Fionn is once again on a hunting expedition, when his party encounters a strange boy who cannot speak. Fionn's hounds once again intervene, and the boy is taken into Fionn's care. As he learns to speak, it is revealed that the boy is the son of Fionn and Sadhbh, cared for over the years by his mother, the red deer. Fionn names his son Oisin, "small deer," and the boy grows up to become an accomplished bard and a distinguished member of the Fianna.

According to legend, Fionn sleeps in a cave, where he will awaken once more to defend Ireland in the time of its greatest need.

CHAPTER THREE

The Mother Goddesses

The most ancient and best-known deity of the Celts was the great mother goddess, who embodied the earth and represented fertility, abundance, and regeneration. She was the mother of the gods and the first ancestor of the people. The Celts were deeply concerned with the command of the female powers in both their aspects—the Celtic goddess could be a loving nurturer and provider, but she was also a violent warrior and a cruel enchantress.

THE THREE MOTHERS

The Celts had special reverence for the number three, and many of their important goddesses appeared in groups of three. One of the earliest groups of "triple" goddesses was the trio of goddesses of motherhood known in Roman Britain as the *deae matres* or *matronae*, the "mother goddesses." Icons of the matres have been found all over northwestern Europe. They invariably appear together, almost always seated in a row, often with breasts bared. The three are usually depicted as a younger woman flanked by older matrons, and they hold in their laps various symbols of nurture: breads, fruits, and meats, or cornucopias. They are also sometimes shown with nursing infants and accoutrements of motherhood such as diapers or bathing sponges.

GODS IN TRIPLICATE

The mothers are not the only deities to appear in threes in early Celtic iconography. The god Lugh was often portrayed as having three faces or even three heads, and the water goddess Coventina is often depicted in triple form. As well, a number of Celtic myths (Diarmaid and Grainne, Culhwch and Olwen) turn on love triangles.

There is some speculation that the three mothers represent three seasons and their fruits—spring, summer, and winter—or perhaps each is a seasonal aspect of a single goddess. The three mothers appear to have been tutelary deities, viewed as guardians of homes and communities.

DANU AND THE PEOPLE OF DANU

Little is known about the goddess Danu, the progenitor of the Irish gods. As indicated earlier, she is sometimes represented as water, an important source of life. The gods are the Tuatha Dé Danann, the "People of the Goddess Danu," yet very little is recorded about her other than her name. Danu might have had little function other than as an ancestress or creatrix, and large parts of her story may thus have been discarded by the Christian monks who recorded the myths of the Tuatha, as they preferred to portray them as ancestral humans rather than as deities in their own right.

Danu is related to the Welsh goddess Dôn, and possibly Anu. The roots of the names *Dana* and *Dôn* have connotations of wealth, abundance, and flowing water.

THE HORSE-MOTHERS

The horse was of incalculable value to the Celts. For 3,000 years, the horse served as a domestic animal in Western Europe and was hunted as a major source of sustenance for thousands of years before that. Horses provided meat, milk, transportation, and labor, and they were necessary to the survival of Celtic culture. Thus the horse was closely connected with divinity and was often venerated as a god on its own.

The mother goddesses had many curious associations with horses, often appearing in iconography astride or alongside horses. This may have a connection with the idea of the goddess as consort to the ancient father god, who was often depicted as a horse. Eventually, however, the goddess herself became more important, and the horse lessened in importance.

EPONA: THE DIVINE MARE

Though a number of Celtic goddesses were connected with horses, the most popular of these was Epona, whose name means "divine mare." Epona is almost invariably depicted with horses—often astride as a rider, sometimes enthroned like the Roman goddess Cybele, and occasionally as a mare and accompanying foal.

While most Celtic goddesses were connected to a specific locality, Epona's worship was widespread. In fact, Epona had the singular honor of being the only Celtic deity to be venerated within the borders of Rome itself. She is connected with fertility and prosperity, but above all, she is a protector of horses, donkeys, and other transport animals. Her name is derived from the Greek word for horse, *epos*, and her image is found in stables everywhere, even in Rome and Greece. Epona was especially popular with the Roman cavalry.

EPONA

Epona may have had early connections to the ancient Greek earth goddess Demeter. There is evidence that in some early forms, Demeter was worshipped in the form of a mare.

Epona makes no appearances by that name in Ireland, but she is similar enough to the goddess Macha that is the two are sometimes assumed to be the same goddess. Macha is best known from the tales of the Tuatha Dé Danann recounted in the Ulster Cycle, but even here she is closely associated with horses. Macha's win in a race against the king's horses precipitates her labor and death and begins the curse of the Ulstermen. Later, it is Macha's own horse who carries the hero Cuchulainn to his death on the battlefield and who mourns him afterward. Macha's name itself means "plain" or "pasture," a grazing spot.

THE MORRIGÁN

These Celtic earth goddesses were not sweet earth mothers by any means. While they represented the fertility of the land and the nurture of its people, they were often portrayed as harsh or even cruel, much like nature itself. A number of goddesses were associated with the sovereignty of the land, and most of these were also goddesses of war and death. They embodied the earth itself in both its positive and negative aspects.

The most famous of the goddesses of sovereignty was the Morrigán, whose name means "great queen" or "phantom queen." The Morrigán was of fearsome aspect, often appearing in the form of a carrion crow. She was a primarily a goddess of war, ruler of the battlefield and the taker of fallen warriors. Despite the seeming contradiction, the Morrigán was also the goddess of fertility, cattle, and crops.

While it may seem a contradiction that a goddess of life and fertility would also be a goddess of war and death, it is actually an insight into the worldview of the Celts, who correctly observed that death was necessary for the generation of life. The Celts were most aware of natural cycles, and they ascribed mystical importance to the necessity of blood and decay as the sustenance of new life.

The rulership of kings was only by proxy, by authority of the goddess. Kings were symbolically wed to the goddess, and their mandate to rule depended on the whim of the earth—if the fertility of the land failed, or natural disasters struck, this could be seen as the goddess herself expressing displeasure with her earthly husband.

The Morrigán's earliest written appearance is in the stories of the Ulster Cycle. She first appears to the hero Cuchulainn, who catches her attempting to steal one of his cows. The hero does not recognize her, and in his attempt to prevent her taking the cow, he incites her to anger. She makes a prophecy of his death in battle, which comes to pass. And when he is about to die, she and her sister Badh in crow form come and sit on his shoulders.

In the Táin bó Cuilainge, or Cattle Raid of Cooley, she first appears in the form of a crow to warn away the brown bull. Later, the Morrigán appears to Cuchulainn as a beautiful girl and attempts to seduce him, but he rejects her advances. This time, it is the scorned goddess herself who attempts to kill him, by first transforming into an eel, then a wolf, then a red heifer.

She is wounded each time by the hero, and finally she reappears in the form of a wounded elderly woman. Cuchulainn shows sudden compassion, and offers milk to the old woman, which heals her wounds. In gratitude, she makes a prophecy of the coming battle. In all versions of the story, the goddess appears as women in different stages of life, from maiden to old woman.

BOUDICCA'S SACRIFICE

It is to Andraste, another form of the war goddess, that the Celtic warrior-queen Boudicca sacrificed hundreds of captive Roman women after her defeat of Roman troops in 61 B.C.E.

The Morrigán's guises of age appear connected with her various functions. As maiden, she appears as sovereignty, the ruling principle, and Cuchulainn's rejection can be seen as a rejection of sovereignty itself—his refusal to couple with the goddess may be directly responsible for his death in battle. As the crone, she is a seer, and a harbinger of death.

In direct contrast to Cuchulainn's encounter with sovereignty is the Dagda's similar meeting. On the eve of the battle of Magh Tuireadh, the god encounters the Morrigán as a beautiful maiden washing in the river. He mates with her, and she predicts he will triumph over the Fomorians. The goddess even aids in that victory, appearing in the battlefield with an incantation that rallies the troops to victory: "Kings, arise to the battle!"

In another telling, as Cuchulainn makes his way to the battlefield, he passes the Morrigán, who in the guise of an old woman is washing bloody garments in the river. When he asks what she is doing, she replies that she is washing the funeral clothes of the hero. In this guise, the Morrigán was called the "washer at the ford," and her appearance presaged death.

The Morrigán and her related goddesses are heavily associated with crows, birds of death and decay. In most versions of the death of Cuchulainn, his death on the battlefield is only recognized when a crow lands upon the hero's upright body. The Morrigán was ruler over the battlefield, and the heads of the slain were euphemistically referred to as "Morrigán's acorn crop," a likely reference to the crows' habit of pecking out the eyes of the dead.

MORGAN LE FAY

A most curious figure in Arthurian legends is Morgan le Fay, or "Morgan of the Fairies," portrayed in the stories as the often-evil half sister of King Arthur. While the names of the two women do not appear to be linguistically related, their similarities are remarkable. Like the goddess, Morgan is filled with contradictions—she is Arthur's healer and protector, yet she tries to kill him on a number of occasions. Both Morgan and the Morrigán are associated with crows, and Morgan takes on many of the initiatory aspects of the Morrigán.

MORE ON MORGAN

Morgan has another connection to the Great Goddess through the Welsh folklore character Modron, "mother." Modron was also married to a Urien and, like Morgan, had a son named Owain. Curiously, a tale of Modron repeats an old legend about the washer at the stream, wherein the lady is said to be under a curse until she bears a Christian son.

Morgan's earliest appearance is in the *Life of Merlin* by Geoffrey of Monmouth in the twelfth century. Though there has been a lot of discussion about Geoffrey's source material, most scholars agree that he got the material for the book from Welsh traditions. In her appearances in the Arthurian cycles, in a parallel of the older myth tales, Morgan assumes the role of sovereignty and mates with the young Arthur. It is Morgan who heals a wounded Arthur and gives him the magical protective scabbard that enables him to succeed in battle, and when scorned, she rescinds the gift, allowing him to become fatally wounded. In the end, Morgan receives the dying King and ferries him to Avalon.

MORGAN'S FAMILY?

Not every version of the legend shows Morgan in such a benevolent light. In some tales, she has an incestuous affair with King Arthur, her half brother. From this union is born Mordred, who later kills Arthur at the battle of Camlann.

THE CAILLEACH

Another of the goddesses of sovereignty was Cailleach. Cailleach in Gaelic means "veiled," a reference to the habitual garb of an old woman. There are numerous appellations to the name Cailleach, such as Cailleach Bheara (Cailleach of Bheare, Scotland) This suggests that the name "Cailleach" may have been a nickname of sorts applied to local sovereignty goddesses.

The Cailleach is similar to goddesses like the Morrigán in many ways. She is connected with lakes and streams, and appears to have also been a goddess of sovereignty. Like the Morrigán, she appears in many stories attempting to seduce the hero, only the scenario is reversed, and Cailleach retains her haglike appearance. Like the other goddesses of sovereignty, Cailleachs are strongly associated with waterways, and she is said to be the source of many rivers and streams, as well as the guardian of wells.

THE LOATHLY LADY

There are many instances in myth tales wherein the hero is challenged to kiss or even marry a hideous old hag, who is a goddess in disguise. The courageous man is rewarded when she suddenly transforms into a beautiful maiden. Such is the story of Niall, son of Eochaid, who is named the rightful high king after daring to embrace the hag who taunts him from her well. This story, too, is carried over into Arthurian lore. In the tale of Peredur and other Arthurian romances, the knight Gawain, in order to save the life of the king, must marry a foul hag. Gawain, however, accepts his fate with good cheer, only to find his acceptance has broken a spell and his hideous wife is transformed into a beauty without parallel. In these tales, the "loathly lady" represents the goddess as sovereignty and all the responsibilities it entails.

CERRIDWEN

Another goddess who varied in aspect from maiden to crone was the Welsh Cerridwen, an enchantress who lived under a lake. Cerridwen's name is from roots meaning "fair poetry," and Cerridwen is a patron of poets and poetry. Cerridwen is also mother to the renowned bard Taliesin. Cerridwen was a trickster of sorts who took the appearance of a hag or a maiden, depending on her purpose, and who also had the power to shape-shift. She was the keeper of the cauldron of poetic inspiration, but guarded it jealously.

BRIGHID

One of the most widely worshipped of the Celtic goddesses was Brighid, a goddess of poetry, fire, healing waters, and inspiration. Brighid was the patron goddess of artisans of all kinds, including poets, smiths, and metalworkers. The name *Brighid* comes from a root with connotations of fire and heat, and may mean "fire arrow" or even "exalted one."

BRIGHID AND THE ARTS

Brighid has a double connection to poets and their art. She is not only the goddess of poetry, but the mother of Oghma, the god of eloquence. Originally, she was Brigantia, the sovereignty goddess of the Brigantes, a powerful tribe of British Celts. It was in this form she was related to Minerva, both as a goddess of craftsmanship and of war. You may also remember from earlier in this book that she had a special relationship with druids.

As mentioned earlier, in many versions of Celtic myth, Brighid is not the Dagda's companion but rather his daughter. And there are other variations. The Irish Brighid was a triple goddess, the name belonging to not one but three daughters of the Dagda, each of whom had a separate specialty. As goddess of poetry, Brighid is sovereign over magic and is also associated with spoken enchantment, seership, and prophecy. Brighid as the goddess of fire ruled over the smith's fire as well as the hearth-fire, and her temples contained a sacred flame watched over by a company of virgin priestesses, much like those of the temples of Vesta in Rome. This tradition was imitated by the nuns at Kildare, who kept a perpetual flame lit in honor of St. Brigid.

The Brighid of water was sovereign over healing baths and wells. In this form, she often appears as a hideous hag and may be related to Cailleach, who is also mentioned in the context of sacred wells. According to some sources, Brighid and the Cailleach are two sides of the same goddess, a young Brighid ruling over the summer months beginning with the festival of Imbolc, and Cailleach ruling the months of winter, from Samhuinn (Samhain) onward.

CHURCH OF THE OAK

The name *Kildare* is from the Irish Cill-Dara, meaning "church of the oak." According to Irish Christian legend, the Abbess Brigid chose a location containing a gigantic oak tree as a site on which to found her abbey.

The ancient town of Kildare, Ireland, was once home to an ancient temple of Brighid. In later times, the site was home to the abbey of Brigid, who may have been a Catholic abbess or simply a Christianized remolding of the goddess. Evidence points to the latter, as the site is home to both a sacred well and an eternal flame, and is sited on the former location of a temple dedicated to the goddess.

Giraldus Cambrensis, Gerald of Wales, gives an account of his visit to Kildare in 1185, in which he describes the perpetual fires kept there in Brigid's honor:

> At Kildare, in Leinster, celebrated for the glorious Brigit, many miracles have been wrought worthy of memory. Among these, the first that occurs is the fire of St. Brigit, which is reported never to go out. Not that it cannot be extinguished, but the nuns and holy women tend and feed it, adding fuel with such watchful and diligent care, that from the time of the Virgin, it has continued burning through a long course of years; and although such heaps of wood have been consumed during this long period, there has been no accumulation of ash.
>
> At the time of St. Brigit, twenty nuns were engaged in the Lord's warfare, she herself being the twentieth; after her glorious departure, nineteen have always formed the society, the number having never increased. Each of them has the care of the fire for a single night, the last nun, having heaped wood upon the fire, says: "Brigit take charge of your own fire; for this night belongs to you." She then leaves the fire, and in the morning it is found that the fire has not gone out, and that the usual quantity of fuel has been used.
>
> The fire is surrounded by a hedge, made of stakes and brushwood, and forming a circle, within which no male can enter; and if any one should presume to enter, which has been sometimes attempted by rash men, he will not escape the divine vengeance. Moreover, it is only lawful for women to blow the fire, fanning it or using bellows only, and not with their breath.

It seems quite certain that the practice which Cambrensis describes is a very ancient one, and almost certainly initiated by the priestesses of the Great Goddess. Especially telling is the prohibition against men near the sacred fires, and the promise of divine vengeance that Cambrensis so innocently attributes to the Christian God.

CHAPTER FOUR

The Gods of the Celts

The Celts had numerous male deities, so many that the names and attributes of only a fraction of their number are known. The gods of the Gauls were various. Although many were bound to localities or tribes, a number were probably viewed as universal and were popular throughout the Celtic territories. The Romans recognized these gods as identical to their own (although the Gauls may not have felt that way). Some of these early Gaulish gods remain mysterious, with little more known about them than their names. A few remained popular and became part of the Gaelic and Brythonic pantheons.

THE DAGDA: THE GOOD GOD

The Dagda, or "the Good God," was the preeminent Irish god, the father and ruler of the Tuatha Dé Danann, although archaeological evidence indicates that he was an older, assimilated deity. The Dagda was also called Eochaid Ollathair, "Great Father Horse," and In Ruad Rofhessa, "The Red One of Great Knowledge," with *red* most likely referring to the Dagda's sunburned complexion. The Dagda is not called "good" in reference to his benevolence but in regard to his many skills in fighting, singing, games, and sport.

The Dagda possessed three magical accoutrements. The best known was his gigantic, phallic club, which had the power to kill with one blow—although when reversed, a strike with the handle could return the dead to life. The club was reportedly so large that it needed to be dragged about on a wheeled cart.

He also owned an equally large cauldron called Coire Ansic, "Undry," which was always filled with whatever one desired to eat and which could never be emptied. This cauldron housed the invincible Spear of Lugh when it was not in use.

The Dagda's third and most prized possession was Daurdabla, his magical harp, which had the power to bring great joy, great sorrow, or profound prophetic sleep.

The appetites of the Dagda were large. When it came to food or women, he was insatiable. During the wars with the Fomorians, the Dagda sought audiences with them in order to stall their war-making plans while the Tuatha Dé Danann rallied to arms. The Fomorians were no fools, and hearing of his great love of porridge, arranged to have a gigantic bowl filled with porridge, into which were thrown many animals—hundreds of sheep, pigs, and cows. A guest was expected to eat all he was offered or risk a grave insult to his host—which the Fomorians were hoping for. The

Dagda had the last laugh, however; he pulled out his gigantic spoon and set to work, devouring every last drop in very little time.

The Dagda liked women as much as he liked food, and he went to great lengths to be with women he desired, even those who belonged to others. One of his great risks was going after the goddess Boann, the wife of Elcmar. To accomplish this, he simply stopped time. Their tryst had an unintended consequence, however, and Boann became pregnant. To avoid being caught by an angry husband, the Dagda had to keep time at a standstill until nine months were up and his son was born. This child was Aenghus, the god of love, who due to the circumstance of his birth was called "forever young."

AENGHUS, THE GOD OF LOVE

The Celtic god of love and health was known by various names. He was Aenghus mac Og, "Son of Youth," to the Irish, and Mabon ap Modron, "Youth, Son of the Mother" to the Welsh.

GOD OF YOUTH

The Welsh equivalent of Aenghus is the youth god Mabon ap Modron, also the son of a water goddess and also associated with love and healing. Mabon was a favorite in medieval Welsh romances and appears as a character in many early Arthurian tales. There is some evidence that medieval Welsh poets identified the youthful deity with the infant Jesus.

Aenghus and his equivalents were very different from the average Celtic god. While the typical Celtic deity, even a poet, was invariably portrayed as a brawny, mustached warrior, the god of eternal youth was depicted as a beardless young man or a small child.

Aenghus was the ruler over the Neolithic tomb at Newgrange, viewed by the Irish as the home of the god and an entrance to the Otherworld. The nearby river Boyne is named for the river goddess Boann, his mother. Aenghus was fostered either by Midir or by Manannan mac Lir, depending on the source.

Aenghus is closely associated with water birds, and both he and his bride Caer have the ability to take on the form of swans.

GODS OF LIGHT AND ART

Of the Gaulish gods who enjoyed wide recognition, only a few remained popular by the time the Celts had receded to the British Isles. These were Lugos, who became Lugh, god of arts and craftsmanship; and Ogmios, who remained throughout the god of eloquence and poetic skill, called Oghma by the Irish.

DIFFERENT AREAS, DIFFERENT ASPECTS

It can often get confusing trying to keep straight which Celtic deities ruled what and to which classical gods they corresponded. It is important to keep in mind that the gods did not always have the same aspects in every area they were worshipped, and that different cultures within the Celtic milieu stressed some over others.

BELENOS

Belenos (sometimes Belenus) was an early Gaulish sun god, about whom very little is known. To the Welsh, he was Beli Mawr. The festival of Belenos was Beltaine, held on the first of May to mark the beginning of summer.

Belenos was identified with the Greek Apollo, as the driver of a vast horse-drawn sun-wagon. The emblems of Belenos were the lightning bolt, the wagon, and the solar wheel. Like many of the early Celtic father gods, Belenos was closely associated with horses. Belenos represented the light and heat of the sun, and in later times he was associated with healing hot springs and baths.

LUGH

Irish mythology often revolves around the forces of light and darkness and their constant struggle for control. Unlike other such worldviews, however, the Irish appear to have embraced both the light and the darkness. One deity who embodies this dualistic view was the Gallic god Lugos, eventually known to the Irish as Lugh and to the Welsh as Lleu.

AN ARCHANGEL

With the coming of Christianity, Lugos was associated with the archangel Michael, who was also been considered to have solar affinities. Many of the sacred places once dedicated to Lugos were rededicated to the angel.

The god Lugos was very popular with the Gauls, and several ancient cities were named for him. Lugos was a god of light and had affinities with both Mercury and Apollo. Lugos could be considered a sun god, but he was also a god of industry and art. Lugos above all the Celtic gods was most often associated with Mercury, to the extent that in some areas, the two gods became completely identified. Lugos's icons were ravens and dogs.

Lugos may have had a triple aspect, as some older images depict him with three heads or faces. Some scholars have even suggested that Lugos was not a single god, but a trinity of sorts—the god Esus, Taranis, and Teutates as one triune deity. There is also a possible connection between an epithet of the Irish Lugh ("fierce striker") and the ancient nameless hammer god.

LUGH'S TRANSFORMATIONS

In Welsh mythology, Lugos became Lleu, the brother of Dylan and the son of the goddess Arianrhod. Lleu's aspects are essentially the same as Lugh's, and both are connected to agriculture and the calendar, but their personal mythologies and relationships differ. Lugh of the Long Hand eventually was referred to as stooping Lugh, or *Lugh-chromain*. This, in turn, transformed into "leprechaun."

In a commentary on the Celtic reverence for a deity he referred to as Mercury, but who was certainly Lugos, Caesar remarked:

> . . . of all the gods they most worship Mercury. He has the largest number of images, and they regard him as the inventor of all the arts, as their guide on the roads and in travel, and as chiefly influential in making money and in trade.

Lugos was one of the few Gaulish gods to transition into the Irish and British pantheons—as Lugh, he became one of the Tuatha Dé Danann. His feast day, Lughnasadh, was held on the first of August. Lugh was a god of intellect, a patron of craftsmanship and skill. In mythological stories he wins many battles of wit and makes many displays of cleverness. The legend of Lugh's entry into the Tuatha Dé Danann tells that he was refused admittance unless he could demonstrate a unique skill. He demonstrated his abilities as a smith, a warrior, a poet, a magician, and a harpist, but each time was told the tribe has someone with each of these skills. Clever Lugh asked if they had one who can do all of these at once, and stumped, the gods had to allow him to join them. Lugh quickly earned their respect, however, and even became their chief.

OGMIOS

Ogmios is a bit odd even in the unusual Celtic pantheon. He was one of the ancient Celtic gods, known as Ogmios to the Gauls and Oghma to the Irish. In ancient times, Ogmios was depicted with the bald-front tonsure of a druid and a grinning countenance, often carrying aloft a gigantic club. In many appearances, he appears with a train of men following behind him, attached to him (often, to his tongue) by chains. He is sometimes called Ogmios Sun-Face and appears wizened or sunburned.

There are further records of the god in medieval Ireland, where he is referred to as the Oghma, a heroic member of the Tuatha Dé Danann and the son of Brighid, the goddess of poetry and fire. Oghma, like his predecessor, was a god of language and a patron of bards. Ogmios's words weren't just useful for leading men, however. Gaulish artifacts invoking the god are often in the form of appeals asking the god to curse enemies and bind lovers. Oghma is credited with the creation of the ogham alphabet, an Irish alphabet used mainly for inscriptions that began appearing around the fifth century. The fourteenth-century Book of Ballymote contains a tract on the letters and their mythological origin.

The father of Ogham was Oghma;
The mother of Ogham was the hand or knife of Oghma.

The excerpt implies that Oghma was a god not only of words but of artistry. It connects the act of speaking with the creative impetus behind craftsmanship and the relationship between word and action. It also calls to mind several instances in mythological tales about the god, where the ogham characters are used magically to locate or bind, abilities ascribed to eloquence of Oghma. In Celtic mythology, magic, artisanship, and eloquence are always linked.

GODS OF BLOOD AND WAR

Several Gaulish gods are generally considered to have been universally worshipped throughout Celtic territories. Caesar also briefly mentions many of them, but instead of calling them by their Celtic names he falls back on the Roman habit of calling foreign gods by Roman names. Caesar refers to six of these gods, three of which he identifies as Jupiter, Mars, and Mercury.

Of the six, three are mentioned in the poet Lucan's epic *Pharsalia*, which describes Caesar's campaigns in Gaul. These are Taranis, Esus, and Teutates, whom Lucan describes as savage and cruel deities whose altars are soaked with blood. Lucan was probably using more than a little poetic license, but the gist of it was true.

TARANIS

Taranis is in all likelihood the Gaulish god that Caesar equated with the Roman Jupiter in his writings on the Gallic Wars. The sole mention of Taranis by name in this context is by Lucan, who mentions him as one of three gods to whom human sacrifices were given. Lucan claims that to each god were given victims, killed in a manner appropriate for that god. Victims sacrificed to Taranis were reportedly burned, as would befit a god of lightning and fire. It is often speculated that the Wicker Man sacrifices described by Caesar might have been carried out under the auspices of Taranis.

Taranis is unmistakably a sky god. While he is often pictured riding across the heavens in a great chariot, he is less a god of the sun than a god of thunder. The main emblems of Taranis are his wheel, which he often holds aloft, and a thunderbolt. The name Taranis comes from a root meaning "thunder," and he is closely related to the Norse god Thor. It was to Taranis that the collected heads of the slain were said to be dedicated.

ESUS, THE LORD

The second of the bloodthirsty gods mentioned by Lucan was Esus or Hesus, whose name literally means "lord." Little is known about this god, but the few remaining images of Esus depict him dressed as a woodsman, usually in the act of cutting down a willow tree. Sometimes, he appears to be emerging from the tree itself. Another emblem associated with Esus is the Tarvos Trigaranus, a bull accompanied by three cranes riding on its back, who appears to be a sacrificial figure associated with the willow tree.

ESUS AND CUCHULAINN

Esus may also be connected to the legend of the Green Man, or forest spirit, the ever-present personification of the wildlands, or, in later tales, to the mysterious character called the "man in the tree," or Derg Corra. Some have also speculated that there is a connection between Esus and Cuchulainn, the hero of the Tuatha Dé Danann. An episode wherein Cuchulainn fells a tree is often cited as evidence of a connection.

Esus was closely connected to trees, and according to the same source, his victims were hung from trees and bled, with the direction of the runoff reportedly interpreted as an omen. This is evocative of rites to the Norse Odin, who may have originated as a Gaulish god. In the Norse Havamal, or sayings of Odin, a similar rite of sacrifice is mentioned, only with a twist—in order to gain the magical rune alphabet, Odin is sacrificed to himself.

Strangely, Esus's appellation "Lord," his self-sacrifice, and his iconic relation to trees caused both druids and Christians alike to associate him with Jesus, a rather strange comparison that continued to be made hundreds of years later. Even more strangely, images of Esus are often littered with nautical images—anchors, sea birds, and so on—and one of the best-preserved monuments in his honor was erected by ancient sailors in France, called the Pilier des Nautes, "pillar of the sailors." Commenters on the *Pharsalia* have equated Esus with both Mercury and Mars.

TUETATES

The third god Lucan mentions is Teutates, a god of war. Teutates (also Teutatis and Teutanos) was often associated with the Roman Mars. Lucan records that those victims sacrificed to Teutates were drowned in cauldrons, bringing to mind the ancient tales of the resurrection of warriors through the waters of the cauldron of life. Teutates is referred to in some accounts in the plural, which has led to speculation that there were multiple instances of the god, who may have been tribal patrons or protectors.

CERNUNNOS AND THE FOREST GODS

The most mysterious of the Celtic deities are the mostly nameless lords of the hunt. Foremost of these is the antlered deity dubbed Cernunnos, a Romanized Gaulish appellation taken from a small handful of inscriptions, only one of which is associated with an image. Cernunnos simply means "the horned one"; his Celtic name or names are unknown, although there are some clues to his identity.

Cernunnos was likely not one but many deities who shared similar attributes. He appears in art almost invariably as a stag-antlered man, seated in a cross-legged pose among the animals and plants of the forest. He is associated with animals of the forest, symbols of the Otherworld. Both snakes and stags are emblems of renewal and rebirth—as the snakes sheds its skin and is reborn, so too does the stag throw off its antlers, only to form new ones in the spring. The horned one then could be viewed as not only a god of resurrection, but also of death, and could be looked upon as a guardian of the Otherworld.

The snake that accompanies Cernunnos and other Celtic deities is something of a mystery. Snakes in general are associated with fertility, death, and regeneration or healing. Cernunnos's serpent is no ordinary snake but a particular oddity known as a horned or ram-head serpent, sporting a pair of curved horns. Horned snakes (in Celtic iconography) are often associated with healing, especially healing springs.

IS CERNUNNOS THE DEVIL?

The depiction of the Christian devil as a horned figure is no coincidence. As Christianity swept westward over the former domains of the Celtic gods, many monuments and temples were abandoned to the elements. In medieval times, these images of a serpent-entwined deity took on a sinister significance and were looked upon as images of Satan.

Cernunnos was a god of fertility and hunting. He appears to have been the most widely worshipped of the Celtic deities, if not a supreme deity—although strangely enough, the body of Celtic mythology that remains is entirely silent on the antlered god. Cernunnos may have been carried over into Irish mythology as Fionn, a deity who is very closely associated with deer and hunting.

One of the most famous depictions of Cernunnos is among the mythological scenes depicted on the Gundestrup cauldron, where he sits cross-legged among birds, deer, and other animals. He wears a torque, a circular choker with open, decorated ends that is an emblem of sovereignty, and holds another in his right hand. In his left, he grasps a horned serpent, an emblem of fertility. The torque suggests a connection with kingship.

DRUIDS' CAULDRONS

The cauldron found at Gundestrup is the most famous example of the druids' ritual cauldrons. It is worked with pictorial narratives of mythological tales, including the Spear of Lugh and the Cauldron of Rebirth.

The worship of Cernunnos may be ancient, as Neolithic burial sites have revealed the bodies of tribal priests interred in antlered costumes, often in the same cross-legged pose in which Cernunnos appears in later stone carvings. Images of antlered men and gods also appear in very early stone pictographs, and some are thought to represent the deity. Figures of (presumed) shamanic figures wearing antlered garb appear in ecstatic poses on cave paintings from as far back as 10,000 B.C.E.

In later Roman-period carvings, Cernunnos appears to be associated with material wealth and prosperity, perhaps a god of commerce. He is pictured as an enthroned character whose lap overflows with acorns, nuts, and even gold coins, or surrounded by overflowing cornucopias. He is often flanked by images of the Roman gods Apollo and Mercury, whose attributes he probably shared.

THE GREEN MAN/DERG CORRA

A mysterious character who appears in tales connected with the god Fionn is Derg Corra ("man in the tree"). He is a symbol of wisdom, closely connected, like Fionn, with the stag. He is described as a curious character who sometimes goes about "on the shanks of a deer," but is described in the tale of Fionn as seated in a tree, with a raven on his shoulder and a deer at his feet. He carries a bronze cup containing a salmon and shares among his companions various fruits of wisdom. Derg Corra is an obvious personification of the forest and its creatures, perhaps an embodiment of the tree of life itself. His creatures represent all of the domains of earth— a bird for the sky, a stag for the land, and a salmon to represent the waters.

There is every reason to believe that this ancient forest deity is directly related to the phenomenon known as the Green Man. Scarcely a medieval building anywhere of any note is without one or more representations of the Green Man in its decorations—in some cases, dozens may be found worked in stone, carved into the woodwork, and hidden among more ordinary decorations. The most common appearance of the Green Man is found carved in wood or stone. He is a great foliate creature, with a face made entirely of leaves and vines, often with wild tendrils sprouting from his mouth. His look is often wild and staring, and he appears to be the absolute embodiment of unfettered natural force.

MANANNAN MAC LIR

Manannan mac Lir, or "Manannan, son of sea," was the Irish god of the sea, and especially connected with the Isle of Man, which is named for him. He was peripherally a member of the Tuatha Dé Danann but most likely predates the majority of the Irish pantheon. Manannan seems to have been something of a psychopomp, a being that escorts newly dead souls to the afterlife, and at one point was counted as a ruler of the Otherworld Mag Mell or Emain Ablach.

THE TRICKSTER GOD

Manannan was a bit of a trickster, often visiting disaster on unsuspecting victims. Most of the stories in which he is a central character revolve around plots of trickery; in one instance, he tricks King Cormac out of his own children. In the end, though, when the lesson is learned, the god returns everything to order.

Manannan's accoutrements include a goblet of truth, which breaks if three lies are told over it and is magically restored when the truth is spoken over it three times. He also owns a magical ship that sails without sails, and a magical cloak of invisibility that can draw down a covering mist. Manannan, like most rulers of the Otherworld, owns a cauldron of never-ending plenty and a magical white horse that can travel as easily over water as over land.

CHAPTER FIVE

The Mabinogion

The story collection called *The Mabinogion* includes some of the earliest prose literature produced in Britain. The first manuscripts appeared in the fourteenth and early fifteenth centuries, but they were based on compilations of much earlier traditions in Wales. There are, in total, eleven different stories. Lady Charlotte Guest, the folklorist who first translated a collection of Welsh prose tales drawn from the fourteenth-century Red Book of Hergest and the White Book of Rhydderch, called those stories *The Mabinogion*. The stories are mostly drawn from earlier literary sources and concern the family of the goddess Dôn, a Welsh variation of the tales of the Tuatha Dé Danann.

Although the stories are of widely varied provenance and age, four of them seem to be a fairly coherent group; they are known as the four "branches" of the Mabinogi. These are:

1. Branch One: The legend of Pwyll, prince of Dyfed
2. Branch Two: The story of Branwen, Daughter of Lir
3. Branch Three: Tales of Manawydan, son of Lir
4. Branch Four: The story of Math, son of Mathonwy

The other tales included in Lady Charlotte's collection are:

✦ Peredur, son of Efrog
✦ The Dream of the Emperor Maxen
✦ Lludd and Llefelys
✦ The Lady of the Well
✦ Geraint, son of Erbin
✦ How Culhwch Won Olwen
✦ Rhonabwy's Dream

Again, it should be stressed that with the possible exception of the four branches, there is no indication that these stories were meant by their original authors to be part of a collection. They were extensively worked over by Christian scribes, who added other elements to them, including, possibly, the Arthurian characters who intrude in many of the tales.

In this chapter, we will discuss the four branches; the story of Culhwch and Olwen can be found in Chapter 9.

THE GODDESS DÔN

The Welsh family of gods were also descended from a goddess, Dôn. Dôn is no doubt related to Danu, the mother of the Tuatha Dé Danann, but there is little mention of either goddess in the entire remaining body of Celtic mythology.

PWYLL

Pwyll, prince of Dyfed, is hunting one day when he takes for his own a stag killed by Arawn, king of Annwfn. To atone for this action, he shape-shifts into the likeness of Arawn himself and goes to the king's house, where he vanquishes the king's enemy, Hafgan.

Later, Pwyll meets a beautiful woman, Rhiannon, whom he pursues and eventually catches. Like so many beautiful women in these stories, Rhiannon has a magical side to her; indeed, in some parts of the Mabinogi she is presented as a goddess. She and Pwyll wed and have a child. However, the child mysteriously disappears, and Rhiannon's maidens, frightened they will be accused of negligence, frame her for murder. Although Pwyll does not banish her or imprison her, he makes her sit at the entrance to the court, telling her story to all those who pass by.

Things end well when the missing child is discovered by a former courtier and is restored to his parents. They name the boy Pryderi, and in due course when his father dies, Pryderi becomes the ruler of Dyfed.

Rhiannon is, in the story, a much more interesting figure than Pwyll, and there have been many studies of her suggesting that she is both a goddess and an example of the "wronged wife" motif that often appears in folklore.

BRANWEN, DAUGHTER OF LIR

In this, the second branch of the Mabinogi, the dominant themes are treachery and death. The hero of the story, Bran Bendigeid, "the Blessed Raven," was a hero of unmatched mythical proportion before Arthur was counted as Britain's greatest champion. Bran was by most accounts the son of Lir, a giant who possessed superhuman strength and abilities.

BRAN THE RAVEN

Both Bran's head and his moniker "Raven" associate him with the early Celtic cult of the head, and possibly with the Morrígán. That Bran's severed head was capable of prophecy also connects him with the ancient Celtic practice of augury, divination through bird flight.

The story of Bran as recounted in *The Mabinogion* begins with the marriage of his sister, Branwen, to Mathowlch, the high king of Ireland. The wedding was held on the shores of Anglesey isle, and giant tents were erected to accommodate the giant's enormous frame. The marriage feast began with much merriment, but it was soon to be soured by the pique of Bran's half brother Efnissyen, who was offended that he had never been asked to consent to the marriage.

Efnissyen took out his annoyance on Mathowlch's stables, mutilating his fine horses. The king, outraged and dismayed by this insult from his bride's family, called off the wedding and prepared to return to his ships. Bran, being a man of honor, quickly stepped in and pleaded with Mathowlch to remain. To remedy his losses, he offered the king a new horse for each one injured, plus a great silver staff and a platter of gold. Mathowlch, still smarting, refused.

So great was Bran's desire to do the honorable thing that he offered the Irish king Wales's greatest treasure: the Cauldron of Rebirth, which could be used to restore the bodies of the dead to full health, but for their powers of speech. Mathowlch at last relented and accepted Bran's generosity. He took his new bride home with him, and she bore him a son within the year, whom she named Gwern, "Alder."

Mathowlch, unfortunately, hadn't forgiven his wife's family for the mutilation of his horses. Once he had a son, Branwen was banished to the kitchen, where she was expected to toil as a common servant. Angry as he was, Mathowlch was not foolish enough to let Bran hear of his deeds, so he took great pains to prevent any word of his cruelty from reaching the giant's ears. Ships were prohibited from traveling to Britain, and ships from Britain were seized as they made landing.

This situation obviously could not hold, but Branwen decided not to wait for her brother to investigate his missing ships. No fool herself, she devised a way to contact her brother in secret. She trained a young bird to carry messages and sent it to find Bran. Bran proved easy to locate, and he immediately mustered an invasion force. He left his kingdom under the care of his son Caradoc and sailed for Ireland with his fleet.

BRAN THE GIANT

Actually, it was only Bran's armies who set sail to meet Mathowlch's forces. Bran was of such tremendous size that he was forced to wade in the ocean alongside his ships.

Meanwhile, Mathowlch was plagued by visions of a forest that appeared in the midst of the sea, flanked by an enormous mountain. Having no one who could interpret this vision, he summoned Branwen to interpret. She informed the king that the forest upon the ocean was Bran's navy, and the mountain was her brother, coming to rescue her.

Now the king knew that his brother-in-law was coming for him and that he would certainly be defeated in battle. So he devised a plan to trick the giant through flattery. He set about at once constructing a house big enough to accommodate Bran. The house was to be so large that it would hold not only the giant but his army as well. It would be the first house large enough to fit Bran, and the giant's first home, certain to impress him and make him forget his anger at least temporarily.

Mathowlch arranged to have a great feast prepared in the hall of the new home. The king expected the giant and his party would get quite drunk, at which time he planned a surprise attack. From the pillars of the great hall, he hung a great many sacks, each one containing an armed warrior, who would drop down among Bran's men and slaughter them.

THE DESTRUCTION OF IRELAND

At first, the giant was quite pleased with his new home, and the ruse was successful. When he asked about the sacks hung from the pillars, Mathowlch explained these were provisions of flour and oats. Bran was satisfied with this explanation. His ever-suspicious brother Efnissyen was not so sure, however, and went about squeezing each sack to assure himself. Because Efnissyen was part giant himself, he managed to squeeze each warrior quite to death, and Mathowlch was forced to reckon a new plan.

Before he was able, however, the hot-headed Efnissyen once again made a mess of things. Upon being introduced to Branwen's young son, Efnissyen was reminded of his anger at the wedding, and in a fit of temper he threw the child into the fireplace.

The feast erupted into warfare, and the battle raged for three days and nights before Bran's armies emerged victorious. The battle had such longevity in large part because the magical cauldron that Bran had given Mathowlch enabled him to continually resurrect his forces. Efnissyen concealed himself among the Irish dead and was able to split the cauldron when he was thrown inside it, and the Irish were defeated shortly afterward. Efnissyen achieved some measure of salvation in this act, as the sacrifice killed him.

The result of the battle was catastrophic. Every Irish citizen but for five pregnant women lay dead, and the armies of Bran were reduced to seven warriors. Bran himself was wounded with a poison dart and lay dying. Branwen, distraught that her discomfort had brought ruin on all, died of grief on the spot.

THE DEATH OF CARADOC

While Bran was battling in Ireland, a rival chieftain overthrew his son Caradoc and enslaved the British chieftains with dark magic. Caradoc, like his aunt Branwen, expired from grief.

THE MIRACULOUS HEAD

The dying giant implored his seven remaining men to cut off his head and return with it to Britain. Upon their return, his men chanced to enter the Otherworld, where they remained for eighty years, having forgotten all of their troubles. The head of Bran remained active and made merry alongside them, until one chanced to open the door leading to the upper world. The men all recalled their mission and the great disaster that had befallen. They returned to Britain and buried Bran's head under the Tower of London, facing the shoreline. The head served as a powerful talisman, protecting Britain from invasion for many generations before it was dug up and turned around by the pious Arthur, who claimed that from that point forward, Britain would be protected by God and by Arthur's armies alone.

THE THIRD AND FOURTH BRANCHES

The third and fourth branches of the Mabinogi are much more filled with magic and magical events than the first two. Both concern Pryderi, son of Pwyll.

THE DEADLY CURSE

In the third branch, a strange curse has come upon the land, devastating crops. Pryderi joins his friend Manawydan in hunting a magic boar, which enters a strange castle. Pryderi follows it and is trapped by a mysterious golden bowl. Manawydan, after waiting for some time, returns to tell Pryderi's wife and mother what has happened. Rhiannon goes to rescue her son but is herself trapped.

Manawydan lives for a time with Pryderi's wife (although he respects her celibacy in the absence of her husband). He plants wheat, but the crops mysteriously fail. When he stays in the field all night, he realizes that the wheat is being eaten by mice. Enraged, he captures one and prepares to hang it from a miniature gallows.

To his surprise, a passing bishop asks him to spare the mouse. When he asks why, the bishop explains that he is a friend of the man Pryderi's mother, Rhiannon, deserted for Pwyll. The mouse is his shape-shifted wife. Manawydan manages to bargain for the release of Pryderi and Rhiannon and the lifting of the curse on the land.

MATH, SON OF MATHONWY

One of the most popular stories from the Mabinogi is that contained in the fourth branch. It concerns the Welsh god Lleu, the Welsh equivalent of Lugh of the Tuatha Dé Danann. Lleu is the son of the goddess Arianrhod, who has cursed Lleu with a *tynged* (geas) that he may take no wife from any human race. Lleu turns to the sorcerer Math for help, and

Math uses a magic wand to create Lleu a bride made entirely of flowers. Lleu's floral bride is named Blodeuedd, which means "bride of flowers."

Unfortunately, although Blodeuedd is beautiful, she has her own will and isn't pleased to become Lleu's wife. One day, while her husband is away visiting, Lleu's bride meets a handsome young hunter named Goronwy, and they soon fall in love. Desperate for a way to be together, the young lovers plot to be rid of Lleu so they will be free to marry.

It is not easy to kill a god, so it takes much conniving to get Lleu to reveal the means by which he can be killed. Through seduction, Blodeuedd learns that Lleu can only be killed by a spear of an entire year's making, and only while keeping one foot in a cauldron of water and another on a goat's back. Lleu's treacherous bride and her lover immediately set to work on the spear, and upon its completion, Blodeuedd convinces her husband to take a bath on a riverbank. She arranges to have a goat set at the base of the tub, and as Lleu steps out, Goronwy hurls his spear.

Lleu is too fast for Goronwy, however, and he escapes death by transforming himself into an eagle. His bride and her lover take his kingdom and rule in his place, but Lleu's friends are quick to discover his fate and are able to restore Lleu to human form. Lleu dispatches his wife's lover with his spear, but Blodeuedd's punishment is more fitting. It is decided that the woman of flowers will be transformed into a bird, but not just any bird. Because she has rejected the lord of light, she will be forced to remain in darkness for the remainder of her days, and so the lady of flowers becomes an owl, mourning forever her wicked deeds.

CHAPTER SIX

The Tuatha Dé Danann

The Tuatha Dé Danann is a mythological race unlike any other. They are the mysterious pre-Celtic inhabitants of Ireland, the gods of the Celtic myth-cycles, and the fairies of Celtic folklore. Masters of magic, craftsmanship, and secret knowledge, they carried the four legendary hallows, or Treasures of Ireland—the magical Sword of Nuada, the Spear of Lugh, the Cauldron of Bounty (belonging to the Dagda), and the Lia Fáil or "Stone of Destiny," which would foretell the succession of Irish kings. The Dé Dananns inhabited the same land as the Celts, shrouded from sight in the mystical Otherworld, and eventually became known as the fey, or fairies.

OLD GODS TO FAIRY-FOLK

Tuatha Dé Danann means the "People of the Goddess Danu." They are a primarily Irish pantheon descended from a great mother goddess, about whom very little is recorded. According to legend, these divine ancestors of the Celts built the Sídhe-mounds, stone circles, and ancient tombs that dot the Irish landscape. When the Celts first arrived in Ireland, they immediately assigned these mysterious, abandoned places to their ancient ancestral gods, imagining these locations as doorways to the Otherworld.

FEAR OF IRON

An old superstition about fairies is that they fear iron, which may be used to ward them off. This may stem from early Iron Age settlers' attempts to explain discoveries of stone weapons and implements left behind by these early Stone Age residents.

The oldest of the Tuatha Dé Danann was the goddess Danu, also called Anu or Anand, or Dôn by the Welsh. Near Tara, the mythical home of the gods, are two raised earthworks resembling breasts, called the "paps of Anu," likely symbolizing the goddess as the embodiment of the land. Even from ancient times, the goddess was closely linked to horses and husbandry, and she is also closely associated with other mother goddesses—Epona, Macha, and the Morrigán.

GODS OF THE DÉ DANANN

The ranks of the Dé Danann are seemingly unlimited in number. Originally, different localities had their own tribal deities, who were often very closely related; over time, many of these blended together, and some took on the aspects of others. The best-known gods of the Dé Danann are these:

- ✤ Im Dagda, "the Good God," the son of Danu
- ✤ Nuada of the Silver Arm, god of war and divine justice
- ✤ Lugh of the Long Arms, "Son of the Sun" and "Lugh the many-skilled," a pre-Irish Celtic god
- ✤ Ogmios, Oghma, or Ogma, god of poetry and eloquence, of Gaulish origin
- ✤ Manannan mac Lir, god of the sea and weather
- ✤ Aenghus mac Og, the son of Boann and a god of love, sometime guardian of Mag Mell or the Blessed Isle

TRIPLE GODDESSES

A number of triple goddesses are associated with the Dé Danann. They are triple in the sense that they are usually portrayed with three aspects or personalities, sometimes portrayed as sisters in later literature. The triple goddesses are related to the Matronae of the European Celts. They are closely linked to the land, and many at one time or another were goddesses of sovereignty, personifications of the earth and the symbolic spouses of its rulers. Triple goddesses of the Dé Danann include these:

- ✤ Epona, a goddess of horses and cavalry
- ✤ The Morrigán, goddess of fertility, war, and death
- ✤ Brighid, goddess of metalworking, poetry, and fire

In the Book of Invasions, the Tuatha Dé Danann are recast as the ancient race who lived in Ireland before the coming of the Milesian Celts. They are described as a race of mystical sorcerers of great skill, whose druids could raise the dead and even conceal the entirety of their people in mist. With these skills, they wrest the island from the grasp of the clumsy and poorly equipped Fir Bolg ("bag men") in the first of two legendary battles at Magh Tuireadh. In the second great battle, they defeat the fearsome Fomorian giants and drive them into the sea. They do not fare as well with the next invaders, who call themselves the "Sons of Míl" and bring their own magic with them.

INTO THE MISTS

Historians gives the name *Milesians* to the "Sons of Míl," a semi-mythical invasion force of Spanish Celts. The Milesians were followers of the Gaulish (some say Scythian) leader Golam, known by his title Míl Espáine, the "soldier of Hispania." Míl's legend tells that he dreamed his descendants would someday rule Ireland, and he fights his way westward with an army, intending to take it by force. Míl is killed in battle before reaching the island, but his wife and sons carry on his quest.

The Tuatha Dé Danann are a powerful race, but the Milesians, with the aid of their powerful bard, Míl's son Amergin, eventually defeat them. The Milesians then settle on the land they call Éire, after the daughter of the Dagda and Brighid. The Milesians are the last of the invaders and the ancestors of the modern Irish.

After their loss at the hands of the Milesians, the Tuatha Dé Danann retreat fully into the Otherworld. Upon reaching a truce with the Milesians, they agree to divide the land between them, with the Milesians taking the visible world and the Dé Danann choosing the Otherworld, which is mysteriously located both to the west and under the earth. The Tuatha Dé Danann are led into the Sídhe-mounds by the Dagda and remain hidden from human view. They occasionally appear in the human world to aid in battles, engage in mischief, or entice mortals into their realm.

PEOPLE OF THE SÍDHE

Over time, the old religion faded away, but the Celtic sense of the Otherworld did not. Even long after Christianity flowed through every acre of Celtic land, the denizens of the Sídhe remained. In many cases they took on a sinister cast and were viewed with great superstition. Sometimes, they were called fey, after the Roman *fata,* or "fates," because to see a fairy was an omen of an impending death—a sign that the veil was thinning, and a journey to the Otherworld was imminent.

THE FAIRY QUEEN

Playwright William Shakespeare's Mab, Queen of the Fairies, is likely none other than Medb, the Danann queen of the Ulster Cycle who contends with Fionn for possession of the brown bull of Cooley. Over time, most of the Irish gods became relegated to the Land of Faerie.

Once a divine race of warriors, the people of the Sídhe were now regarded as supernatural, tricksy folk who often worked mischief on mortals, which ranged from pranks like souring the milk of cows to stealing children or causing disease. They were superstitiously referred to as the "fair folk" or "good people," in hopes that such an utterance of respect would deflect mischief.

NUADA OF THE SILVER HAND

Nuada was the first king of the Tuatha Dé Danann, who brought his tribe to Ireland and contended with its inhabitants for possession of the island. (Other versions of the legend say he was the son of the Dagda.) At the first battle at Magh Tuireadh, Nuada's warriors clash with the Fir

Bolg. The battle is carried out as a series of single combats, one warrior against another, until Nuada is matched with a Fir Bolg champion,
Streng. Nuada fights fiercely, but he suffers a great loss—the enemy warrior slices off his left hand at the wrist. Even so, the Fir Bolg are eventually driven back, and they retreat to the western province of Connacht.

Because sacred law decrees that a king of the Dé Danann must be whole
in body and mind, the maimed Nuada is forced to step down as ruler of the
gods. A council is convened, and a new king is appointed by vote, a half-
Fomorian named Bres the Beautiful. Bres, despite his dashing figure, proves
a very unpopular king. He identifies with his Fomorian side and treats the
Dé Dananns terribly, levying large taxes and forgoing the usual hospitality
and entertainments a king is expected to provide. A solution is sought, and
finally, the Danann physician Dian Cecht uses his healing skill to fashion
for Nuada a fantastic silver hand, which functions as well as a human hand.
Restored to wholeness, Nuada seeks to regain his position.

Bres, however, is having none of it. He enjoys being king and naturally refuses to step aside. All seems hopeless until a bard, Cairpre, seeks
the hospitality of Bres's court and, like so many before him, is refused.
The offended Cairpre composes the first bardic satire of legend, a scath-
ing indictment of Bres's stinginess:

> No meat on the plates;
> No milk of the cows;
> No shelter after sunset;
> No money for minstrels:
> May Bres's cheer be what he gives others!

The poem embarrasses Bres so greatly that his face breaks out in
gigantic boils, a disfiguration great enough to force Bres to abdicate the
throne according to the ancient rules. In short order, Nuada is once
again king of the Tuatha Dé Danann.

The dethroned Bres has no intention of going quietly. He complains of his humiliation to his Fomorian relatives, and the Tuatha Dé Danann soon face a wave of invaders. Unlike the rather conventional Fir Bolgs, the Fomorians are, like the Dé Dananns, a magical race, described as misshapen one-eyed giants who live under the waves.

LUGH THE LONG-ARMED

As the Dé Dananns prepare to meet the Fomorians on the battlefield at Magh Tuireadh, a stranger comes to the court, an arrogant man who dresses like a king and declares himself to be Lugh, a master of all arts. King Nuada invites the man to come to court and display his many skills. After witnessing Lugh's abilities as a warrior, a smith, a hunter, and a bard, Nuada is so impressed that he declares that Lugh should be king in his place, and that he should lead the warriors to battle against the Fomorians.

THE EYE OF BALOR

In Irish folk belief, the "eye of Balor" was the term given for a curse received from a baleful look, akin to the "evil eye" in Italy and Greece.

The second battle of Magh Tuireadh begins with the usual custom of single combat, with Fomorian champions paired against the best Dé Danann warriors. The Fomorian paired with Nuada is Lugh's own grandfather, the giant one-eyed Balor, whose gaze is fatal to all it falls upon. Nuada cannot escape Balor's glare and is killed, but Lugh possesses a magical spear that never fails to hit its target. He kills his grandfather with one blow to his terrible eye. The eye is pushed clear through the giant's head, killing the Fomorian forces arrayed behind him.

As the Fomorians are driven back, Lugh pursues Bres and corners him. The deposed leader begs for his life, offering in return any secret Lugh wishes to possess. Lugh agrees to the terms and asks Bres to tell him the correct days for plowing, sowing, and reaping crops. Bres obliges, and the Tuatha Dé Danann become masters of agriculture.

THE FOUR HALLOWS

The Tuatha Dé Danann were possessed of four magical talismanic weapons, or hallows, which are probably the most famous mystical objects of all time. Although many other magical items occur in Celtic legends, these four receive the most attention and notoriety.

All four symbols were of obvious importance to the Celts, and long before they appeared in literature, they were depicted on a variety of ritual artifacts. Although later mythological accounts of the sacred weapons appear on the surface to be little more than imaginative tales, they hint at much deeper meanings.

These are the four hallows:

1. The Sword of Light, attributed to the god Nuada, which could not be escaped
2. The Invincible Spear, attributed to the sun god Lugh, which never missed
3. The Cauldron of Bounty, belonging to the Dagda, a source of endless sustenance
4. The Stone of Destiny, or Lia Fáil, which would cry out when walked over by a true king of Tara

Each of the four legendary weapons was said to have originated in a different city of the Otherworld, each ruled by one of the powerful druids who had taught the secrets of magick and poetry to the Tuatha Dé Danann. The four hallows are also obviously chosen because they are associated with the elements of the cosmos—air, fire, water, and earth.

THE SWORD OF LIGHT

The most famous account of the hallows is found in the Book of Invasions. The first of these was the magical sword of the Danann king Nuada, the Celtic god of divine justice and truth. The sword is called the Sword of Light or the Sword of Truth. Nuada's weapon was otherworldly, forged in the city of Findias in the land of Tir na Nog. Nuada's sword was irresistible. When pulled from its scabbard, no enemy could flee from it, and its blow was always fatal.

THE SWORD OF NUADA

The Sword of Nuada is the prototypical magical sword that inspired many literary magical swords, among them Arthur's Excalibur and Narsil from J.R.R. Tolkien's *Lord of the Rings*. A magical sword also makes its appearance in the Harry Potter novels: the sword of Godric Gryffindor, with which Harry slays the basilisk in *Harry Potter and the Chamber of Secrets*.

Swords were a very important part of Celtic culture, and, along with the spear, they were the ever-present symbol of the warrior class. The weapons of the warrior were not simply tools but deeply important spiritual symbols that stood for the ideal qualities of the warrior. The makers of weapons were highly regarded artisans, metalworkers whose skills were literally perceived as a gift of the gods. As a consequence, a sword was not simply an implement but an emblem of a higher spiritual truth, an emulation of the attributes of the gods.

SWORD OF ILLUMINATION

A sword is a slicing instrument, one that dissects, divides, and cuts away. Symbolically, Nuada's sword is a sword of illumination, and it can be viewed as an attribute of wisdom. It represents the quality of discernment, the ability to cut away the irrelevant and make judgments and correct divisions—to get to the heart of a matter. Thus, the sword symbolizes justice, truth, and the application of the law, concepts dear to the Celtic heart.

NUADA AND OSIRIS

The story of Nuada has a curious parallel to the story of the Egyptian god Osiris. Both are gods of the underworld and judges of the dead. Like Nuada, Osiris was maimed and restored, losing his left eye in battle with his brother Seth.

A clue to the meaning of the sword can be found in the story of Nuada, who loses his ability to rule when he loses his hand. The loss of the hand symbolizes imbalance, and without balance, a Celtic king cannot justly rule. With the creation of his silver hand, balance is restored, and Nuada is once again fit to rule. Clues to the cause of Nuada's imbalance are also given, as it is his left hand that is severed, and its replacement is a hand of silver. Both the left hand and silver are attributes of the moon, a symbol of femininity and intuition. The implication is that Nuada's martial male side has overcome his feminine, lunar side, and the new hand represents the restoration of the two forces to their proper balance.

Nuada's sword is the embodiment of justice, from which no one, not even a king or a god, can escape. Celtic mythology is filled with tales of divine justice catching up to those who thought they could avoid it; this tale illustrates that even a god needs balance.

THE INVINCIBLE SPEAR

The Spear of Lugh, also called the Spear of Victory or the Invincible Spear, has properties similar to the Sword of Nuada—when thrown, it unerringly hit its target. The spear was blazingly hot, and it became hotter the longer it was used. It was stored in a vat of water at night to keep it from catching fire and scorching the earth.

Lugh of the Long Arms (sometimes, "Long Hands" or even "Artful Hands") was the Celtic sun god, who predates even the Tuatha Dé Danann. The name *Lugh* means "light" or "bright," and both the spear and the epithet "long armed" are symbolic, representing the penetrating qualities of sunlight.

BALOR

The Spear of Lugh makes its appearance in the myth cycle at the second battle of Magh Tuireadh, when Lugh uses it to pierce the eye of the giant Balor and prevents his magic from wiping out the Dé Dananns. Lugh and Balor in this story could be seen as two opposite aspects of the sun. Lugh is the beneficial solar energy, the source of fertility, nourishment, and illumination. Balor, on the other side, represents the harmful solar aspect as the scorching glare that withers crops, dries up lakes and streams, and causes drought and famine. Lugh's precise aim, which destroys Balor's withering gaze, is the application of knowledge. Another clue comes from the traditional ending of the story—it is the knowledge of planting and sowing that harnesses the sun's energy for human benefit, so radiant Lugh with his spear replaces the death-dealing giant.

THE CAULDRON OF REBIRTH

Cauldrons figure heavily in Celtic art, ritual, and mythology. Cauldrons were an ever-present ritual item in Celtic religious practices. Many beautifully worked examples have been found intentionally deposited in the bottoms of lakes, springs, and wells as offerings to the gods of water.

In Celtic daily life, the cauldron was the most important item a household possessed. It was used for cooking and brewing, for dyeing, and working leather. The cauldron's usual place was in the center of the home, and so it was associated with the axis mundi, a symbolic representation of the center of the cosmos. The cauldron itself was a microcosm of water, a miniature representation of the abundant well at the base of the world tree.

Cauldrons were also an essential accoutrement of the druid, and there is much evidence of their ritual use in temples, where the cauldron would have been used for divinatory purposes, for collecting the blood of a sacrifice, or for holding sacramental meals.

THE DAGDA'S CAULDRON OF PLENTY

The Cauldron of Bounty belonged to the Dagda, or "Good God." The Dagda was the son of the goddess Danu, one of the eldest of the Dé Danann. The Dagda was a god of excess and abundance, and also of music and inspiration. He was especially associated with the craft of the bards and is often depicted in statuary with a harp in his hands.

According to the later legends of Dagda's Cauldron of Plenty, it contained an endless supply of sustenance and could never be emptied. Symbolically, it is the sea, with its endless supply of fish, water for the rains, and the source of healing springs and pools. The cauldron is also related to the cornucopia, a traditional mythic symbol of plenty.

REBIRTH AND REGENERATION

Many stories revolve around the Cauldron of Rebirth, which is another form of the Dagda's cauldron. In innumerable mythological stories, the cauldron is used to resurrect warriors slain on the battlefield. (We noted one of these stories earlier in the second branch of the Mabinogi.) Indeed, many early examples of Celtic ritual art depict warriors patiently standing in line as the god dips them, one by one, into the cauldron.

REBIRTH AND BAPTISM

The importance to druid ritual of immersion in cauldrons may be one of the reasons the Celts readily accepted Christianity. Resurrected gods and rebirth by watery immersion were already an integral part of Celtic spirituality when Christian missionaries arrived in Ireland with their own ideas about baptism.

In this aspect, the cauldron is closely related to Celtic ideas of the afterlife and rebirth. The gods of water were themselves continuously reborn, and the waters of the cauldron have obvious parallels to the watery environment of the womb, the passageway to new life.

In the story of the cauldron of Bran, related earlier, in which slain fighters are placed during a battle, the warriors emerge overnight from the cauldron unharmed, save for the loss of their powers of speech. This is a probable reference to the reborn soul as an infant incapable of speaking.

The womb analogy carries over in the role of the cauldron as a source of inspiration. Artistic and poetic inspiration arose from the depths of water, and the bards and poets attributed their ideas to the guardian of the waters.

THE STONE OF DESTINY

The Stone of Destiny, or Lia Fáil, is the most famous of the four hallows and the only one believed to exist outside the Otherworld. The stone was for untold years used in the inaugurations of Irish kings at the hill of Tara, the legendary seat of the kings of the Tuatha Dé Danann. According to one Irish legend, the Lia Fáil was "borrowed" by the Scottish king Fergus and never returned. The stone was moved to England in 1300 and resided for many years in Westminster, where it has been an integral part of the coronation of British kings and queens. It is now called the "Stone of Scone" after its one-time home in the Scottish city of Scone. On the other hand, a standing stone on top of the Hill of Tara in County Meath in Ireland is also often identified with the Lia Fáil.

The stone was stolen in 1950 by a group of young Scottish nationalists and transported to Edinburgh and then to Arbroath. After police located it, it was returned to Westminster, but in 1996, as a concession to growing nationalist feelings in Scotland, the British government agreed the stone should be kept in Scotland. Today, along with the Scottish crown jewels, it is on display at Edinburgh Castle.

Stones were long associated with the Tuatha Dé Danann, who the Celts believed were responsible for the multitude of stone monuments scattered about Europe. The Celts also believed these monuments to be the doorways the Tuatha Dé Danann used to travel to and from the Otherworld. The Celts themselves used stones for altars and as markers of boundaries, roads, and areas sacred to the gods. In the story related in the Book of Invasions, the Stone of Destiny served a singular oracular purpose, which was to identify a destined king of Tara. Before the election of a king, the candidates would step on the stone, which let out a great cry when the true, destined king set his foot upon it.

JACOB'S PILLOW

A Christian version of the stone's history posits that the Lia Fáil was once the pillow of the Old Testament patriarch Jacob, who laid his head on it before dreaming of a stairway to heaven. Joseph of Arimathea, a follower of Jesus, was believed to have sailed to Ireland using the stone as a boat.

STONES AND SOVEREIGNTY

The Stone of Destiny is not the only one that could identify kings. Arthur, the legendary High King of Britain, learns of his destiny when he pulls a sword from a stone. The Arthurian stone is, of course, an echo of the ancient Celtic ritual of kingship.

Symbolically, the stone represents the earth, and its significance harks back to the ancient tradition of Celtic kings, whereby a ruler was not vested in his power until he had performed a symbolic marriage with the goddess of the earth. This ritual ensured the fertility of the land and the prosperity of his people.

KING STONES

The legends of kingmaking stones have some origin in actual practice; several outside observers of Celtic culture noted the druids' use of stones as sacrificial altars and divinatory tools. Rites of kingship among the Celtic tribes often involved sacrifice and divinatory rites. In one account, a horse, the animal sacred to the goddess, was slaughtered on a stone altar. Wrapped in the horse's skin, the diviner then spent the night on the stone altar in order that the identity of the new king might come to him in his dreams.

CHAPTER SEVEN

The Druids

D ruids held a high place in Celtic society. While Celtic kings held secular power, druids ruled all functions of religious life, acting as priests, judges, and seers. The druids were the repository of sacred lore and the intermediaries between the gods and man. Besides presiding over religious ceremonies and sacrifices, the druids were the guardians of genealogies, complex legal codes, healing lore, and mythology. The druids also acted as astronomers, keeping the calendars by which the timing of festivals and auspicious days were determined. Upon the death of a king, druid seers conducted ritual divination to determine the next ruler.

WHO WERE THE DRUIDS?

The exact origin of the druid class is unknown, although, at least in some form, they likely preexisted the Celts in Europe. The Irish historical record isn't very clear on the matter. Every tribe of people that figures in it are said to have had their own druids, from the Fir Bolgs to the Gallic Milesians; even the mythical northern homeland of the Tuatha Dé Danann was reputedly ruled by powerful druids. In reality, the druids are probably in some way descended from the Neolithic tribal shaman-priests.

Adding to the aura of mystery around the ancient druids was the Celts' seeming abhorrence of the written word. The Celts were neither ignorant or unlearned, prizing wisdom and learning above all things. While writing was eventually used for lesser purposes such as marking roads or keeping monetary records or contracts, Celtic history, law, and religion were instead preserved through an elaborate system of memorization and oral transmission. The priestly classes charged with the keeping of this great body of knowledge and lore were the druids, who commanded tremendous respect among the Celts and constituted a societal class equal in stature to the nobility. The druid ability to mediate between worlds afforded them a great deal of secular power as well; having the ear of the gods gave them influence over nearly every aspect of Celtic society.

DRUIDS THROUGH FOREIGN EYES

Most of what is known about the Gallic druids is drawn from the writings of Roman and Greek observers, most notably from the pen of Julius Caesar, who gave a detailed (if flawed) account of Celtic culture in his history of the Roman incursion on Celtic territory. Other important biographies of the druids come from the Roman author Pliny the Elder and Greek historians Diodorus Siculus and Strabo. While the Roman account tends to be hostile, the Greek writers tended to be more sympathetic to the druids, praising them for their wisdom and intellect. Diodorus praised their preference for austere living conditions, and Strabo referred to druids as "the most just of men."

While all of these are valuable sources, Caesar created the best record of the druids, outlining their rank in society, their inner hierarchies, their methods of training, and the manner of their rituals and sacrifice. Although Caesar regarded the Celts as barbarians, he too affords the druids some admiration for their intellectual pursuits, even if he recounts with horror their sacrificial practices. It is of course important to remember that Caesar is writing about a culture he has been at war with, and that he never personally witnessed any of the events he describes.

BECOMING A DRUID

The ranks of druidry were not closed. Any who managed to complete the rigorous training required could become a druid and thus a privileged member of society, exempt from paying taxes or going to war.

The druids also undertook the role of educators, and druid schools enjoyed a fine reputation. Classical writers often praised druid schools, where sons of the noble classes were taught alongside aspiring druids.

Caesar notes that the druids were heavily organized, with a chief "archdruid" above all the others. When the leader died, a successor was elected by committee. Each tribe had its own complement of druids, with some acting as advisers to the king while others might have held roles as physicians or musicians. Likewise, each sacred shrine or grove had its priests and attendants. Again according to Caesar, the druids held annual meetings in the "land of the Carnutes," a tribe that lived near what is now Chartres, France.

IMMORTALITY

Druid theology centered on the doctrine of metempsychosis, the transmigration of souls. Unlike many other reincarnation doctrines, the druids did not appear to believe there was any hierarchy of souls. Rather, one could move from man to animal and vice versa, in an endless cycle of rebirth. One could be a king, a peasant, a warrior, or even, it appears, an animal or bird.

The Roman poet Lucan, in a diatribe against the druids, remarked sourly:

> It is you [druids] who say that the shades of the dead seek not the silent land of Erebus and the pale halls of Pluto; rather, you tell us that the same spirit has a body again elsewhere, and that death, if what you sing is true, is but the midpoint of a long life.

Caesar surmises, with some disgust, that the druid doctrine of reincarnation was largely responsible for the fearlessness of the Celtic warriors. The Celts' general attitude of "eat, drink, and be merry" may also be attributed to this easygoing attitude toward death.

THE KEEPERS OF WISDOM

As noted earlier, the origin of the word *druid* is thought by many to be a combination of two roots, *dru*, meaning "oak," and *vid*, meaning "knowledge" or "knower." Other Celtic scholars reject this definition. *Dru*, they argue, more properly translates as "firm" or "solid," and relates to concepts of truth and steadfastness, while *vid* or *weid* means "to see." The word *druid* therefore denotes one who sees well or truly: a seer or prophet.

TRAINING A DRUID
Becoming a druid was a huge undertaking; some observers claimed the process took up to twenty years of intense study and memorization.

The number of years of training one underwent to join the ranks of the druids varies from one early historian's accounts to the next. However, most agree it was somewhere between twelve and twenty years.

THE DRUID CLASS

Druid was both an institution and a title. The druids, along with the bards and the filidh, together made up the druid class. The Gallic druids held to a similar categorization of druid, bard, and vate, with the latter holding a position equivalent to the later Irish filidh.

The early chroniclers of the druids generally agree that the druidic class was divided into three categories: druids, vates, and bards. The Irish referred to these as drui, faithi or filidh, and baird. These three groups had overlapping responsibilities. The druids were priests, magicians, and adjudicators who shared the role of seer with the filidh. The vates were diviners and poets who specialized in magical singing and satire. The bards were poets also charged with the much larger responsibility of keeping the records of the tribe. Within these three divisions were further specializations, encompassing numerous types of song and poetry, musical instruments, and so on.

THE DRUID CLASS

Priests were by far the most powerful members of the druid class and the highest in rank. They oversaw the annual festivals of the gods and presided over the sacrificial ceremonies that were the main rite of worship in Celtic society. As keepers of the sacred calendar, priests were also charged with determining auspicious days for planting and harvesting, for going to war, and for the coronation of kings.

In addition to their religious duties, the druids were the chief administrators of the Celtic legal system. They were called upon to arbitrate all kinds of disputes, presiding over civil matters such as boundary disputes or the division of estates, as well as negotiating treaties and agreements between groups, tribes, and even kings. Their intense training gave them immense authority in legal matters, and they were always on hand to advise their rulers on matters of law. They also acted as ambassadors, often traveling great distances to enact treaties and trade agreements among tribes.

THE GEAS

One of the powers the druids had over kings was the geas, or sacred taboo. We have already seen some of these in action. The geas was a magical obligation or injunction that the recipient was bound to honor. Failure to honor a geas could bring dishonor, misfortune, or death.

WISE JUDGES

The Celtic legal system over which the druids presided was complicated, arranged around an intricate system of balances. Punishments for crimes varied according to the severity of the offense, the relationship between the parties involved, and the class of both the offender and the victim. Both civil and criminal offenses usually involved fines, which were paid either by the offender or his kin.

Druids were also responsible for deciding the fate of criminals and for carrying out whatever punishment the gods decreed. Some crimes carried the penalty of death, and executions were carried out as an offering to the gods. The discovered remains of such killings show various methods of execution, all highly ritualistic.

DRUID SPECIALTIES

There were many further divisions of responsibility among the druids of the priestly class. These included the *gutuater*, or "father of voice," the chief ceremonial chanter who gave the invocation of the gods in ritual, and the *cainte* ("chanter") who was a master of religious chants. The *liaig* ("leech") acted as physician and was trained in surgery and the use of healing plants and medicines. The *deogbaire* ("cup bearer") was a sort of wine-steward who was also trained in the use of psychotropic drugs.

FILIDH: SEERS AND POETS

A special class among the Continental druids was the filidh, the poet-seers, who also acted as composers, counselors, diviners, and healers. Where the druids functioned as high priests and judges, the filidh were more accessible to the people.

THE FILIDH'S LEGACY

The filidh kept their high status in Celtic society, even as their ancient religion faded away. The filidh continued to command respect after Christianity was firmly established in Ireland, even into the Renaissance.

There is also evidence of further specialties within the ranks of the filidh. In addition to their duties as repositories of sacred songs and stories, they composed, divined the future, and even entertained with riddles and political satire.

A fili made his (or her—female filidh were not unheard of) living composing heroic songs or satires or performing divination for his patrons; patrons who neglected to pay might even be satirized themselves. The satire of the filidh was not looked upon as simple social commentary—it was potent magic that could cause all sorts of misfortune for the recipient of the fili's withering songs.

According to ancient sources, divination was one of the most important roles of a druid. They give many examples of divination styles, especially augury, interpreting the flight of birds or the movement of animals. Some writers also mention a form of divination involving reading omens into the entrails of freshly sacrificed animal—and, occasionally, human—victims.

BARDS: THE WISDOM KEEPERS

To the Celt, words were potent magic, and no words were more potent than those of the bard. The duty of the bard was also that of a poet, but the bard's specialty was the heroic eulogy. One of the ways a Celtic warrior achieved immortality was through valorous acts on the battlefield. Without the bard to memorialize his heroism, the warrior would be forgotten by his people.

In later times, the lines between bard and fili became somewhat blurred, and the terms were sometimes used almost interchangeably.

Another specialty of the bard was genealogy, the history of the people of his tribe and their deeds. As such, the bard was the guardian of his tribe's identity. Without their bard, the people would have no sense of who they were or where they had been.

The training of a bard was lengthy and required the memorization of a vast amount of material. In addition to memorizing hundreds of songs, bards learned complicated genealogies, ancestral stories, and histories by heart.

FEMALE DRUIDS

There are numerous written references to female druids, who appear to have filled a variety of roles in Celtic religious life. There are many mentions of *ban-drui* ("female druid") and *ban-fili* ("woman-poet") in the historical records, and Celtic myth stories are of course filled with references to female magicians, seers, and wise-women. The great hero Cuchulainn is trained by Scáthach ("shadowy"), a legendary warrior in her own right who teaches Cuchulainn his legendary battle-leap and, in her capacity as seer, predicts his eventual misfortune.

BOUDICCA

Women with political power were often described as priestesses of religion. One of the most famous of the purported female druids is Queen Boudicca, who was a priestess of the war goddess Andraste. Records of her victories include the brutal sacrifice of hundreds of female Roman captives. At the same time, Boudicca is often cited as an early British hero, and a statue of her was erected in the nineteenth century near the Houses of Parliament in London.

The Roman historian Tacitus makes note of female druids attending meetings at the druid sanctuary at Mona, where they reportedly encouraged the Britons to rebel against the Roman armies.

Another Roman story claims that the ascent of the emperor Diocletian was predicted by a druid seeress. It seems the young emperor, while still a soldier in the Roman army, was quite rude to his druid hostess, failing to pay adequately for food and board. She upbraided him for his stinginess, to which he joked that he would be more liberal with his money when he was emperor. At this, the druidess drew herself up and warned Diocletian not to make jokes, for he would indeed be emperor, after slaying "the boar." True to her prediction, Diocletian did rise to throne after slaying the Roman prefect Arius, whose surname was Aper, meaning *boar.*

Tacitus also gives an account of the Veleda, a powerful oracle of the Germanic Bructeri tribe, who ruled over a large portion of Germany and was considered semi-divine. The Veleda was involved in political negotiations and was known to have successfully arbitrated several conflicts between tribes. She was eventually captured by the Romans around the year C.E. 77 for her involvement in rebellion against the Empire.

SACRIFICE

The druid religion was closely tied to the natural world, which was the domain of both humans and the gods. All of nature not only flowed from the gods, but made up their substance as well. The creatures and growing things of the earth had communion with the gods; they functioned as messengers between man and the Otherworld, even embodying the gods themselves. Animals provided meat, milk, and clothing; the trees of the forest offered shelter and nourishment; and plants provided not only food but medicine for the healers—all gifts of the gods requiring gratitude and repayment.

The Celts thus had great respect for both animals and plants. That which was sustenance for the body was also the body of the gods and therefore deserving of propitiation and respect. Sacrifice in return for what was received kept the cycle of life continuous, and ensured fertility and abundance.

THANKS TO THE GODS

Because the Celts viewed animals and plants as the embodiment of the gods, they sought to maintain balance between the worlds. As the living creatures gave of their substance for the nourishment of the people, the people gave of theirs for the sustenance of the gods. Sacrifice was an integral part of the spiritual lives of the Celtic tribes. Gifts of weaponry and art, trophies of war, even the blood of animals and humans were given in return for what the gods gave. As in many other early cultures, the form of these sacrifices could appear quite brutal. The Celts may have felt close connections to the earth, but they were hardly sentimental.

SACRIFICES

Caesar remarks on the practice of sacrifice, "[W]hen they have determined on a decisive battle, they dedicate as a rule whatever spoil they may take. After a victory they sacrifice such living things as they have taken, and all the other effects they gather into one place."

Offerings of wealth were also common. Large deposits of unused, high-quality weapons, adornments, and implements have been discovered buried deep in earthen shafts, in peat bogs, and in sacred wells and waterways. The spoils of war also belonged to the gods—captured weapons, treasures, and even livestock were offered en masse as sacrifice for a victory.

HUMAN SACRIFICE

The issue of human sacrifice is the dark shadow that haunts the legacy of the druids. Many outsiders' accounts of druid ritual describe the brutal, bloody sacrifice of criminals and prisoners of war, and bodies of many apparent victims have been uncovered preserved in peat bogs and earthen shafts.

Historical accounts of human sacrifice among the Celts are not unbiased, and they tend to be secondhand accounts filled with exaggeration. Most accounts of druid sacrificial custom come from the pens of Roman chroniclers who made little attempt to conceal their contempt for their subjects.

The Romans made much of what they deemed druidic savagery, but the customs they deride are not so different from Roman treatment of criminals, and they are probably far less brutal than the customs of the gladiatorial arena, for example, or the feeding of Christians to lions.

In any case, it is well known that to the Celts, matters of justice were paramount. As the gods were the source of the legal system, it naturally follows that the dispensation of criminals would be a matter of religion as well. Druid law was based on the Celts' deeply held belief in the balance of forces and the necessity of maintaining that balance. Where breaches of the sacred law created imbalance in the natural order, punishment restored that balance. It is also important to keep in mind the religious beliefs of the Celts that death was not the end of life, but was, in fact, a birth into the next world.

A criminal was likely sacrificed to the god he had offended, in repayment for what was upset. Adding to this view is archaeological evidence that the method of sacrifice varied according to the deity receiving the sacrifice. Those sacrificed to Esus (called "Lord," a deity who was similar in many ways to the Norse Odin) were reportedly strangled or hung from trees; those sacrificed to Teutates (a god of war and healing comparable to the Norse Tyr or the Roman Mars), were drowned in a cauldron or body of water, a ritual closely linked with regeneration in mythical tales of war.

Some remains of sacrificial victims of the druids show signs of highly ritualized death, wherein the victim is killed three ways—usually by blows, strangulation, and drowning. One such victim is called the Lindow Man, a mummified Celt uncovered in the remains of an English peat bog in 1984. Lindow Man's perfectly preserved body shows every sign of ritual execution— he had been struck, his throat was cut, and he had been strangled.

VOLUNTARY SACRIFICE?

One theory of druidic sacrifice claims that in addition to convicted criminals and prisoners of war, some sacrifices consisted of special emissaries to the Otherworld. These would be members of the priestly class, either volunteers or victims chosen by a special lottery. Some researchers have speculated that the victim would not be an offering per se, but a messenger who was chosen to communicate directly with the gods of the Otherworld.

One such sacrifice has been deduced from circumstantial evidence uncovered from the bodies of victims such as the Lindow Man, and related customs still practiced in rural Celtic communities. The evidence suggests the use of a lottery system, whereby a bannock cake (a cake of wheat, barley, oats, and hazelnuts) would be deliberately scorched in one corner, and then broken into bits and passed blindly among the candidates. The recipient of the burned portion would be ritually dispatched to the Otherworld. Forensic testing of the contents of Lindow Man's stomach contents—burned bannock and mistletoe pollen—bear out these theories. Because Lindow Man died during the time of the Roman invasion, some speculate he may have been chosen as a special emissary to the gods, in a desperate attempt to stave off destruction.

THE DECLINE OF THE DRUIDS

From about the first century, under heavy Roman influence, the institution of druidry began to fade away, and with the establishment of European Christianity, it disappeared almost entirely. The influence of religion, however, was not responsible for this decline, which instead was largely an issue of language, law, and, ironically, religious tolerance.

What contributed the most to the druids' disappearance was language. Romans were generally religiously neutral. They were not terribly interested in eradicating Celtic religion, except where druid power influenced uprisings and disturbed their carefully planned social order. Further, the Romans identified the Celtic gods as simply foreign versions of their own deities. They encouraged syncretism between the pantheons, which of course benefited the Roman rulers more than the druids.

The Celts under Roman rule were Roman citizens, and they were encouraged (sometimes by force) to make use of the Roman legal system, whose operative language was, of course, Latin. Latin eventually supplanted the Gallic languages, which the druid oral tradition relied on. Druid schools crumbled, and the hierarchical structure of druidry failed. What remained of druidry was pushed into Ireland and Scotland, outside the reaches of the Roman Empire.

THE DRUIDS AND THE CHRISTIANS

With the coming of the Christians, the use of Latin became a matter of religion as well. The old languages were relegated to the pagans and derided as the tongue of uneducated peasants, and so whatever remained of the druidic intellectual structure declined rapidly.

There are still reports of druids operating all the way into the twelfth century. But because the ancient institutional structures were gone, the initiatory teachings of druidry passed from one individual to the next. Eventually, druids were viewed as little more than solitary healers, wizards, or even common fortune-tellers.

The Christians in Ireland were of a different sort than those who had earlier conquered other parts of Europe. They were primarily scholarly monks. Although they were largely disdainful of the pagan religions, they retained enough respect for the institution of druidry that many elements of Celtic theology became intertwined with Celtic Christianity.

TRANSITION

In their histories, the Christian monks painted an often-contradictory view of druidry. Druids portrayed in the monk's accounts of Ireland's ancient heroic past are stern, powerful, and dignified. Many are even portrayed as wise prophets, foretelling the coming of Christianity to the island. Later, reflecting real-life political power struggles, druids were depicted more as devious wizards or scheming, superstitious pagans. This strange dichotomy persisted into medieval times—Irish ancestral pride perhaps at odds with proper Christian sentiment.

PREDICTING ST. PATRICK

Lochru and Lucat-Mael, the druids of the court of King Lóegaire, made a dark prediction that a "shaven-headed foreigner" would appear and seduce the people and that this stranger's new doctrine would forever supplant the religion of the druids. This stranger of course was St. Patrick.

Not everything was peaceful, however. The conversion of the Celts, whose spirituality already gave them a unique understanding of Christian ideas of trinities, baptisms, prophets, and resurrected gods, were not too resistant to the new faith. Many of Ireland's druids, on the other hand, faced a loss of power, prestige, and property under the new regime, and conflicts between local druids and Rome's bishops were inevitable. This was not helped any by the animosity that St. Patrick exhibited toward the druids.

CHAPTER EIGHT

Celtic Storytellers

Of all the classes of druidry, singers and poets had the greatest longevity. While by most accounts the earlier continental druids
divided themselves into priests, musician-poets, and seers, the latter two
became somewhat interchangeable to the Brythonic Celts. The bards
and the filidh took on overlapping functions and in later times were
almost interchangeable. As Christianity came to prominence, the bards
even absorbed many of the remaining functions of the druids. Ironically,
the last refuge of the Celtic bards was in the monasteries of Britain and
Ireland.

MUSIC AND MAGIC

By the time Christianity was firmly established in the British Isles, the druid priesthood had been largely forced out. Many of the duties they had previously fulfilled were absorbed by the filidh, high-ranking bards who functioned as singers, poets, satirists, and diviners. In a time when entertainments were few, the fili was in high demand, despite his pagan origins.

DIVINE SEEING

The name *fili* comes from a root meaning "to see," an apt description of the function of the fili, whose "sight" ranged from divinatory seership to the sharp insights he relied on to write effective poetry and satires.

A fili was not a poet or singer in the sense of a modern-day entertainer. While filidh of lesser rank and reputation may have been relegated to such pursuits, the compositions of the higher ranks of the filidh were infused with magical potency. A patron for whom a song of praise was written was magnified in reputation and fortune. On the other hand, one who had been satirized faced more than embarrassment; in fact, the satire of a fili could be dangerous to one's fortunes. Needless to say, it was not considered prudent to anger or insult a poet, and the filidh enjoyed the best hospitality and accommodations wherever they went.

The filidh were highly trained poets and musicians, learned in literature, writing, meter, and composition. Poets of lower rank were referred to simply as "bard," but they received no training. These lesser poets were expected to rely on their inborn talents alone.

Celtic law divided the filidh into a hierarchy of seven ranks, each with its own honor price and allotted retinue. The highest rank among the filidh was ollam dana, or "highest of art," whose honor price was equal that of a king. The lowest-ranking fili was the fochloc, with a retinue of two. Many of the filidh were eventually absorbed into the ranks of ecclesiastical scholars, and in later times, some of the best-regarded bards were Christian monks. The remainder continued in much the same vein as before, only now as secular poets and petty magicians who functioned outside any religious context.

These later "secular" filidh are sometimes derided as spin doctors of a sort. Without the ancient traditions and highly specialized training of the druids and their support systems, the filidh became reliant on the favor of the kings and nobles who patronized them, with the implication that the once-independent poets were beholden to the whims of the patrons who supported them.

SHINING BROW: TALIESIN

Of all of the bards of the Celts, none was as celebrated as Taliesin. Taliesin was by most accounts a genuine historical person about whom many myths and legends have sprung up. He is counted variously among the bards of King Arthur's court, in the company of the hero Bran, or in the court of Urien.

The historical Taliesin lived around the sixth century and was most likely a member of the court of Urien of Rheged. Little else is known of the true details of his life, except that he was of such reputation that he came to eventually be regarded as a semi-divine character of almost unlimited talent. By the twelfth century, he was a romantic figure of legend rivaling Merlin and even Arthur.

The name Taliesin means "shining brow," meaning *beautiful*. The common story of his birth explains that he received the name from his foster father, the prince Elphin, who discovered the child sealed in a leather bag in the bottom of a fish-weir.

An older tale of the events leading up to this discovery tells that the young man, the son of a bard named Henwg, was kidnapped and later abandoned by Irish pirates. The later, more romantic legend recounts Taliesin's birth as divine.

THE BIRTH OF TALIESIN

The mythological account of Taliesin's birth begins with a young farm boy named Gwion Bach, who was chosen by the goddess Cerridwen to tend to her cauldron of knowledge, in which she is preparing a draught of wisdom for her son, a hapless ugly boy called Avagddi. The potion was complex and had to be stirred for a year and a day. Its first three drops would confer priceless wisdom and insight, while the rest would be deadly poison.

Gwion was to stir the pot, while Cerridwen's blind servant Morda was to tend the fire beneath it. At first, Gwion tended to his business without incident, but one day, as Morda added wood to the fire, the cauldron bubbled up, overflowed, and then burst, sending three precious drops flying out to land on Gwion's hand. Gwion (like Fionn before him) unwittingly stuck his burned hand in his mouth and received wisdom and foresight, instantly becoming the wisest man in the world.

When Cerridwen returned and found that her precious gift of prophecy had been usurped by her young servant, she was furious and vowed to kill him. Gwion fled, with the goddess in pursuit. Gwion called on his newfound wisdom and transformed himself into a rabbit, but the goddess became a hound and stayed hot on his heels. Gwion then became a salmon and leaped into the river. Cerridwen became an otter and followed. Gwion became a wren, and the goddess pursued him in the form of a hawk. Finally, Gwion spied a farmstead, and concealed himself as a kernel of corn among many others. Undaunted, Cerridwen became a hen and gobbled up all of the corn, including Gwion.

Gwion had the last laugh, however, as the goddess soon found herself pregnant. She vowed to kill the child, but as she gave birth, she saw the child's great beauty and found herself unable to do the deed. Instead, she tied him up in a leather sack and disposed of him in the ocean, where he was eventually discovered by the son of Urien, king of Rheged.

THE SONG OF TALIESIN

In a portion of the famous Welsh poem attributed to Taliesin, the bard recounts his magical transformations in a manner very similar to Amergin's invocation of Ireland:

> A second time was I formed.
> I have been a blue salmon.
> I have been a dog; I have been a stag;
> I have been a roebuck on the mountain.
> I have been a stock, I have been a spade;
> I have been an axe in the hand;
> I have been a pin in a forceps,
> A year and a half;
> I have been a speckled white cock
> Upon hens in Eiddyn.
> I have been a stallion over a stud.
> I have been a violent bull,
> I have been a buck of yellow hue,
> As it is feeding.
> I have been a grain discovered,
> Which grew on a hill.
> He that reaped me placed me,
> Into a smoke-hole driving me.
> Exerting of the hand,
> In afflicting me,

> A hen received me,
> With ruddy claws, (and) parting comb.
> I rested nine nights.
> In her womb a child,
> I have been matured,   ·
> I have been an offering before the Guledig (Prince),
> I have been dead, I have been alive.

The earliest mention of Taliesin is in the poem "Spoils of Annwn," which refers to an (assumed) older legend, in which Taliesin is one of the few to survive an Otherworld quest for the cauldron of immortality. In the second tale (or branch) of *The Mabinogion*, Taliesin among one of seven survivors of a host who battled Matholwch, and it is he who returns the head of Bran to England.

MYSTICAL THREES

In Celtic mystical lore, no number was more sacred or magical than three. When Christianity arrived on Celtic shores, the Celts recognized the doctrine of the trinity to be their own, and so they embraced the new religion and made it their own. Even long after the triad gods of the pagan Celts had lapsed into myth/obscurity, the sacredness of threes remained.

Likewise, there were Three Illuminations, mysterious skills that were required to reach the highest ranks of the filidh: the *imbas forosnai*, or illuminating wisdom; the *tenm laida*, "cracking open the nuts of wisdom," and the *dichetal do chennaib*, "illumination by song." Both the imbas forosnai and tenm laida rituals were reportedly banned by St. Patrick as expressions of dark magic, although the dichetal do chennaib was tolerated as a scholarly exercise.

Other instances of the number three in bardic lore include these:

* The three cauldrons that give inspiration to the poet: warmth, wisdom, and knowledge
* The three enchanting powers of music: joy, sleep, and sorrow
* The three faces of the triple goddess Brighid, the patroness of poetry, fire, and water

THE CELTIC HARP

The clarsach, or Celtic harp, is the most beloved emblem of Ireland, chosen to represent the country as its national symbol. The iconic Irish harp, however, only dates to around the ninth century, when its image began to appear in Scottish stone carvings. Earlier Irish examples depict a squarish-shaped stringed instrument, probably a lyre adapted from the Greeks. Although the Celtic harp has become almost synonymous with the Irish bards, the harp itself did not become a common instrument in Ireland until around the fifteenth century.

THE DAGDA'S HARP
The Irish father god the Dagda, a patron of the Irish bards, possessed the magical harp Daurdabla, "oak of two greens." With the harp, the Dagda could play music that could move men to deep sorrow, profound joy, or prophecy. It was this magical ability to control emotion through music that the Irish bards attributed to their patron.

The harp is magically bound to the Dagda. One tale tells that it was stolen in the heat of battle by the Fomorians; he was able to retrieve it by singing to it its own name.

The Dagda's harp was also called Coir Cethair Chuir, which means "four-angled music," a name that reflects the belief that the Dagda used the harp to invoke the seasons. It has been theorized that the four angles may refer to the solar cross that is the basis for the Celtic calendar.

The harp's songs are referred to as the Three Noble Strains of Ireland, songs of enchantment from which none were immune. These are Goltrai, or the "Strain of Lament," which would invoke the deepest sorrow; Geantrai, the "Strain of Joy," which provoked merriment and foolishness; and Suantri, the "Strain of Sleep," which caused the hearer to fall into a deep, prophetic sleep. These songs are said to originate with the goddess Boann, the wife of the Dagda's harpist Uaithne and the sister of Aenghus, in connection with the birth of her three sons:

- ✣ Goltraiges, whose birth caused the goddess great pain
- ✣ Gentraiges, whose birth was joyful
- ✣ Suantres, whose birth consumed her with fatigue

Some combination of the three strains were believed to comprise the whole range of bardic music.

AMERGIN AND AMERGIN

The archetypal bard of the Irish, who was called Amergin Glungel, "White Knee," was also Amergin of the Milesians, the first Celtic tribe of Ireland. Amergin was the chief of eight sons of the Spanish ruler Míl Espáine (literally, "soldier of Spain"), by legend, the conquerors of the Tuatha Dé Danann. Amergin was a druid poet of supernatural ability and talent.

According to mythological accounts of the founding of Ireland, it was with the supernatural aid of Amergin and his power of song that the Milesians won Ireland from its divine inhabitants.

As the legend goes, an uncle of Míl, named Ith, sets out on a journey of exploration that brings him to Ireland. He is welcomed there by the three kings of Ireland, Mac Cuill, Mac Cecht, and Mac Gréine, who offer him hospitality and think him wise. After Ith has been in their company a time, they ask him to settle a dispute between them, about which nothing is related. Ith responds with a paean to Ireland's beauty and bounty, which for some reason infuriates his hosts. Ith is attacked and mortally wounded, but he manages to reach his ship and relate his misfortunes before he expires. His countrymen return to Spain with stories of the treachery of the Dé Danann kings and also of the bounty of their kingdom.

The eight sons of Míl gather their arms and, along with forty chieftains, set sail for Ireland. The Tuatha Dé Danann call up a magical mist with which to shroud the island, but after three days, the Milesians discover a patch of land. They meet with the wives of the three Irish kings, Banba, Éire, and Fótla, and battle them in succession. Each time they are victorious, and each queen in turn demands of Amergin that her name be given to the island after her. Amergin agrees and demands battle with the Dé Danann kings who have been concealing the island. The queens agree, and they nominate the wise Amergin as judge, to set the terms of battle between the two races.

The Dé Danann, of course, are supernatural beings, and they attempt to defeat the Milesians through trickery. They request that the Milesians retreat "beyond the ninth wave" while they prepare their defenses for battle, to which the sporting Amergin agrees. The Milesians return to their ships and sail away from the island. However, when they attempt to return, they are confounded by a magical storm raised up by the Tuatha Dé Danann's powerful druids. They are no match for Amergin, however, who calls upon the island itself:

I invoke the land of Ireland.
Much-coursed be the fertile sea,
Fertile be the fruit-strewn mountain,
Fruit-strewn be the showery wood,
Showery be the river of water-falls,
Of water-falls be the lake of deep pools,
Deep pooled be the hill-top well,
A well of the tribes be the assembly,
An assembly of the kings be Tara,
Tara be the hill of the tribes,
The tribes of the sons of Míl,
Of Míl be the ships the barks,
Let the lofty bark be Ireland,
Lofty Ireland darkly sung,
An incantation of great cunning;
The great cunning of the wives of Bres,
The wives of Bres of Buaigne;
The great lady Ireland,
Eremon hath conquered her,
Ir, Eber have invoked for her.
I invoke the land of Ireland.

At the conclusion of Amergin's song, the sea becomes as smooth as glass, and the Milesians are able to easily land their ships. Numerous battles follow, during which each of the Danann kings is bested in single combat by the three surviving sons of Míl. Amergin then divides the isle among his brothers, and each portion is named for one of the queens of the vanquished kings, as promised. Afterward, the remnant of the Tuatha Dé Danann was led underground by the Dagda, destined to become the fairy rulers of the Sídhe. They remained in Ireland, inhabiting the ancient tombs, and making occasional appearances to help or hinder the descendants of Míl as they saw fit.

Amergin's most famous song has become Ireland's most famous poem and invocation. The "Song of Amergin" is sung when his ships have landed and he first sets foot upon Ireland's shores:

> I am a wind on the sea
> I am a wave of the ocean
> I am the roar of the sea,
> I am a powerful ox,
> I am a hawk on a cliff,
> I am a dewdrop in the sunshine,
> I am a boar for valor,
> I am a salmon in pools,
> I am a lake in a plain,
> I am the strength of art,
> I am a spear with spoils that wages battle,
> I am a man that shapes fire for a head.
> Who clears the stone-place of the mountain?
> What the place in which the setting of the sun lies?
> Who has sought peace without fear seven times?
> Who names the waterfalls?
> Who brings his cattle from the house of Tethra?
> What person, what god
> Forms weapons in a fort?
> In a fort that nourishes satirists,
> Chants a petition, divides the Ogham letters,
> Separates a fleet, has sung praises?
> A wise satirist.
> He sang afterwards to increase fish in the creeks:
> Fishful sea—
> Fertile land—
> Burst of fish—
> Fish under wave—
> With courses of birds—
> Rough sea—
> A white wall—
> With hundreds of salmon—
> Broad whale—
> A port song—
> A burst of fish.

With his song, Amergin proves the Milesians worthy of occupying the land, and the magic of the Tuatha Dé Danann is lifted.

SUPERNATURAL CHILD: AMERGIN MAC ECCIT

Amergin of the Milesians was one of two poets who went by that name. The story of Amergin mac Eccit's childhood, as told in the Book of Leinster, is a typical Irish tale of the wise child. It tells that Amergin, the son of a smith, is born ugly and mute, never speaking even into puberty. He sits in rags and filth, eating table scraps and amusing himself with empty nut shells until one day a servant of the poet Athirne startles him, and he utters a spontaneous verse.

BARD-CRAFT AND SMITH-CRAFT

That Amergin mac Eccit is the son of a smith is telling. Both bard-craft and smith-craft were considered by the Irish to be magical arts, and both fell under the patronage of the fire goddess Brighid. Under her tutelage, the smith fashioned with metal and earthly fire, and the bard worked with words and Otherworld fire.

Word quickly spreads of the boy's gilded tongue, until the tale reaches the ears of Athirne. Athirne, fearing for his position as King Conchobar's bard, conspires to kill his young competitor. He is, however, tricked into assaulting an earthen copy of the boy instead, and afterward he is forced to compensate the smith. This he does by adopting the boy as his foster son and teaching him the poet's craft. Amergin mac Eccit goes on to become the chief bard of Ulster in Athirne's place.

The poems of the semi-legendary Welsh poet Taliesin have similarities to those attributed to Amergin.

THE FILIDH

At the decline of druidry, the filidh gradually began to take over from the druids, and absorbed many of their ritual functions, serving as poets, judges, magicians, and seers. With the coming of Christianity, many of the filidh were associated with monasteries, even though the poems they wrote often betrayed their druid roots. Although the relationship between the druids and the Christians was often antagonistic, the scholarly refuge of the monastery proved popular with the druid remnant. Likewise, the monasteries could scarcely refuse learned lawmakers, historians, and composers. While many of the religious trappings of the filidh were dispensed with, their orders of rank and social status remained strong until the Protestant Reformation, when many of their associated monasteries were destroyed. Ironically, association with pagan institutions added fuel to Protestant attacks on Catholicism.

THE WELL OF INSPIRATION

Welsh bards were called Cerddorion, "sons of Cerridwen," after their patron Taliesin, and those who were especially wise or gifted were said to have drunk from the cauldron of wisdom as he did.

To the ancient tribes of Europe, the cauldron, representing a microcosm of the sea and the sacred well, has long been a symbol of wisdom, inspiration, and immortality. The source of the bards' poetic inspiration was said to be a figurative well or cauldron, from which the gods dispensed poetry and insight to the deserving.

A seventh-century poem that has come to be called the "Cauldron of Poesy," attributed to Amergin Glungel, describes the creation of poetry as the product of three figurative cauldrons, which dwelled inside a man

and dispensed warmth, wisdom, and knowledge. The poem describes
the three qualities required to create poetry and alludes to the supernatural abilities of the accomplished poet:

> My perfect cauldron of warming
> has been taken by the gods from the mysterious abyss of the elements;
> a perfect truth that ennobles from the center of being,
> that pours forth a terrifying stream of speech.
> I am Amergin White-knee,
> with pale substance and grey hair,
> accomplishing my poetic incubation in proper forms,
> in diverse colors.
> The gods do not give the same wisdom to everyone,
> tipped, inverted, right-side-up;
> no knowledge, half-knowledge, full knowledge—
> for Eber Donn, the making of fearful poetry,
> of vast, mighty draughts death-spells, of great chanting;
> in active voice, in passive silence, in the neutral balance between,
> in rhythm and form and rhyme,
> in this way is spoken the path and function of my cauldrons.

The poem describes the three cauldrons as gifts of the gods, given to
every man in varying measure. It goes on in subsequent verses to explain
that for some, the cauldrons may only flow if stirred by "great sorrow
or great joy." In other words, some are born with wisdom, but it only
blossoms to greatness in the few whose experiences unleash the flow of
inspiration:

> The Cauldron of Incubation is born upright in a person from the
> beginning.
> It distributes wisdom to people in their youth.
> The Cauldron of Motion, however, after turning increases.
> That is to say it is born tipped on its side in a person.
> The Cauldron of Wisdom is born on its lips and it distributes wisdom
> in every art besides poetry.

WISDOM OF THE PALMS

Access to the well of inspiration was closely linked with seership; in fact, both prophecy and poetry were said to derive from the same source. The chief method for obtaining magical sight for Irish filidh was said to be a practice called *imbas forosnai*, "wisdom that illuminates," or more literally, "wisdom of the palms." The technique, one of three magical skills of the poet, was described somewhat scornfully in the tenth century by glossarist Cormac mac Cuilennan:

> Thus then is that done. The poet chews a piece of the red flesh of a pig, or a dog, or a cat, and puts it then on a flagstone behind the door-valve, and chants an incantation over it, and offers it to idol gods, and calls them to him, and leaves them not on the morrow, and then chants over his two palms, and calls again idol gods to him, that his sleep may not be disturbed. Then he puts his two palms on his two cheeks and sleeps. And men are watching him that he may not turn over and that no one may disturb him. And then it is revealed to him that for which he was engaged till the end of a nómad (three days and nights), or two or three for the long or the short that he may judge himself (to be) at the offering. And therefore it is called Imm-bas, to wit, a palm on this side and a palm on that around his head.

The symbolism Cormac describes gives every indication that the imbas ritual is descended from earlier druid rites of seership. Early accounts of druid divinations recall the use of trance-sleep in combination with sacrifice—for instance, when a new high king was to be decided, a complex divination ceremony would be enacted. This involved the sacrificial slaughter of a horse, sacred to the goddess Sovereignty, after which the chief seer would be sealed inside the skin of the sacrificed animal. In the darkness, he would fall into a trance, and in that trance-sleep, he would receive the word of the goddess's choice of spouse—the new high king.

CHAPTER NINE

The Heroes

To say that the hero is a central figure in Celtic mythology and culture is a great understatement. The gods of the Celtic pantheons are warriors, adventurers, and accomplished poets to a one—even the most sensitive poet was also a fearsome warrior. It was not simply bravery and fearlessness that was expected of the hero, but also learning, skill, cleverness, and loyalty. A lack of any of these qualities spelled the tragic downfall of many a great Celtic hero.

THE CULT OF THE HERO

Many outside observers remarked admiringly on the fearlessness of the Celts, a reputation that very often kept them safe from invasion. Even though it lacked a central government, Celtic society's cult of the hero provided the glue that held disparate tribes together, offering the Celts a common mythology.

Heroes of particular bravery and importance might become kings, and extraordinary heroes might even become gods. Heroes were very highly regarded as cult figures in Celtic society, praised in song and story, and were laid to rest in lavish tombs when they died. It has long been supposed that many, if not all, of the deities of the Celtic pantheons were heroic ancestors whose great deeds made them immortal in song and story. And even as the ascendancy of Christianity demoted the gods, the hero remained an important fixture in the Celtic imagination.

With the coming of Christianity came Christian heroes, whose deeds of bravery and magic for a time eclipsed in importance even the heroes of the Bible. Celtic warrior-kings were eventually eclipsed by the likes of Arthur, Gawain, and Peredur. Irish saints could perform feats of druidic magic, travel to the Otherworld and back, and were even credited with converting many of the ancient divine heroes to Christianity.

HERO TALES

The Celtic tradition of heroic stories is the direct ancestor of the so-called fairy tale. Although the popular stories have evolved over time to reside in the realm of make-believe, they are firmly rooted in Celtic spiritual traditions. Named for the fairy-folk who inspired them, they contain all of the elements associated with the genre.

CULHWCH AND OLWEN

Earlier we mentioned the story of Culhwch and Olwen, one of the great Celtic love tales, which forms part of the story collection *The Mabinogion*. Culhwch was by most accounts the son of Goleudydd, who was overcome with madness, causing her to wander the countryside over the course of her pregnancy. She recovered her sanity as her labor began in a pigsty, but without sufficient time to remedy the situation. And so the hero was born among the pigs, and named Culhwch, "son of pig." Culhwch's mother returned home but died shortly afterward.

Culhwch's father remarried a powerful woman who wished Culhwch to marry her own daughter. Culhwch refused, and his stepmother placed him under a curse, requiring that his future wife must be a girl named Olwen, the daughter of Yspaddadden, the dangerous chieftain of the race of giants. As far as love went, this was not a terrible curse, as Olwen's great beauty and demeanor were legendary, but her location was unknown and her father was a terrifying tyrant.

To locate his future spouse, Culhwch gathers together a band of skilled men, including Cei and Beddwyr, heroes who emerge later as transplants into tales of King Arthur (their names changed to Sir Kay and Sir Bedivere). The party wanders in search of Olwen, and they are unsuccessful until they reach the home of a shepherd whose wife admits to being Olwen's hairdresser.

Although terrified of the giant Yspaddadden, the woman reveals that she is related to Culhwch and will arrange for him to meet his future bride. When Olwen arrives for her usual appointment, the woman introduces her to Culhwch. Olwen is immediately charmed, but she warns Culhwch that she cannot marry him without her father's consent. She further warns him that he must accede to any condition whatsoever her father may set and that flinching from any request will be fatal.

Culhwch and his party immediately set out for the giant's property. Unbeknownst to Culhwch, Yspaddadden labors under a curse of his own—that should his daughter marry and beget children, the giant will die. When Culhwch and his party arrive at the giant's castle, the giant attacks them with poisoned stones, which Culhwch and his band are able to catch and return to the giant. After this cycle repeats for three days, the giant relents and admits Culhwch to his court. He agrees to the marriage of the hero and his daughter, but sets strict conditions on the marriage, which cannot succeed unless Culhwch completes three impossible tasks.

The first task laid upon Culhwch is to sow flax for Olwen's bridal veil. Culhwch is led to a barren field, which the giant informs him was sown when he first took Olwen's mother for a bride. The field has so far failed to sprout. Culhwch is ordered to retrieve nine bushels of flaxseed from the field, burn the field, till it, resow it, and harvest nine more bushels of flax—all to be accomplished in one day. The giant is certain that Culhwch cannot accomplish the task, but Culhwch remembers his betrothed's warning, and assures that he can easily accomplish the task.

THE HUNT OF TWRCH TRWYTH

The second task laid upon Culhwch by Yspaddadden is the accumulation of a great dowry, consisting of thirteen great treasures, including the magical sword by which the giant is destined to die. Culhwch affirms that these, too, will be easy to gather. The giant's final request is for a shave and a haircut, which can only be accomplished with a special razor, scissors, and comb, which conveniently reside between the ears of the great boar Twrch Trwyth, who, in parallel to the tales of Cuchulainn, can only be hunted with the aid of a magical hound that happens to belong to the long-disappeared Mabon ap Modron.

At this point in the cycle, King Arthur and his men inexplicably make an abrupt appearance to carry on the remainder of the tasks, although many of these tales have either vanished or been left to the imagination.

The flax is recovered by ants grateful to Arthur's companion Cei, who performs heroic deeds on their behalf. Arthur and his party locate and rescue the imprisoned Mabon, and the grateful demigod allows them the use of his magical hound.

The culmination of the story of Culhwch is in the hunt for Twrch Trwyth, the great boar. Like any proper boar in Celtic mythology, Twrch Trwyth is exceedingly large, powerful, and clever. Several attempts to acquire the barber tools through trickery are foiled. The magician Menw takes on the form of a bird and attempts to steal them but is nearly killed by the boar's poisonous barbs.

THE ORIGINS OF THE TALE

Although the first written versions of the tales of Culhwch date from the early medieval period, there is evidence that the basic elements of the story are drawn from much earlier mythology. In some areas, early stone carvings illustrate elements of the tale, including the great boar with his razor and comb. The recurrence of the sacred numbers three and nine also hint at the deeper meaning of the story.

Twrch Trwyth proves impossible to do away with. All of Culhwch and Arthur's forces are unsuccessful in killing even the piglets that accompany him. Arthur himself then battles the great boar for nine days without making any progress. At last, they attempt to negotiate with Twrch Trwyth, who informs them that his annoyance is now so great he intends to venture into Culhwch's lands and destroy them. The warriors follow him from one coast to another, and at last they manage to drive him into the sea, where they recover the scissors and accoutrements with the aid of Manannan mac Lir.

Quests fulfilled at last, Culhwch returns to Yspaddadden's castle, but instead of welcome, he is met with hostility. The foolish giant informs him that because his daughter's marriage spells his death, he will never allow her to marry. But Culhwch is now in possession of the sword that can kill the giant, and he promptly cuts off Yspaddadden's head.

FANTASTIC VOYAGES

An important genre of Celtic hero stories is the travel myth, the tale of a heroic voyage. This kind of tale is called an *imram* ("journey"), and these contain similar elements of Otherworld journeying, usually by sea. According to tradition, there are seven great imrams, but only three tales survive in their entirety. These are the Voyage of Mael Duin, the Voyage of St. Brendan, and the Voyage of Snedgus and Mac Ríagla.

MAEL DUIN

The saga of Mael Duin is the earliest known Celtic travel myth. Many later tales, such as "The Voyage of Brendan," are based on this legend.

Mael Duin was the son of a renowned warrior, Ailill Edge-of-Battle. His father was killed on the battlefield before Mael was born, and his mother became a nun. Mael was fostered with his sister's family, raised never knowing the truth of his origins.

When Mael grows to maturity, he discovers his true background and makes a pact to avenge his father's death. Not knowing where to begin, he consults a druid, who tells him his enemies can be found across the sea. But in order to reach them, Mael must accept a geas and take with him a crew of exactly seventeen men.

Mael prepares his ships and selects his crew of seventeen, yet as he prepares to set sail, his three foster brothers beg to come along. When Mael demurs, they attempt to swim after Mael's boat. Fearful they will drown themselves in their stubbornness, Mael at last relents and pulls his brothers on board.

After many days of vigorous rowing, Mael and his party encounter two small islands, their destination. However, when they prepare to disembark, a sudden storm blows up and tosses the boat far out to sea. Mael berates his foster brothers for their sudden misfortune, which must be due to their disregard for the druid's geas.

They continue to sail for days, even weeks, as the storm rages around them. Eventually, the winds recede, and the adventurers find themselves in the sea of the Otherworld, populated with many strange islands. These islands contain many strange and wonderful things, including an island filled with giant ants, another filled with giant horses, another by flaming pigs, and even one populated by phantom horsemen.

On one of the islands, Mael discovers an enchanted apple tree, from which he steals a branch containing three apples. These are the sort of Otherworld apples that can never be fully consumed, and they feed his crew for many days. Eventually, Mael and his crew encounter a walled island. The island contains a fabulous palace at its center, with many treasures on display. Oddly, it is deserted but for a great many cats that wander about. In the kitchen, Mael and his crew find an abundance of food and drink, of which they eat their fill.

As they prepare to return to their ship, one of Mael's brothers suggests they gather some of the treasure that is arrayed about the castle. Mael cautions against it, lest it anger the feline occupants of the palace. Mael's brother cannot resist entirely, however, and snatches a necklace as they depart. At this, the cats begin to glow like embers. They pursue Mael's brother, and when they catch him, they leap on him, and his body is reduced to ashes. Mael grieves, but he returns the stolen treasure and apologizes to the cats before departing once more.

Mael and his companions continue from isle to isle, seeing many more strange, wonderful, and frightening things. One island they encounter is populated with a great number of dark-skinned people, who sit along the beaches weeping terribly. When one of Mael's brothers leaps from the ship to inquire what they sorrow about, he is overcome with sadness and sits among them weeping inconsolably. When he refuses to return to the ship, the others continue without him.

Eventually, the crew encounters the island's counterpart, whose population is filled with immense joy and whose fields ring with laughter. Mael's remaining brother, in his grief, finds the isle irresistible and cannot be prevented from leaving the ship. At last unburdened of his extra passengers, Mael finds himself free to leave the Otherworld. A falcon appears in the sky and leads the sailors back to Ireland, to the small isles where Mael was first blown off course. There, Mael encounters the men responsible for his father's death. When he prepares to confront them, however, they greet him as a great hero on account of his journeys. At this, all of Mael's anger leaves him, and he no longer desires vengeance.

In the course of their island wanderings, it is said that Mael Duin and his companions encounter an island populated with Otherworld women who offer them eternal youth and happiness. Mael marries the island's queen, and he and his men are happy there for the span of a year. Eventually, they become homesick and wish to leave. As they row away from the island, the queen throws Mael a length of string, and when he catches it, she uses it to draw the boat back to shore. This cycle is repeated several times, until Mael's exasperated crew cuts off his hand to prevent a recurrence.

THE VOYAGE OF ST. BRENDAN

The legend of St. Brendan of Clonfert, otherwise known as Brendan the Navigator, represents the Christian entry into the imram tradition. Brendan was rumored to have been born in the late fifth century. He was a student of St. Brigid of Munster (an altogether different Brigid from the renowned goddess/saint) and went on to found a number of monasteries. While most historians agree that Brendan probably did conduct some sort of sea expeditions, many of the elements of Brendan's tale are identical to elements of earlier legends, especially the story of Mael Duin and the Voyage of Bran. The story resembles the ancient tales, with much religious allegory and scenes evocative of Dante's "Inferno."

THE PATRON SAINT OF TRAVELERS

Brendan's story did not go unnoticed by the Church. Shortly after he was made a saint, he was adopted as the patron saint of travelers and sailors (along with the more famous St. Christopher).

Brendan's legend tells that he began his voyage as penance for burning a religious book containing accounts of many fantastic miracles. An admonishing angel declares that as punishment, Brendan will spend seven years journeying to Tir na Nog ("land of youth"), to witness his own miracles and record them in the place of those he had destroyed. Brendan sets sail with an improbable sixty companions in a small Irish boat called a coracle, a primitive leather craft traditionally popular with traveling monks.

Brendan's recorded adventures sound very much like Mael Duin's. He travels to many small islands, each with unique inhabitants, and sees many bizarre and strange sights. Like Mael, he takes on three passengers at the last minute, who all meet fated ends. Also like Mael, he and his men encounter an uninhabited palace filled with food and laden with jewels—although in this version, it is Brendan himself who denounces the thief and prevents any misfortune from befalling the party.

The most fantastic element of Brendan's story concerns an island that is seemingly unremarkable until the sailors build a campfire to warm themselves and cook their supper. The island suddenly begins to quake and quickly sinks beneath the waves, allowing the party barely enough time to scramble back to their boat. It soon becomes evident that the island is not an island at all but an enormous serpent or dragon, whose name Brendan reveals to be Jasconius. The resemblance of Jasconius to the fabled Jormungandr, the Norse serpent of Midgard, is well recognized.

FOOD FOR THE CREW

Instead of magical apples, Brendan and his sailors feast on bread and water delivered in answer to the abbot's pious prayers. The party acquires a mysterious "Provider," an old hermit who appears at will and keeps them stocked with food, water, and fish for the best part of their journey.

In another oddly pagan encounter, Brendan encounters an island, called the "Eden of the Birds," inhabited by birds. The cheerful creatures reveal to Brendan that they are an ancient tribe of people whom God has caused to take the shape of birds for eternity, in order to testify to the glories of creation. It is a curious passage. The theme of warriors returning as divine messenger-birds is an ancient pagan idea, but Brendan's story is clearly intended for a Christian audience—another sign of the unusual amity Celtic theologians had with the old pagan ideas. The story disappears from later versions, perhaps due to discomfort with this similarity.

The adventures continue in like vein, with more monsters and sea creatures, demonic encounters, and even a visit to Judas, who is stranded on an outcropping of rock, much like Prometheus, suffering eternal, repeating torments. At one stop, Brendan and his crew are forced to flee as they are pelted with flaming rocks and molten metal hurled by a giant from the entrance of a great cave. It seems clear that Brendan and his men, although at sea, are also in hell, and that this version of hell is very much like the ancient Otherworld.

Eventually they come to a place of complete darkness, through which they travel for many weeks. At last the darkness lifts, and they encounter a beautiful paradise—an island filled with fruiting trees and precious stones, where it is eternally daylight. Here, they encounter a monastery, from which appears a mysterious, shining youth, who calls all of them by name and informs the adventurers that they have reached their destination, the Blessed Isle. He exhorts them to fill up their ship with all they can carry and to return home.

When Brendan inquires whether the island should ever be known to mankind, the youth promises that it would one day be known to all. Brendan and his party remain on the island for three days and nights. As they prepare to leave, they seek a blessing from the monastery. Upon exiting, they discover themselves miraculously returned to their own monastery.

Brendan's tale proved incredibly popular and encouraged many to visit his monasteries. Many people attempted to recreate his journeys in order to locate "Brendan's Isle." In modern times, there has been much speculation over the veracity of the story and whether many of the seemingly fanciful details of the story may describe real locations.

Some theorize that the giant hurling rocks from his cave may in fact describe volcanoes of Iceland, or that the isle of birds may describe one of the Danish Faroe Islands. Various encounters with sea monsters are said to describe whales and other unfamiliar creatures. There is even an unlikely but persistent belief that the Blessed Isle visited by Brendan was in fact the shore of Newfoundland, which would place Brendan as the first European in America.

SNEDGUS AND MAC RIAGLA

The Voyage of Snedgus and Mac Riagla was another late addition to the imram tradition, one that is more overtly Christian than earlier stories. Both heroes were priests of Columcille, and they begin their journey for reasons that are never revealed. After an encounter with a miraculous spring, they decide to leave the fate of their journey in the hands of God, and they throw away their oars. Their adventures aren't terribly remarkable; in close parallel to the earlier tales, they come upon magical isles filled with birds, creatures, and the like. What is unusual about the story is that among the saints and biblical characters they encounter are ancient kings and mythological figures, including Merlin—who is mentioned as an equal to Patrick, and credited with helping the great saint to intercede with a wrathful God on behalf of Ireland.

CHAPTER TEN

Fairies and Fey Folk

Otherworldly creatures were active in the Celtic imagination. The spread of Christianity among the Celts transformed the Otherworld from a place of happiness and eternal youth and health into a sort of hell where fairies and devils were sometimes indistinguishable. The fair folk dropped by to come to human aid now and again, but in the main they were viewed with superstition, as capricious characters who were usually up to no good. Fairies were blamed for just about anything that went wrong, from sour milk to infant death, poor weather, or failed crops.

FAIRY AVOIDANCE

Although nowadays one might see many methods promoted to encourage fairy sightings, in ancient times it was considered seriously bad luck—even potentially fatal—to spot a fairy. Even if a sighting wasn't an omen of death, one always risked pranks or disfigurement, or one might even be spirited away to the fairies' underground lair.

One way of avoiding fairies and their magic was to wear ones' clothing inside out, which would confound them. Fairies were also reputed to be terrified of iron or steel, so even a single pin could prove effective against them.

THE FAIRY COURT

Fairies in Celtic lore include not only the dignified Dé Dananns, but also phantoms and strange elemental creatures of air, water, and earth, including all manner of goblins, mermaids, leprechauns, and the like. In Christian times, fairies were divided into two classes, the "Seelie court," or the more noble fairies, which included the ancient Dé Dananns, and the "Unseelie court," made up of goblins, spooks, and phantoms.

Fire and embers were also effective at repelling fairies, although these were impractical in general because with fire, the cure could be more damaging than the fairy mischief it was intended to prevent. Other common charms against fairies included holy amulets, knots and pentacles inscribed on doorposts, or even urine sprinkled about one's property.

CHANGELINGS

Changelings were fairy children, substituted in the cradle for human children spirited away by fairies. A changeling was often distinguished by its wizened looks, by precocious behaviors or talents, or because the child was sickly or disfigured or of poor temperament. Sometimes, all it took was an unusually hungry baby to prompt suspicion of a swap. Fairy abductions were often blamed on parents or other relatives. Too much attention or praise paid a baby would attract unwanted attention from the fairies, who coveted beautiful or congenial babies.

As a result, "changeling" was a common explanation for anything from crib death to behavioral problems, and medieval chroniclers made much mention of the phenomenon.

Charms against fairy abduction were the same as those against other fairy mischief. Parents might put the child's clothes on inside out, or they might dangle needles or scissors from the child's cradle to dissuade the fairies from entry.

Fear of fairy abductions was persistent in Christian times, and all sorts of extreme measures were taken to prevent substitutions. If a child was believed a changeling, he or she might be subjected to all sorts of bizarre treatment, sometimes even cruelty or abuse. One common method of identifying a changeling was to place the child on a shovel held over the hearth-fire. Reports of parents' cruel treatment of sup-posed changeling children continued well into the Victorian era.

SPIRITS OF THE EARTH

The ancient Celts were animists, finding all of nature to be inhabited by the divine. In Irish folklore, fairies and supernatural creatures inhabit nearly every corner of the natural world, and then some. There are the true fairies, the Sídhe, the fair immortals of the Tuatha Dé Danann who live in large tribes under the earth. There are all manner of household spirits, as well as spirits who inhabit lakes and streams, trees and flowers, mountains and mines. Some were helpful, or at least benevolent with regard to mortals, but some were quite malevolent. Fairies were never referred to by name, but were called instead the "good people."

LEPRECHAUNS

One of the best-known characters of Irish folklore is the leprechaun, a fairy creature of short stature and shorter temper. Eternally, the leprechaun evades the treasure seekers who covet his horde of gold, which tradition states he keeps at the "end of the rainbow."

THE GOOD SIDE OF LEPRECHAUNS

While the stereotypical leprechaun in the Americas is a coarse mischief maker, the Irish have traditionally viewed the leprechaun as a well-spoken, intelligent, and hard-working creature who likes nothing better than to be left to his work in solitude.

The leprechaun is often depicted as a miniature cobbler, a tricky elf who can be made to divulge where his treasures are buried if he is caught. However, if his captor can be fooled into taking his eyes off the leprechaun for even an instant, he can vanish without a trace. In most tales, the leprechaun is victorious, outwitting his erstwhile human captors.

The legend of the leprechaun probably sprang up to explain the hoards of treasure and grave-goods buried and dropped into lakes and streams by the pagan Celts. A thieving fairy probably seemed the best explanation for the mysterious caches.

THE LURIKEEN

The lurikeen of Kildare is nearly identical to the modern concept of the leprechaun. He is a tiny goblin shoemaker, as most tales recount, who is so industrious that he is caught unaware and forced to reveal the location of his hoarded treasure. In order to do so, however, one must keep an eye on him every moment, lest he escape, a feat that is notoriously difficult to do, as the lurikeen is an exceedingly clever creature.

THE CLURICHAUN

A creature who is closely related to the leprechaun is the clurichaun. Unlike the industrious leprechaun, the clurichaun is a surly, sneering drunk who ruins livestock by riding on them in the night. Clurichauns are also known to torment habitual drunks and raid wine cellars.

The clurichauns aren't completely useless, however. Being a possessive lot, they will protect their favorite wine cellars from thieves and dishonest servants.

THE BROWNIE

The brownie was a creature particular to Scotland, a tiny, wizened brown goblin with large eyes and oversized, pointed ears. A usually benevolent household elf, the brownie was a nocturnal spirit who would venture out at night to tidy up and do household chores. The brownies did, however, expect payment for their services, usually in the form of milk or food left for them. If they weren't rewarded, they would retaliate by souring milk, breaking things, or letting the livestock loose to roam. A particularly unhappy brownie might desert the household altogether.

A gift of clothes would rid a house of a brownie forever, being perceived as a great insult.

A version of this legend may be seen in the Brothers Grimm fairy tale about the elves and the shoemaker. An impoverished shoemaker gains himself a pair of tiny helpers, who spend their nights laboring without compensation. When the shoemaker attempts to reward his small benefactors by creating them their own shoes and clothes, they promptly vanish.

DOBBY THE HOUSE ELF

The character of Dobby the House Elf in the Harry Potter series is undoubtedly based on the Scottish brownie, one of a number of supernatural creatures from the books based on Celtic mythology. Curiously, although both are freed by gifts of clothing, J.K. Rowling portrays this as a positive event in her books.

PIXIES

Pixies are a creature particular to the area near Devon and Cornwall, in England. They are usually described as small, wizened creatures, with wrinkled brown skin, bald heads, and pointed ears. They are sometimes described as ancient druids who refused to convert to Christianity and were doomed to roam the earth, rejected by both heaven and hell. Other descriptions attribute childlike qualities to them.

Pixies are largely viewed as harmless pranksters who like to play pranks on unsuspecting mortals, but sometimes they are more malevolent. It is often said that if a curious traveler follows a pixie, he will be lured into the fairy realm, never to be seen again.

TROWS AND SEA TROWS

Trows are creatures peculiar to the areas around the Orkney and Shetland isles. The name *trow* is most likely a corruption of the imported Norse word *troll*, although trows were most often described as rather small in size, albeit grotesque looking. The trows were called "good folk," calling to mind the fairy epithet "fair folk." Like trolls, trows cannot be exposed to sunlight, as they will turn to stone. Trows come in several varieties, from tiny creatures who live under toadstools in the forest, to humanlike fairies who take human wives.

TROWS AND BARROW-WIGHTS

J.R.R. Tolkien's fearsome barrow-wights, the tomb-dwelling phantoms from the *Lord of the Rings* trilogy, were most likely modeled after the trow.

Like the fairies, the trows were rumored to live in barrows and tombs under the earth, where they created treasures of gold and silver and threw merry, boisterous parties to which human fiddlers were occasionally invited—and from which they sometimes never returned. Trows were nocturnal, venturing forth only by night, usually to cause mischief of one form or another.

Sea trows, resembling the Irish selkies, are nocturnal creatures that take the form of fish or seals but venture on land at night, shedding their animal skins to appear in human form. Unlike most trows, the sea trow is attractive in appearance; folklore is filled with tales of lucky fishermen who are able to capture beautiful trow brides for themselves by taking their discarded skins. (To be fair, other sources call them ugly. One sixteenth-century source describes them as looking like a horse whose body was covered in seaweed.)

SPIRITS OF WATER

In druid times, water gods and spirits were often benevolent. Lakes and springs were ruled over by gods of warmth and healing. Rivers, wells, and streams were often ruled by goddesses, often the local goddesses of sovereignty. Over time, the darker aspects of those deities became prominent, while their divine features receded. Many water spirits slowly evolved into bogles, terrifying beasts whose specialty was lying in wait for unsuspecting passers-by.

Not all of the water spirits are bad. Some, such as the selkie, are tragic, water-bound creatures that can be redeemed through their interactions with humanity. Most water-bound creatures, good or evil, can be captured and pressed into service and/or marriage to humans.

KELPIE: MALEVOLENT SEA HORSE
The kelpie was a malevolent creature, a shape-shifter that could take on the appearance of a man but most often appeared in the form of a fine horse with a silken coat and gleaming eyes. The telltale difference between this supernatural creature and its earthly look-alike was the kelp or rushes clinging to its mane. To see a kelpie was an omen of death by drowning; to meet one might mean instant death.

The kelpie's malevolent behavior took a number of forms. Most commonly, it would lurk near docks or ferries, in the form of a lovely horse. A passerby foolish enough to attempt a ride on the horse would find himself stuck tight as the kelpie returned to the water, drowning the unfortunate victim and devouring him. This wasn't the kelpie's only trick, however. If a potential victim chanced by on horseback, it might take the form of a hideous old man, leaping onto the saddle. The kelpie also liked to appear as a handsome young man and seduce young women to their deaths.

One could capture a kelpie and put it to work. If one was clever enough and quick enough, a harness could be tossed over a kelpie's neck, rendering it docile, after which the creature was reputed to make an exceptionally strong workhorse.

The water horse is a very ancient motif in Celtic territories that may have originated in the ancient horse-cults of Celtic Europe. Early images of water horses appear to have been benign in aspect and are related to water deities such as Manannan mac Lir.

A Scottish variation of the kelpie was the shellycoat, so called for the shells and seaweed that dangled from his mane. The shellycoat was of malevolent character but not as evil as the kelpie. The shellycoat's favorite prank was to mimic the cries of a drowning person, distracting travelers who would frantically search for a crying victim but, after finally reaching the source of the cries, would discover only a hysterically laughing phantom.

HARVEY

In the Jimmy Stewart classic movie *Harvey* (1950), the titular character is a pooka, a six-foot-three-and-a-half-inch rabbit only Stewart's character is able to see. A similar character but with much more sinister aspects appears in *Donnie Darko* (2001).

THE POOKA

The pooka (or sometimes phooka) is an obvious relation to the kelpie. Like the kelpie, he appears as a horse, usually a colt, but can also be spotted in the form of a goat, dog, or rabbit. Sometimes he appears as a wizened goblin. He is typically hung round the neck with heavy chains and loiters about on the edges of marshes and lakes. Like the kelpie, the pooka enjoys luring mortals and leaping astride riders' horses, but unlike the kelpie, the pooka is in it for fun, and usually the victim of his pranks comes to no harm.

That is not to say the pooka is a harmless creature. He has been known to roam the countryside at night, destroying crops, scattering livestock, and souring milk. It is traditional for Irish farmers to leave a portion of their crops behind after harvest for the pooka, in order to be spared his mischief. The pooka's special night is at Samhain, when special precautions must be taken to prevent mischief from befalling one's household.

Many a human reported being ridden by the capricious pooka, but only one man was ever known to have returned the insult. This was the legendary Brian Boru, the greatest of the high kings of Ireland. Brian accomplished this feat by stealing three hairs from the pooka's tail, with which he wove a bridle that he was able to use to control the magical creature. The king rode the horse to exhaustion, after which the pooka agreed not to destroy the property of good Christians or to attack Irishmen unless they were intoxicated. The pooka being what he was of course ignored his promise, but he does seem to have a preference for drunks.

HEADLESS HORSEMAN: THE DULLACHAN

The notion of capricious rides doesn't end with magical horses. The Irish dullachan ("dark man") is the original headless horseman, a wild spectral rider who haunts the countryside, carrying his severed head under one arm as he rides. The head is not useless but is gifted instead with supernatural sight, allowing the phantom to see for miles. Woe to anyone who happens to be near, because when the dullachan reins his horse, it is certain that someone nearby will die. The dullachan's visit is unpleasant for anyone who attempts to thwart his mission as well, for they often find themselves doused with a bucket of blood.

SELKIES: THE SEAL PEOPLE

Selkies ("seals") are the mysterious sea-people who inhabit the waters around the Orkney and Shetland isles. The selkies are a type of trow who take the form of seals and live in caverns underwater. Selkies, like most trows, can leave their animal forms on land and have even been known to take human spouses.

FALLEN ANGELS?

A common legend regarding the selkies claims they are fallen angels; specifically, they are angels unwelcome in heaven but too pure for hell, thus doomed to haunt the coastline in their tragic animal skins. They are also sometimes said to be the transformed souls of the drowned.

Irish and Scottish folklore is filled with stories of humans who take selkie spouses. In most, it is a sort of involuntary enslavement, wherein the would-be husband gains a selkie bride by stealing her sealskin and concealing it so that she may not return to sea. On other occasions, a selkie may fall in love with a human of its own accord, but such love matches are said to be doomed to tragedy. Eventually, selkies must succumb to the lure of their former home, after which they can never return.

Selkie men are another matter. Unlike selkie females, who often must be tricked or captured, male selkies have been known to conceal their own skins in order to seek out human lovers. A woman who wished to attract a selkie would do so by shedding seven tears into the ocean. Women who drowned or disappeared were often said to have been spirited away by selkie lovers.

Causing harm to one of the selkie-folk was to be assiduously avoided, as the death of a selkie is believed to cause furious storms at sea. The selkies are also known as roane, or seals.

MERROWS: THE IRISH MERMAID

The merrow is the Gaelic variety of the mermaid and merman: human from the waist up, with the torso and lower body of a fish. Celtic mermaids were quite lovely and are usually depicted preening with a mirror and comb. The Celtic merman, on the other hand, fares nowhere near as well, being hideously gnarled, with razor-sharp teeth and green-hued skin.

Merrows, like other supernatural sea creatures, can become espoused to humans, either by love or by trickery. To take a mermaid or merman spouse, one must steal his or her magical feathered cap, or *cohuleen druith*, without which the merrow is unable to travel under the waves. The trapped creature would then be forced to agree to remain, in hopes of retrieving this magical possession.

WRAITHS AND SEDUCTRESSES

An unfortunate consequence of the Christianization of the Celts was that the spirits of the earth, especially female ones, began to take on a sinister cast, becoming evil seductresses, wraiths, and monstrous hags. The tests of the goddess became mere blood sport for monsters who inhabited the forests, lakes, and streams.

THE BANSHEE

Originally, the banshee, or *ban Sídhe*, was at one time simply a female of the Sídhe, of fairy-folk. Over time, however, the name came to signify a very specific type of unlucky spirit. Because an encounter with a fairy meant that one was literally "walking between worlds," she came to be viewed as an omen of death.

In later folklore, the banshee evolved into a sort of wraith or ghost, often attached to a particular house or family, whose bloodcurdling wail meant the impending death of a member of the household.

THE WASHER-WOMAN

A related spirit to the banshee was the *ban nighe*, or "washer-woman," a character encountered in Irish and Welsh mythology who also came to be viewed as a shade. The ban nighe was originally a particular aspect of the goddess of sovereignty, who symbolically washed the garments of a warrior and warned him of his impending death. In Christian times, she lost her divine aspect and became an apparition who would appear beside the river, washing the grave-clothes of those about to die.

OWAIN AND THE WASHER-WOMAN

An early version of the washer-woman myth concerns the Welsh sovereignty goddess Modron, who is inexplicably cursed to wash at the riverside until she bears a son by a Christian. That son is the hero Owain.

Romanticized tales of the washer-woman give a more benevolent aspect to the water goddess. In many cases, she is a mysterious lady who guards a well, stream, or fountain, and whose function is to test the hero or provide him with a task, quest, or geas.

THE KORRIGAN

While the banshee and the ban nighe were not viewed as malevolent, there were creatures who could cause the death of any unfortunate enough to cross their paths. The most malevolent of these was the korrigan, originally thought to be the spirit of female druids who opposed the conversion of Celtic lands to Christianity. She is especially associated with water, and may be another aspect of the Morrigán. There are generally said to be nine korrigans in all.

The korrigan was a wicked spirit, with a number of vile habits. She was fond of sitting by the lakes or wells, combing her long, beautiful hair, and she would attempt to seduce any man who chanced by. Those who spurned her advances would be cursed with death.

Men weren't the only victims of the korrigan. It was she who was largely credited with the kidnap of human infants, replacing them with changelings, and raising the human children as her own.

SINGULAR PHANTOMS

Some members of the fairy-folk were so infamous they had no peers. Most of these solitary fairies belonged to a particular locale, although some appear to have had no boundaries to their haunts. To a one, these creatures are mischievous or malevolent.

One such creature was the fearsome Amadan Dubh, the "Black Fool," also known as the "Stroking Lad." The Amadan lived in a ruined castle and ventured out at random looking for prey, which he enchanted with his pipes before touching them—a touch that rendered his chosen victim crippled, disfigured, or paralyzed. The Amadan's choice of victims was capricious, although occasionally he served as a means of dispensing a sort of divine justice, serving his touch on men and women who blasphemed or broke social etiquette.

CHAPTER ELEVEN

The Otherworld

The Celtic Otherworld was unlike most others of the ancient world. The Celtic Otherworld was at the same time the abode of the gods and the land of the dead. It was a contradictory place, existing both in the world and far from it. It was a place of happiness and eternal youth, yet it was sometimes perceived as transitory, a temporary abode between mortal lives. It was a place of joy and plenty to the dead who dwelt there, yet it was a curse to mortals who chanced to stray beyond its borders because they would find themselves enchanted, while the outside world passed them by.

BEYOND THE VISIBLE

In earlier times, the Otherworld was described as a land of origin, the magical homeland of the divine ancestors of the Irish people. The Irish Otherworld was Tir na Nog, the "Land of Youth," which was originally located on an island far to the west, and from which the Tuatha Dé Danann came when they migrated to Ireland. It was a land of powerful magic, inhabited by powerful druids who were the source of the gods' tremendous skill and learning.

ENTRANCES TO THE OTHERWORLD

The entrances to the Otherworld were said to be hidden throughout the landscape, an idea that persisted long after the coming of Christianity and even lingers today. One could stay too long in the forest, or slumber too long beneath a particular tree, and find oneself in the realm of fairy—yet the Otherworld was remarkably resistant to intentional attempts at trespass.

In later accounts, the Otherworld was said to exist concurrently alongside the mortal realm, inaccessible to most by virtue of the powerful magic that made it invisible to mortal eyes. A veil of invisibility kept all but the most determined from finding its entrances, although some occasionally found their way in by happenstance. Many a tale tells of the hero who penetrates the veil, only to return to discover friends and family long dead and the world unrecognizable.

ANNWN

To the Welsh, the Otherworld was Annwn, also a land of youth and plenty. Annwn was ruled by Arawn or Gwyn ap Nudd, equivalent to the Irish Nuada. Annwn was said to be accessible only through death or through a single door accessible one day a year, said to be located at Glastonbury Tor.

SAMHAIN

The door to Annwn may of course be an allusion to the feast of Samhain, the solar feast day on which the doorway to the underworld was believed to lay open. The name Annwn means "deep" or "under earth."

The chief treasure of Annwn was its cauldron, which overflowed with an abundance of plenty, an object similar to the Irish Cauldron of Plenty. One of the earliest Arthurian tales, "The Spoils of Annwn," concerns a fateful quest for the cauldron, from which only seven men return.

The Welsh story of Annwn was probably the genesis of the Arthurian legend of Avalon, and the cauldron appears to be an early pagan version of the tale of the Holy Grail. Christians seem to have some difficulty with the concepts of the Otherworld, as many tales attempt to reconcile belief in the old pagan concepts of the afterlife. In one Christianized tale of Annwn, Gwyn ap Nudd is given dominion over the demons in order to prevent them from overtaking the earth.

Annwn came to be called Avalon, the name by which the Otherworld is most commonly known today. The name *Avalon* is believed to derive from the Welsh *Ynys Afallach*, "Isle of Apples," a reference to the abundant fruit of the Otherworld. According to Arthurian legends, Avalon was both a place of healing and the final resting place of the King. Strangely, Arthur is accompanied to his final rest by his treacherous sister Morgan le Fay—who may be a version of the Morrigán, the Celtic goddess of death—a fitting escort for a king who ends his life in battle. Arthur is first connected to Avalon by twelfth-century chronicler Geoffrey of Monmouth, who also identifies it as the birthplace of Arthur's magical sword Excalibur.

GLASTONBURY

Another tradition claims Arthur's burial to be at Glastonbury, an idea not as contradictory as it seems. Avalon was, after all, conceived to be an island, and Glastonbury at one time had the appearance of an island, with its great tor arising from a wetland. Also notable is the continued presence of ancient apple orchards at the site. In the late twelfth century, the monks of Glastonbury Abbey announced they had found a grave in which were buried a man and woman; the man was of exceptional size. The monks instantly leaped to the conclusion that this was the grave of Arthur and Guinevere. And just in case there was any question of their identity, a leaden cross bearing the convenient Latin inscription *Hic jacet sepultus inclitus rex Arthurus in insula Avalonia* ("Here lies interred the famous King Arthur on the Isle of Avalon") lay above the stone cover. Glastonbury increased greatly in importance afterward, becoming the second most powerful church in England for a time. In 1278, the bodies were reburied with much pomp under the foot of the altar, with King Edward and Queen Eleanor in solemn attendance. However, the bodies were later lost in the confusion and disruption that accompanied the English Reformation of the sixteenth century.

THE SÍDHE-MOUNDS

When the Iron Age Celts came upon remnants of their Stone Age predecessors, they imagined their imposing monuments and tombs as doorways to the underworld. These tombs and earth-mounds were referred to as Sídhe, and eventually, the name for these ancient sites became synonymous with the gods who inhabited them. These were the Tuatha Dé Danann, the race of gods led underground by the Dagda upon the arrival of the conquering Milesian Celts.

With the ascendancy of Christianity, the Otherworld gods passed into legend. They metamorphosed into the fairy-folk, and their domain became a place of enchantment and even trickery, where mortals were enticed to neglect their responsibilities for idylls from which some never returned. Eventually, the land of eternal youth came to be viewed as a pitfall, a danger to be avoided, inhabited by malicious spirits and even demons.

TIR NA NOG

The chief Irish Otherworld was called Tir na Nog, "land of youth." Tir na Nog was difficult to reach, at least for humans—animals could seemingly cross over at will. Tir na Nog is described variously as a distant land, far over the western seas, and as one that was also located in the same place as the ordinary world, but magically hidden so that it was only accessible through magic or chance, or by invitation from one of its residents. In Tir na Nog, there is no illness, no aging, and no death. Everyone is eternally young and beautiful, and there is an endless supply of food and drink.

MAG MELL

Another variation of the land of the dead in Ireland was Mag Mell, the "plain of joy," an underwater realm ruled by the sea god, Manannan mac Lir. Like Tir na Nog, Mag Mell was inhabited by the spirits of the dead and visited by the living, even an occasional Christian monk. Mag Mell features in tales of the hero Bran and in the adventures of St. Brendan.

BREASIL

A later name for the Irish Otherworld was Breasil, or Hy-Brasil, "princely isle," or "the isle of the blessed." According to Irish myth, the island belonged to the sea god, Manannan mac Lir. Like the Greek Elysium, Breasil was a place of rest and eternal youth.

THE UNDERWATER ISLAND

According to legend, Breasil spent most of its existence underwater. It appeared above the surface only once every seven years although it could be fixed in place by fire. A typical tale recounts that the island was forced to remain in place for a time after being pinned by a fiery arrow.

During the Middle Ages, it was generally accepted that Breasil was a real island to the west of Ireland, and it was even added to a number of maps. There were numerous accounts of visits there, all filled with fanciful detail.

OISIN AND NIAMH

Oisin, or "small deer," the son of the hero Fionn and the doe Sadhbh, was a legendary hero and poet in his own right. Oisin played a peculiar role in Irish mythology, a reconciler of pagan and Christian wisdom. It is Oisin who recounts to St. Patrick the glories of the Otherworld and the heroics of the Fianna, long after they have passed. He tells Patrick of his journey to the Otherworld, where he has lived 300 years while time has passed him by.

Oisin's journey begins while he is on a hunting trip with his father, Fionn. The hunting party spies a strange, beautiful queen astride a white horse. She announces that she is Niamh, the daughter of the king of Tir na Nog, and has traveled a long distance, all to declare her love for Oisin. Oisin, struck by her beauty, is instantly smitten. He agrees to follow her anywhere she might go, even before she describes her home as a place of beauty, abundance, and eternal youth and wellness:

> Delightful is the land beyond all dreams,
> Fairer than anything your eyes have ever seen.
> There all the year the fruit is on the tree,
> And all the year the bloom is on the flower.
> There with wild honey drip the forest trees;
> The stores of wine and mead shall never fail.
> Nor pain nor sickness knows the dweller there,
> Death and decay come near him never more.

Oisin accompanies his fairy bride on her magical horse to the Otherworld, which is reached by sea. The Otherworld is just as she has described, a place of eternal merrymaking and pleasures, but after three years, Oisin grows weary of the place. Homesick, he tells his bride he desires to return home. She acquiesces, telling him that time has passed much more quickly in the mortal realm. She gives him her horse to ride and warns him never to dismount. He returns to find his father's estates a ruin and the Fianna no more than a legend. Saddened, he makes ready to return to Niamh, when he spies some men struggling to move a great stone from their cropland. He stoops to assist, but his saddle breaks, and he is thrown to the ground, whereupon he instantly ages 300 years. Niamh's horse returns to Tir na Nog without him, and the astonished farmers bring the now-feeble old man to St. Patrick, who shelters him. Oisin is not easily won over, either. When Patrick observes him pining, Oisin snappishly remarks that he will convert if Patrick's heaven is half as good as his own Otherworld.

ST. PATRICK'S PURGATORY/ THE JOURNEY TO PURGATORY

Parts of the pagan faith of the Irish may have faded fairly quickly, but belief in the Otherworld remained strong. A popular pilgrimage for Irish Catholics through the Middle Ages and even today is to a tiny island on Lough Derg ("red lake") in the northwest of Ireland, where pilgrims flock to visit "St. Patrick's Purgatory," the place where St. Patrick reputedly experienced visions of heaven and hell. The usual legend of Lough Derg and the saint claims that Patrick received a vision of purgatory while sleeping in the island's cave. The story is probably apocryphal, as there were no known connections to the island until long after the saint's death.

Originally, the tale of the purgatory cave, right down to the details of the epic struggle with the sea monster, was attributed to St. Brendan. The protagonist of the story was later switched to St. Patrick, as it probably made the then-lucrative pilgrimage more attractive.

Every year, pilgrims visit the lake's tiny Station Island, site of an ancient monastery, where they fast and pray while walking circuits around the ruins of the ancient hermits' cells. The actual site of Patrick's alleged vision, however, is believed to be a cave on nearby Saints' Island.

The earliest known reference to St. Patrick's purgatory is in *The Treatise on St. Patrick's Purgatory,* the late twelfth-century work of

Gilbert, a Cistercian monk who recounts the tale as told to him by a fellow monk named Owain who has visited the Otherworld on the site and survived to tell of it.

According to Gilbert's tale, Owain was once a knight of ill repute who has lived a life of greed, violence, and immorality. He journeys to the island to repent of his sins. After many days of rites and preparation, he enters the cave, where he stumbles around in the dark until he eventually spies a glimmer of light. He follows the light as it brightens, and passes through to what is described as purgatory but is more reminiscent of the Otherworld. There he encounters two men in white robes and shaved heads—it is unclear if they are monks or even druids—who tell him how to prepare for an onslaught of evil spirits to come. Most importantly, they warn, he must not turn back before the journey is complete.

FORTRESS OF GLASS

Among the Christian imagery are more hints of the story's ancient pagan origins. Patrick's purgatory is accessed not through death but via a mysterious mode of travel. The most telling detail is the appearance of paradise. It is a fortress of glass, an idea with no parallel in Christian mythology but with plenty in Celtic paganism. The traditional entrance to the Otherworld in Welsh mythology was Caer Wydr, the Tower of Glass.

Owain continues onward and encounters a nightmare landscape filled with devils, demons, and anguished souls in torment. Owain follows the instructions of his mysterious teachers, using prayer to save himself from one peril after another, as the demons torment him and continually urge him to return home. Eventually, Owain encounters the gates of paradise, and his experiences there leave him wishing to be a new man. He not only repents of his former life but abandons it wholly to enter the monastery.

The story of Owain's journey is followed by many others, most of which follow the same basic formula. A penitent would enter an underground cave or chamber on the island, and in the dark he would be overcome by sleep, during which he would have visions of purgatory and its inhabitants. Many of these followed the formula of Dante's "Inferno," with successive levels of punishments for different degrees of sinfulness.

In later times, the tale of purgatory was conflated with the legend of St. Patrick, and Owain was all but forgotten as the island became a hugely popular destination for pilgrims wishing to recreate the visionary experience.

Purgatory is not the island's only connection to the Otherworld. According to local legend, it was in this lake that St. Patrick fought and defeated a water monster placed there by Fionn mac Cumhaill himself. The blood of the monster supposedly gives the lake its red coloration. By some accounts, Patrick was said to have driven the infamous snakes of Ireland to this lake—at the same time, it was also supposedly the last colony of Ireland's druids.

These stories, very odd for Christian tales, are almost certainly reworked from older legends. Even if the loch was the site of a showdown between Christian and druid, the connotation of the place as otherworldly has remained. Lough Derg is also where the children of Lir were said to have ended their enchantment (as detailed in Chapter 13), and some Celtic scholars speculate that rites in honor of the god Aenghus were conducted on the island in ancient times. The spot crops up in a number of Arthurian stories as well, where it is conflated with the pagan Otherworld.

Near the end of the fifteenth century, the cave was sealed, on the order of the pope, after a Dutch monk complained he had visited the site and found it to be an ordinary cave. Ironically, the cave was closed on St. Patrick's Day, 1497. Pilgrimages continue to a neighboring island, but the current location of the cave is unknown. Curiously, visitors today are not permitted to bring cameras or recording equipment on the lake.

THE WILD HUNT

A particularly persistent Otherworld legend that survived into Christian times was the theme of the Wild Hunt, or "fairy raid," a myth that appeared in numerous European cultures. The Wild Hunt was led by a hunter whose identity varied from one region to the next—sometimes it was Gwyn ap Nudd, sometimes a goddess, sometimes even King Arthur. The hunt is a wild stampede of horses, dogs, and riders who tumble out of the Otherworld in a wild procession, followed by animals of the forest, fairies, and spirits of the dead. The procession is spectral and fierce, with its participants often described as red eyed, flaming, even flesh devouring.

One particularly detailed account of a local legend comes from twelfth-century historian Walter Map, who recounts the appearance of the ghostly host under the command of a former king:

> The nocturnal companies and squadrons, too, which were called of Herlethingus, were sufficiently well-known appearances in England down to the time of Henry II, our present lord. They were troops engaged in endless wandering, in an aimless round, keeping an awe-struck silence, and in them many persons were seen alive who were known to have died. This household of Herlethingus was last seen in the marches of Wales and Hereford in the first year of the reign of Henry II, about noonday: they traveled as we do, with carts and sumpter horses, pack-saddles and panniers, hawks and hounds, and a concourse of men and women. Those who saw them first raised the whole country against them with horns and shouts, and . . . because

they were unable to wring a word from them by addressing them, made ready to extort an answer with their weapons. They, however, rose up into the air and vanished on a sudden.

The Wild Hunt is sometimes called "the fairy raid," but the basic elements are pretty much universal. A seated rider, be it goddess, wild man, ghost, or fairy, leads a wild procession of animals and specters that kills, destroys, or devours everything in its path.

The hunt retained its appeal through Christian times, and later versions of the hunt include cursed or damned characters from Christian legends, from biblical villains to kings or priests who made poor choices in life. One such tale describes the misfortune of Hans von Hackelnberg, a huntsman for the Duke of Brunswick, who is condemned to lead the wild ride until Judgment Day, as punishment for hunting on Sundays.

HERNE THE HUNTER

One leader of the hunt was the British wild man called Herne the Hunter. Herne was a forest spirit, strongly associated with deer. He was almost certainly related to the ancient fertility gods of the forest, perhaps even Cernunnos himself. Herne is portrayed as a male rider with the antlers (and sometimes even the head) of a deer.

The leaders of the hunt can be viewed as fertility spirits, representations of unrestrained sexuality. In earlier times, the Wild Hunt was associated with fertility cults, but in Christian times it became a symbol of the devil at work, which perhaps highlights the differing sexual attitudes of pagans and Christians. To the former, the sexual urge is wild, chaotic, and celebrated, while to the Christians it is fearsome, demonic, and strange.

CHAPTER TWELVE

The Tree of Life

The Celts held the natural world as the giver and keeper of life, and no emblem better represents the intertwined destinies of man and nature than the spreading branches of the tree of life. The tree was regarded as an ancient ancestor of mankind, and is a universal emblem of the macrocosm. The tree was a natural symbol of the three domains, with branches that reach into the sky, its body in the earth, and roots reaching deep into the sacred streams below the earth.

THE WORLD TREE

In the Celtic world, the tree was the original denizen of the natural world. Trees provided everything needed to sustain life—fruit and acorns for eating, wood for shelter and weapons, fuel for warmth and cooking, and bark for medicines and tanning of leather. Without trees, life would have been very difficult, if not impossible.

Trees were not viewed as only being good for utilitarian purposes or even simply as sacred. The trees were literally gods, the venerated ancient ancestors of mankind. Each tree had its own sacred purpose. Some provided wood for making strong, flexible weapons; some provided life-saving medicines and healing salves. Many were shelter to sacred animals or birds, and some were regarded literally as doors to the Otherworld.

HOLY GROVE

The word *nemeton*, meaning "sacred or holy grove," was the generic name given to the forest sanctuaries of the druids. The root *neme* is connected with many ancient European place-names. Some connect the name of Nemed, a Celtic ancestral deity, to the naming of the sacred groves.

Communities had their own sacred trees, called *biles*, which usually stood on a plain or in the center of a clearing, where they represented the axis mundi, or center of the cosmos. The tree chosen as the bile was usually older and well established, and preferably was located near a well or stream. Assemblies would be held under this tree, and harming or cutting it was restricted under the strictest of taboos. The sacred tree represented the soul of the tuath, and its harm or destruction could mean fires, illness, or other disasters.

TREE WORSHIP

Druid worship took place in forest sanctuaries and around sacred lakes and pools. There can be no doubt that trees were especially important in the Celtic religion, and they were a central feature in druid worship. The druid's sanctuary was called the *nemeton*, or grove, wherein rituals and sacrifices would be performed. The Greek chronicler Strabo describes the assembly-place of the druids in Galatia as Drunemeton, the sacred oak grove.

NINE SACRED WOODS

Druid tradition held nine trees as particularly sacred. Wood from the nine was required to light the annual Beltane fires to usher in the summer season. An old song preserves the names of eight of the nine:

> Choose the willow of the streams, choose the hazel of the rocks
> Choose the alder of the marshes, choose the birch of the waterfalls
> Choose the ash of the shade, choose the yew of resilience
> Choose the elm of the brae, choose the oak of the sun

The ninth is not mentioned but is presumed to be the thorn, or hawthorn, tree. The smoke from the sacred fire, called the need-fire, would be used to purify croplands and cattle, and embers from the fire would be used to relight the hearth-fires of every home. Each tree described in this chapter was prized for a different reason. All were sacred to one or more gods, providing an invaluable resource for both practical and magical purposes.

THE OAK

The druids were especially connected with the oak and the mistletoe that grew on its branches. The word *druid* is derived from the same root as the word for oak, *dru*, and it is often suggested that druid means "oak wise" or "oak dweller." The ancient Celts viewed the oak as the axis mundi, the tree of life at the center of the world. From ancient times, the fruit of the oak provided sustenance for human and animal alike; the acorn was the food of the sacred deer and the boar.

The oak was viewed as a doorway to the Otherworld and was associated with death and rebirth. Both oak branches and mistletoe were commonly placed in graves, and the wood was used in mortuary houses and in the construction of tombs.

DOORWAYS TO THE OTHERWORLD

The notion that the oak was a doorway to the land of fairy was a persistent one. An oft-repeated old Irish proverb reflects this belief: "Fairy-folks are in old oaks." The oak tree was sacred in several other mythologies as well, including Norse, Baltic, and Greek.

Trees were often assigned to one of the gods according to their uses and attributes, and in groves, likenesses of the gods were carved from the trees they embodied. Lugh, the sun god, who was also associated with the underworld and death, was especially connected to the oak, where he dwelled in his eagle form. The god is frequently depicted in art wearing a crown of mistletoe, in which case he can be viewed as a personification of the oak itself.

Sacred oaks were held in such esteem that many Irish saints were attached to sacred oaks or groves. In fact, the names of many ancient monastic communities show their origins as sacred oak groves, including

Derry ("oak," a common place-name in Ireland) and Durrow ("oak plain"). The church of St. Brighid was not coincidentally founded at Kildare (Cill-Dara), whose name literally means "church of the oak." The druid-turned-saint Columcille founded his monasteries in oak groves. Columcille was so fond of the grove at the Kells site that he refused to fell any of its trees to build his church and was even said to have spoken an invocation to save it from a threatening wildfire.

A further tale linking Columcille with the sacred oak tells of a man who took bark from the tree under which the saint lived to tan leather for a pair of shoes and was stricken with leprosy for his folly.

THE ASH

The ash tree was very highly regarded as sacred, often serving as the prototypical world tree. To the continental druids, it was second in importance only to the sacred oak, and to the Irish druids, it was the world tree. The name of the ash tree comes from the ancient Saxon root *aesc*, meaning "spear"—and indeed, saplings of ash were preferred by the Celts for the construction of spears. Druids' wands were also constructed of ash, which was prized for its powers over fire and water. Because it was regarded as a solar tree, it was a suitable wood for healing purposes.

The ash was regarded as the world tree by both the Norse and the Irish. The ash grows in open spaces and only thrives in full sunlight. It prefers to be near a source of water so is common near lakes and streams. The ash is sacred to the gods of lightning, and its mere presence was believed to invite lightning and fire. In medieval times, the ash was considered effective as a charm against black magic.

THE THORN (HAWTHORN)

The thorn tree in particular is sacred to the fairies, especially when accompanied by the oak and ash. The thorn tree is a low-growing, prickly tree most commonly used as a protective fence to repel invaders or to keep livestock in check.

The thorn tree was closely associated in bardcraft with the art of satire; the never-ending barbs and pricks of the thorn were an apt analogy to the effects of a good satire. Hawthorn was also a favorite of the birds, giving it a reputation as an otherworldly tree. In later times, the thorn tree was thought to be inhabited by fairies and generally avoided.

THE YEW

Yew trees are relatively short, broad evergreens, bearing dark-green needles and bright red berries. Almost every part of the yew is highly poisonous. The yew is one of the longest-lived trees in existence, with some specimens living as long as 4,000 years.

Yew was also prized as a magical wood, the material of choice for rune-spells, and it was probably used for divination. The wands of the Irish druids were reportedly made of yew wood, and credited with transformative powers. The yew has traditionally provided wood for weapons, especially bows for archers.

The ancient connection between the yew and seership is echoed in Shakespeare's *Romeo and Juliet*, wherein, after slumbering under a yew, Romeo's servant Balthasar has a vision of the death of Paris:

> As I did sleep under this yew-tree here,
> I dreamt my master and another fought,
> And that my master slew him.

The yew is another tree closely associated with death and rebirth, another guardian of the path between the Otherworld and the waking world. Yew boughs were placed in pagan graves and were planted atop ancient burial mounds. Even centuries after the coming of Christianity, the tree remained sacred, and even churchyard burials took place under the branches of ancient yew trees.

A tale from the Book of Invasions tells of the Queen Etain, who loves a Sídhe lord named Midir and runs away with him. Her enraged husband enlists the aid of the druid Codal, who finds her using four yew-wands engraved with ogham letters. Curiously, Etain is linked mythologically with the Caer, the lover of Aenghus, whose name means, literally, "yew-berry."

Yews remained sacred even into Christian times, and in certain parts of tenth-century Wales one faced a very steep fine for harming or cutting one down.

THE HAZEL OF WISDOM

To the Irish druids, hazel was regarded as a source of wisdom and was connected with sacred springs and wells. In the story of the divine hero Fionn mac Cumhaill (Finn MacCool), the salmon of wisdom becomes imbued with strong magic after eating the nuts of the nine sacred hazel trees that surround his well. Fionn, whose surname not so coincidentally means "son of hazel," receives the power of prophecy when he accidentally consumes a morsel of the fish. Chewing hazelnuts was a folk-charm to attain knowledge or inspiration.

NINE AND THE HAZEL

The hazel is especially connected to the sacred number nine. Many tales relating to the hazel figure the tree as appearing in groves of nine. The hazel grows for nine years before it flowers, and in the druid ogham alphabet, it is the ninth letter.

According to legend, the hazel was once a poisonous tree because it was in the fork of a hazel that Lugh hung the head of the giant Balor after defeating him in battle. The tree remained poisonous until felled by the sea god Manannan fifty years later, and the felled tree was made into a shield for Fionn, who called his magical weapon "dripping ancient hazel."

A hazel wand was the mark of authority of the messenger and the judge, an emblem of balance and wisdom. Later, the hazel became associated with witches and the dowser's art, which possibly influenced the name "witch hazel."

THE WILLOW

The Latin botanical name for willow, *Salix*, is derived from the Celtic *sallis*, meaning "near water." The willow, by virtue of its nearness to water, is associated with aquatic and healing gods.

The god most closely connected to the willow is Esus, whose iconic image is depicted in the act of cutting down a willow tree. The smoke of willow was used in rites of seership.

THE BIRCH

The birch provides bark for making boats and flexible coverings. The birch in particular is considered an effective charm against evil. Its wood, particularly when burned, was believed to drive out evil spirits, especially those that plagued the livestock.

THE ELM

The bark of elm was used to make cord and other flexible products and was prized for its ability to withstand moisture and splitting. Like the yew, the elm was associated with death and passages, and it often grew atop burial mounds. In the earliest stories of Arthur, the king is felled by a spear of elm wood.

THE ALDER

Alder was a popular wood among the Celts, and its wood was used for making charcoal for blacksmiths. The alder also produced colored dyes, in particular a red hue associated with warriors, blood, and battle.

The alder was associated with the hero Bran, and it is sometimes personified as a mythological king, who is sometimes referred to in poetry as having the branches of an alder. One ancient Celtic tribe was even named for the tree—the Arverni, or "alder people." Because of its associations with fire, alder wood was used as a charm against flooding. The hollow twigs of alder were tied together to make charms for calling the wind.

APPLES OF AVALON

Apples, or *quert*, were sacred to the Morrigán, and the apples of Annwn (Avalon) healed all wounds. Many Celtic mythological tales feature apples from the Otherworld that confer upon their owner immortality and endless satiety. Welsh legends of Arthur relate that the king seeks out Avalon to heal from grievous battle wounds, and it is there he returns when near death.

Apples also figure in the story of Lugh and in the source of Lugh's appellation "Long Arms." Lugh's father Cian is a supernaturally skilled gardener whose apple trees bear fruit as soon as they are planted. Cian offered his gardener's skills to Lugh's grandfather, the giant Fomorian Balor, in a bargain for the return of a cow he has stolen from Goibnu, the Dé Danann smith. Cian brings the young Lugh along to help with the harvest. The giant observes the young god reaching for spilled apples, and mistaking him for a gardener's assistant, dubs him "little long arms."

On many legends of visits to the Otherworld, an outsider requires a special token to ensure safe passage to and from the land of fairy.

This token is most often a branch of the Otherworld apple tree, a silver bough bearing blossoms and fruit that make music when shaken, often luring humans into enchanted sleep. This idea seems to come from older druidical practices, as early descriptions of the bards often mention the ritual use of silver branches hung with bells.

MISTLETOE AND IVY

Anyone who has spent any time at all studying the ancient druids has learned that the druids held the mistletoe plant in very high esteem. Classical writers, especially Pliny the Elder, point out that of all the plants of the forest, the druids most revered mistletoe. He describes a mistletoe collection ritual, where, on the "sixth day of the moon," the plant is cut with great ceremony using a sickle-bladed knife:

> For they believe that whatever grows on these trees is sent from heaven, and is a sign that the tree has been chosen by the gods themselves. The mistletoe is very rarely to be met with; but when it is found, they gather it with solemn ceremony. This they do above all on the sixth day of the moon, from whence they date the beginnings of their months, of their years, and of their thirty years cycle, because by the sixth day the moon has plenty of vigor and has not run half its course. After due preparations have been made for a sacrifice and a feast under the tree, they hail it as the universal healer and bring to the spot two white bulls, whose horns have never been bound before. A priest clad in a white robe climbs the tree and with a golden sickle cuts the mistletoe, which is caught in a white cloth. Then they sacrifice the victims, praying that the gods will make their gifts propitious to those to whom they have given it.

The mistletoe grows high in the branches of trees, especially the sacred oak, with no visible source of sustenance. For this reason, and because of its golden hue and waxy white fruit, the mistletoe was believed to literally sprout from the sperm of the sun. Because of this solar association, mistletoe was held to be a healing plant and attributed power over numerous ailments. It was so highly regarded as a magical plant that even centuries after the last druid vanished from the earth, the herb was known as "all-heal" and served as a charm against fires and lightning.

BANNING MISTLETOE

After a time, even the church intervened to try and stem the enthusiasm for mistletoe, and it was banned from use in churches. Nevertheless, the plant remained a popular charm and is still part of holiday traditions to this day.

While ivy isn't usually considered to be a tree, it was counted as one among the Celts. To the ivy was given the reputation as the strongest of all the trees. Although it appeared unassuming, it was hardy and persistent, and although its growth was slow, it could eventually strangle even the strongest oak. Ivy was also counted among the sacred evergreens and was associated with resurrection and the Otherworld.

TREE OGHAM:
THE SACRED ALPHABET

The ogham alphabet is a bit of an anomaly in the Celtic world. Writing was a very late addition to Celtic society. When the Celts first began writing religious inscriptions, they usually used the Roman alphabet. So what, then, to make of this mysterious alphabet, found most often on roadside markers and memorial inscriptions? Incidences of the alphabet might appear to be utilitarian, were it not for a few small but intriguing clues.

The Celts' aversion to committing religious learning to writing was noted by several observers. Caesar remarked on this taboo:

> They commit to memory immense amounts of poetry . . . they consider it improper to commit their studies to writing . . . lest it should be vulgarized and lest the memory of scholars should become impaired.

This characteristic reticence remained even after years of Roman rule. Although the Gaulish Celts eventually learned to make written correspondence and keep written records of mundane public affairs, this was always done using Roman or Greek characters. These languages were also used to inscribe the names of deities, often Roman-Celt hybrids and, occasionally, to record Roman-style curses or other invocations to the gods.

FENIUS AND THE OGHAM ALPHABET

The eleventh-century monks who penned the Book of Invasions also refer to the ogham alphabet. However, they record it as the invention of the Scythian King Fenius, who is claimed to have created the script shortly after the fall of the Tower of Babel, by collecting together the best of the world's languages.

The druids, however, remained steadfast in their refusal to make religious records. Curiously, however, they do seem to have developed their own sacred alphabet, which was used publicly mainly between the fourth and eighth centuries, almost exclusively for funerary inscriptions.

The alphabet is called ogham and is most thoroughly recorded in the medieval Irish Book of Ballymote, where it is credited as the invention of Oghma, the Irish god of eloquence. The alphabet recorded in the Book of Ballymote has twenty letters, with five vowels and three sets of five consonants, although the book refers to numerous variations, each with its own letters and styles.

Very little is known about the exact origins of ogham or its possible religious or ritual uses, but there are many hints that the alphabet had mystical meaning and may have been used for divinatory and other ritual purpose. The Book of Ballymote describes its use as a secret sign language by druids and other elite members of society, who may have used it to communicate with one another when open speech would have revealed secret knowledge to outsiders.

It is perhaps not coincidental that written ogham appears only as the great colleges of druidry began to decline and the practice of druidry became more open and prone to vulgarity. Written inscriptions in the ogham script are found most often in Ireland, almost invariably in funereal inscriptions.

Although ogham appears only relatively recently in the archaeological record, it appears to be quite ancient. The letters are similar in construction to the Norse rune alphabet, and the two are referred to in older texts as somewhat interchangeable. Mythologically, the ogham is associated with the gods of the Tuatha Dé Danann, where it is used for communications, curses, and divination. In the story of Midir and Etain, Etain's husband is aided by the druid Codal, who uses ogham letters carved into yew-staves to discover the whereabouts of the runaway wife and her lover.

Another indication of the ogham's age is its association with the druid's sacred trees. Each letter of the alphabet is named for a different tree, not all of which are native to Ireland.

Ogham letters are formed using combinations of vertical diagonal strokes placed on a midline, written bottom to top (left to right in written manuscripts), with each letter comprising one to five strokes. The midline was not always inscribed but was often created using an edge of the inscribed object.

The following letters, with their corresponding trees, compose the ogham alphabet:

LETTER	TREE
B	Beith (birch)
L	Luis (rowan)
F	Fearn (alder)
S	Saille (willow)
N	Nuin (ash)
H	Huath (whitethorn)
D	Duir (oak)
T	Tinne (holly)
C	Coll (hazel)
Q	Quert (apple)
M	Muin (vine)
G	Gort (ivy)
NG	Getal (broom)
Z	Straif (blackthorn)
R	Ruis (elder)
A	Ailm (pine tree)
O	Onn (furze)
U	Ur (heath)
E	Edad (aspen)
I	Idad (yew)

In the sixth century, the following group (*forfeda*) containing an additional five letters was added to the alphabet, most likely reflecting changes in the language:

LETTER	TREE
EA	Eabab (aspen)
OI	Oir (spindle)
UI	Uillend (honeysuckle)
P; later IO and IA	Iphin (gooseberry)
X or hard Ch; later AE	Emoncholl (double hazel)

The Celtic tree ogham has been and is still used as a tool for divination. How it was used by the ancients is unknown, but the method may have been similar to Norse divination using runes. Later mythological stories mention divinations made by carving ogham letters into staves of yew, but they are silent on the details.

CHAPTER THIRTEEN

Sacred Beasts

A recurring feature of Celtic myth tales is the theme of the god, poet, or hero who can transform seemingly at will, taking on the shape of animals or birds. At the root of these tales are the anthropomorphic animal gods of the ancient Celts, deities of forest, lake, and stream who eventually took on human characteristics. Many of the gods of the Irish pantheon have animal forms or origins. The hero Bran, for instance, takes on the form of a hound and is associated with Fionn, who is almost certainly the same personage as the antlered god Cernunnos.

MAGICAL METAMORPHOSIS

A persistent theme in Celtic myth tales was that of metamorphosis, the ability to change from one form to the next. There is also an element of transmigration in the tales, and one persistent theme is the god or hero who takes the form of one animal after another. For example, the druid Finntan survived for a great stretch of time by taking the form of many animals until he was able to relate the ancient history of Ireland to St. Patrick. This may be an allusion to reincarnation, or simply an implication that Finntan absorbed all of the knowledge of the natural world.

The myth of the shape-changer may have very ancient roots. Cave paintings and pictographs left behind by the ancient ancestors of the Celts depict shamanic priests in animal garb, often in the process of transformation into animal forms or perhaps illustrating the assumption of animal characteristics or abilities. The belief that these magician-priests could take on the appearance of animals is echoed in these later stories of transformation.

Other Celtic ideas about animal transformation came from observance of nature. Unusual behavior in animals often took on supernatural meaning. For instance, goddesses of war would assume the form of ravens or carrion crows to carry off the souls of the dead, while gods of healing and rebirth might appear as snakes or stags—animals who are continually reborn through the shedding of skin or antlers.

One of the best-known tales of magical transformation is the story of Taliesin, the Welsh poet-god. The story is typical of metamorphosis stories, with themes of reincarnation and magic, and has many parallels in the story of Fionn.

THE LOVE OF AENGHUS

A number of tales with themes of supernatural transformation as rebirth concern Aenghus mac Og, the Irish god of youth and love. In one story, Aenghus dreams of a beautiful girl. After awakening, he becomes ill, falling into a depression so deep that he cannot be roused from his bed. After several days of this behavior, his concerned friends call for his mother, the goddess Boann. She diagnoses Aenghus' illness as love sickness—Aenghus is literally pining for the girl of his dreams.

At his mother's behest, messengers are sent to the corners of Ireland to look for the mystery girl of Aenghus' dream. At the end of a year, she is at last discovered in a neighboring kingdom. She is Caer, the daughter of the chieftain Ethal. Unfortunately, she is not to be easily won, as she is a shape-changer and lives as she wills. She tells Aenghus that for one year, she takes on the form of a woman, and for the next, that of a swan—and that he may marry her if he can recognize her among the other swans.

He discovers that she will appear at a particular lake on Samhain eve, and he awaits her there. When she appears in her swan form, she is accompanied by hundreds of other birds. From his dream he recognizes the necklet she wears. He calls out to her, but she does not wish to leave the water—so Aenghus himself transforms into a swan, and meets her in the lake. Most versions of the story of Aenghus conclude with the pair remaining swans and singing songs so sweet they could enchant people to sleep for "three days and nights."

VARIATION ON AENGHUS'S TALE

In another tale, it is the brother of Aenghus, Midir, who falls for the maiden Etain (a goddess herself associated with death and rebirth), and takes her for a wife. Unfortunately, Midir is already married, and his first wife does not take kindly to the usurper. She uses magic that causes the maiden to take on the form of a fly although she is such a magical and beautiful fly that Midir does not mind.

Eventually, Midir's wife catches on that the fly that accompanies her husband is Etain, and again she uses magic, this time to cause a great wind to rise up and blow her away. The hapless fly falls into a wine cup, and is swallowed by the wife of the chieftain Etar. Etar's wife becomes pregnant, and gives birth to a baby girl, whom she of course names Etain. The girl grows up ignorant of her origins, until one afternoon she chances to be bathing in a river. Midir, riding by on his horse, recognizes her. The girl instantly remembers her past and her love for Midir.

CREATURES OF THE WOODLANDS

To the Celts, the deer was the most revered of all creatures. Before the advent of agriculture and the keeping of cattle, venison was a staple food of the Celts. The ancient Neolithic ancestors of the Celts revered the deer, and long after its necessity was reduced by the advent of agriculture, the deer remained an important figure in Celtic mythological tales. Stags were associated with gods of the underworld, and they frequently appear in tales as gods or humans in animal guise. Deer frequent the sacred springs and wells and are associated with wisdom and knowledge.

THE MISCHIEVOUS BOAR

Unlike the deer, the boar is often seen as an agent of mischief or malevolence. The famous division between Northern and Southern Ireland is said to have been caused by the mischievous magical boar.

THE BOAR

The boar is a universal symbol of fertility, masculine aggression, and warrior spirit. Boars are known for their fearlessness, aggression, and stubbornness, but they were also revered for their cleverness and intelligence. The Celts believed the boar originated in the Otherworld, and boar meat was always on the menu in Otherworld festivities.

The boar appears many times over as an agent of mischief and a presage of death—he symbolizes the strength of the hero but is also present at his death. At the beginning of the tale of the Táin bó Cuilainge, Friuch and Rucht are the swineherds of the gods, and their names—meaning "bristle" and "grunt," respectively—belie their true nature. These two anthropomorphized boars, through their own mischief, set into motion the sequence of events that leads to great disaster—and the death of the hero Cuchulainn.

We've talked about the tale of Culhwch and Olwen in which there appears a great boar, Twrch Trwyth, who terrorizes the countryside. In order to marry his love Olwen, Culhwch must hunt the great boar and retrieve the magical comb, scissors, and razor he carries in his poisonous bristles. The boar of course is no ordinary animal but a Welsh king who was transformed by a curse.

The boar is frequently associated with royalty, especially the burden of royal hospitality. There is evidence that the boar was once regarded as a deity in its own right—the worship of a boar-god of the Gauls, called Moccus, seems to have been associated with the Roman Mercury, and it may be this or a similar god who inspired many of the later mythological boar tales.

THE FATE OF DIARMAID

The life of the Celtic hero Diarmaid was magically bound up with that of a boar, as recounted in the Fenian Cycle. Diarmaid was the son of Donn, a member of the Fianna. Diarmaid's mother had another son, his stepbrother and constant companion, who was the son of Aenghus's steward, Roc. Donn despised the boy, who was evidence of his wife's infidelity.

One evening, while visiting with Fionn and Aenghus, Diarmaid and his half brother played. The younger son ran between Donn's legs, and without hesitating, Donn broke the boy's neck. To hide his crime, Donn blamed the death on Fionn's hounds, which would have put Fionn in a very bad position. Fionn exposed the truth of the matter and revealed Donn as the killer. The boy's father demanded vengeance, but Fionn prevented him from killing Donn. The anguished father instead produced a magic wand, which he used to transform his dead son into a boar. The boar was a giant, invulnerable to any weapon. The steward declared that the life of Diarmaid was now tied with that of the boar, and that they would die together. Fionn, however, drove the boar into the forest, and a protective geas was placed on Diarmaid, preventing him from hunting boar.

Ironically, Fionn's act of protection was also Diarmaid's undoing. When Diarmaid was grown, he became one of Fionn's warriors, but eventually, he fell in love with Fionn's wife, Grainne, and stole her away. An enraged Fionn relentlessly pursued the couple, but when the company of the gods saw that the two were truly in love, they persuaded Fionn to forgive Diarmaid—or at least to declare peace between him and his former friend.

Diarmaid and Grainne prospered for many years and had many children, and one day, they decided to visit their friends in the company of the Fianna. They were welcomed, but as they slept, Diarmaid was continually awakened by the sound of hounds. He realized he was missing a hunt and rushed out to find Fionn and company in pursuit of the magical boar. When he asked Fionn why he had been excluded from the hunt, Fionn told him of his geas and the events behind it, which had occurred when Diarmaid was too young to remember. Diarmaid shrugged off the danger and set off after the boar, but he could not kill it—each weapon shattered as it struck the boar. Finally, in a fit of frustration, he struck the boar's head with the hilt of his shattered sword, and broke the boar's skull. Unfortunately, the dying animal ran straight for Diarmaid, fatally wounding him with its tusks.

THE TIE THAT BINDS

On a deeper level, the story of Diarmaid reflects and illustrates the Celtic conviction that the fate all things are tied to one another—the hunter and his prey, two ends of the same thread of life.

Diarmaid knew that Fionn could bring him water and so heal him, and Fionn obliged—however, as he neared Diarmaid with the water, his anger returned, and he let it run from his fingers. He tried again, and again, and each time, he was overcome with fury as he neared his dying friend. Diarmaid died, and Aenghus took his body home.

BIRDS: MESSENGERS OF THE GODS

Birds play an enormous role in Celtic mythology, figuring as divine emblems and as messengers of the gods. Chief among the sacred birds of the Celts were the raven, the swan, and the crane, although numerous other birds including geese, ducks, and even owls were held sacred at various times. Many early images of Celtic deities depict them with birds in the place of hands, emphasizing the importance of the birds as divine servants.

THE RAVEN

Because of their dark color and gruesome dietary habits, ravens were especially connected with gods of war and death. But those same gods were also associated with growth and fertility, so ravens were also symbols of new life. It was the raven that accompanied the souls of the dead to the afterlife, and portraits of the deceased often depicted them with the bird. Ravens were sometimes viewed as reincarnated warriors or heroes—the Welsh hero Owain had an army of invincible ravens, which are sometimes interpreted as an army of reincarnated warriors.

The raven was the ruler of the domain of air and therefore of communication; the cry of the raven was often interpreted as the voice of the gods. Images of the gods Lugh and Bran often depict them with birds alighting on their heads and shoulders, symbolizing this divine communication. (The Norse god Odin, who is sometimes compared to Lugh and Bran, has as his companions two ravens called Huginn ["thought"] and Muninn ["memory"].) For this reason, ravens were favored by the druids for use in divinatory ritual.

THE SWAN

The swan was revered by the earliest Celts, as far back as the Urnfield and Hallstatt cultures (circa 800 B.C.E.–500 B.C.E.). Although they are creatures of water, swans were, oddly, connected with the sun, sometimes even appearing as bearers of the chariot of the sun god. Swans and other water birds adorned numerous religious artifacts of the period, including many small statues and masks.

Many of the later Celtic gods appear in tales as swans or with the ability to change into swans. The ability seems closely connected with women, although in some stories male gods have the same power, invariably with a female of the same ability. As seen in the tale of Aenghus, both the god and his magical lover have the ability to transform into swans during the festival of Samhain. Sometimes it is Dechtire, the mother of Cuchulainn, who takes the form of a swan. Yet another tale of Cuchulainn tells of a young girl who pursues the hero in the form of one of the great birds, but she is badly wounded when the god mistakes her for a potential dinner.

SWAN CHAINS

Curiously, virtually every Celtic tale of magical swans share another theme, a chain or chains of precious metal by which a magical swan is identified. In some tales, the chains are of gold and silver; in others, the chain is made of common metals. Many times the birds appear linked together in large groups. The theme is an ancient one, which is reflected by the appearance of chained swans on ancient Celtic and pre-Celtic artifacts.

One of the best-known stories involving swans is the legend of Lir, the Irish sea god, whose beautiful wife dies giving birth to his children and leaves him bereft. Lir marries the sister of his deceased wife, but she is jealous of the attention he lavishes on his children and decides to do away with them. She accomplishes this by sending the children to swim and, while they are in the water, using a druid's wand to transform them into swans. The children are thus tragically enchanted for 900 years, yet they retain their intelligence and powers of speech.

DOMESTIC ANIMALS

The horse has a long history with the Celtic people and at times was a deity unto itself. Horses were associated by the Gauls with both gods and goddesses and were emblems of the sun. The horse was a tremendously important animal to the Celtic tribes, and its domestication transformed their culture from a society of hunters to a community of powerful warriors, traders, and farmers. Horses were not only a source of meat and milk but also provided labor for agriculture and transportation for people and goods, and allowed huge improvements in hunting and war-making capability.

CELTIC HORSEMANSHIP

By the time the Romans took notice of the Celts, they were already accomplished riders, and the Romans even borrowed many Celtic techniques from the Celtic cavalries for their own armies. The Romans were likewise impressed with the Celtic horse goddess, Epona, who was the only Celtic deity to have a temple within the boundaries of Rome.

The horse was of such importance to the Celts that it was associated with the sun itself. In some ancient cult statues, the god Taranis appears as a horse with a human face. The horse is also linked to a number of ancient goddesses, particularly those of warfare. The best known of the horse goddesses is Epona. The god Teutates, "Father of the People," was often portrayed as a bearded horse, and one of the names of the Dagda, "Eochaid," comes from a root meaning "horse."

The Welsh revered a goddess similar to Epona, called Rhiannon. Rhiannon, whose son Pryderi/Peredur is also linked to horses, makes appearances as a riding goddess in many later tales. A curious story of Peredur's birth related in *The Mabinogion* tells that he is abducted at birth and left alongside a foal in a farmer's barn. His mother is accused of his murder, and she is sentenced to carry visitors to her husband's estate on her back. She continues in this manner until her son comes to the gate and is recognized. In this tale again are echoes of transformation, rebirth, and redemption through recognition of the true nature.

THE HOUND

Hounds were another domesticated animal the Celts found invaluable. The hound was the companion of hunters and even of the gods. Hounds were prized emblems of courage and loyalty and were frequently given as gifts by nobles. When bestowed on a courageous warrior, the appellation "hound" was a badge of honor rather than an insult, and the name was even applied to gods, most notably Cuchulainn, the "Hound of Culann."

Hounds were also protective creatures, and a Celtic home seldom went without. Hounds were so well regarded that they were even believed to accompany the souls of the dead to the Otherworld.

THE BULL

The bull was an emblem of fertility, potency, prophecy, and regeneration. The bull was important to the druids, an important element in sacrificial ritual and seership. According to numerous accounts, a druid seeking prophetic or poetic inspiration would slumber under the skin of a sacrificial bull, a ceremony also employed in the elections of kings.

The bull was connected to the sacred crane and was the emblem of the mysterious Gallic god Esus, "lord." Several mysterious Gallic monuments dedicated to Esus contain images of a divine bull figure with the inscription *Tarvos Trigaranus,* or "bull with three cranes," an image of a bull or bull's head with three cranes perched atop his head or back. The symbolism has never been adequately explained and defies any attempt to decipher it, although some have made very tenuous connections between the iconography and the stories of the divine hero Cuchulainn. The bull is the central symbol of Cuchulainn's story, the Táin bó Cuailnge, or Cattle Raid of Cooley, wherein the countryside is laid waste and the god killed, all over a prized magical bull.

DRAGONS AND SERPENTS

The serpent was a symbol of wisdom and fertility. A particular dragon/snake hybrid referred to as the horned serpent was connected to the torque, a collar that is a symbol of sovereignty and status, and to the horned god Cernunnos. It was not until medieval times that dragons began to be viewed negatively; this was probably due to their associations with pagan gods—which is probably why so many tales pit brave Christian knights against wicked dragons.

The serpent was especially connected with healing waters, and the Roman authority Pliny the Elder noted in the first century that the druids especially revered for its healing powers an item they referred to as the "serpent's egg" or "Druid's egg." The serpent's egg was not an egg per se but an egg-shaped stone considered to possess certain magical properties.

MERLIN'S DRAGON

The dragon, a creature inherited by the Romans, was featured in early tales of the Arthurian magician Merlin, where it was a symbol from prophetic visions and invariably a sign of bad omen. Dragons were not all bad, however. The Welsh so revered the protective red dragon that it became their national symbol.

ANIMALS IN CELTIC CHRISTIANITY

Celtic Christians seem to have continued the traditional pagan reverence for animals. Seemingly endless varieties of animals are depicted in Celtic scriptures, and these creatures can be seen cavorting about with their hunters even on religious stone carvings/crucifixes. One exception to this rule, however, would be the snake, whose prominence as a villain in Judeo-Christian mythology made it unsuitable as an object of reverence. The serpent was also viewed as a symbol of druidry and eventually seen as evidence that the druids were in fact demon-worshippers—or at the very least, that they were deceived by the devil. That devil was found among the ancient gods in the form of the horned Cernunnos, whose visage became the emblem of the dark one for centuries to come.

CHAPTER FOURTEEN

Sacred Places

The sacred landscape left by their ancient ancestors had a profound effect on the spiritual and cultural development of the Celtic people. In modern times, people ascribe little if any significance to the landscape; today, the outdoors is rarely considered a necessity of everyday life. The Celts, on the other hand, found themselves intertwined with their surroundings. The land was not simply raw material for exploitation but an intelligent, living presence. The fabric of the land was home not only to man and animal, but also to the spirits of the forest and the crops, the underground dwellings of the ancestors, and the gods themselves.

PORTALS TO THE OTHERWORLD

While the many ancient stone monuments, passage tombs, and barrows that dot the ancient landscape belonged not to the Celts but to their ancient ancestors, the Celts nonetheless regarded them as highly significant. The real meaning of these ancient sites can only be guessed at because there are no written records, no myths, and few clues of any kind to tell how they were used. Long after the culture that built these monuments had passed out of memory, their descendants attributed their origin to the gods. Although there seems to be some continuity of thought and symbolism between the Celts and their ancient predecessors, definitive evidence remains tantalizingly out of reach.

There are several types of megalithic tombs. These are generally divided among four types:

+ Court tombs or court cairns are multichambered generational tombs that resemble underground houses covered with earth.
+ Passage tombs are complex tombs built to resemble elaborate houses and covered over with earth and stones, some with elaborate doorways or courtyards. Passage tombs in Ireland often contain cremated remains rather than bodies.
+ Portal tombs, cromlechs, or dolmens are doorlike stone structures that resemble passageways. Some of these are simply court cairns whose earthen coverings have worn away.
+ Barrows or tumuli are earthen mounds containing burial chambers covered with earth; these have the appearance of hills.

Court tombs are some of the oldest Neolithic gravesites. They were most often built on an east/west axis, and might have been used by a single family for several generations. The graves known as dolmens ("table") or portal tombs (cromlechs, or "crooked stone" to the Irish) appear to be simple stone monuments. However, they are more likely the remains of early barrows from which the earth and contents have long worn away.

PASSAGE TOMBS

The underground chambers known as passage tombs were regarded by the Celts as the homes of the gods, entrances used to travel from the Otherworld to the world of mankind. Although they are commonly called tombs, the so-called passage tombs are not simply tombs but also temples.

Passage tombs are named for their long, tunnellike entrances. Both the symbolism and positioning of the entrances of the chambers of many of these monuments show that the sun played a vital role in the ritual use of the chambers. Most passage tombs are decorated with elaborate carved designs, sometimes with elaborate astronomical calendars, which probably played an important role in the timing of rituals.

SOLAR GATES

It is quite possible that the solstice rituals conducted in the passage tombs were the origin of the Celtic concepts of solar gates, the idea that the solstices and equinoxes represented passages, or "gates," by which the Otherworld could be accessed.

The famous tomb at Newgrange, for example, is replete with solar symbolism. Like many of its kind, the entrance of Newgrange is a long passage leading to an inner chamber. At the first light of the winter solstice, both the passage and the inner chamber are illuminated.

Similar monuments nearby are aligned on the same axis, but they lack the precise alignment of Newgrange. The astronomical alignments, combined with the solar symbolism and presence of cremated remains, have led to speculation that the rituals conducted in the tombs were not simple funerals but ceremonies designed to facilitate the passage of the dead into rebirth—making the moniker "passage tomb" quite appropriate.

THE HOLLOW HILLS: SÍDHE-MOUNDS

The earthen mounds known as barrows, long-barrows, or tumuli are examples of one of the oldest known burial practices, dating back to classical antiquity. The barrows of Europe date mostly from the Neolithic era, but often continue into the Bronze Age. The graves themselves generally contain the bodies of the deceased and a variety of grave goods, including food, utensils, and weaponry. These are covered over with stones, and there are stones covered with earth. Over time, they take on the appearance of an artificial hill. In some areas, many barrows crowd close together, creating a very unusual landscape.

The elaborate barrow tombs of the ancients were also perceived as homes to the Tuatha Dé Danann. They were referred to as the "hollow hills," and it was believed that one could hear the music and conversations of the fairy courts from within. Superstitious travelers even into modern times were reluctant to venture too close to one for fear they may be kidnapped by its inhabitants. The persistent belief that the hills were the homes of divine ancestors was based on a kernel of truth. Possibly, the Celts had some memory or intuition about the real purpose of the burial mounds—in a sense, they were indeed the dwelling-places of their ancient ancestors. The name by which the Tuatha Dé Danann or fairy-folk were commonly known—Aes Sídhe, "barrow people"—is derived from their association with these mounds.

STONE CIRCLES AND ALIGNMENTS

The ancient stone circles of Britain, Ireland, and Scotland represent one of Europe's most enduring enigmas. In their design and function, they are clearly related to the passage tombs that preceded them, but they are not tombs. Hundreds of stone circles of varying complexity can be found throughout the British Isles and beyond, first appearing during the Neolithic period and continuing well into the Bronze Age. While some show signs of use as tombs, it is obvious that they served a larger purpose, possibly as temples, calendars, or even astronomical observatories. In many cases, they appear to be all three.

The earliest form these ancient monuments took was the henge, which consisted of a circular or ovoid ridge surrounding an inside ditch or circular pit. These were sometimes surrounded by wooden posts arranged in circles and, later, by stones. Most were relatively small, around 60 feet in diameter, although larger examples could be as large as 1,200 feet. Most consist of a single ring of stones, although as time passed, the circles grew in size and complexity, with some having as many as three concentric rings. Another popular style of stone monument is called an alignment, consisting of rows of menhirs (standing stones).

Literally thousands of stone circles, alignments, and monuments are scattered throughout Europe. Here are some of the best known:

* Stonehenge, a prehistoric ring of large standing stones, is thought to have been erected around 2200 B.C.E.
* Avebury Henge, a ritual complex located in southwest England, is a monument that rivals Stonehenge in size and importance.
* Hill of Uisneach, the "navel" of Ireland, in County Westmeath; it is also called the "Stone of Divisions." Uisneach represented the

symbolic center of Ireland and was the legendary location of the first Beltaine fire.

* The Ring of Brodgar is a prehistoric stone circle in Orkney, Scotland.

* The Carnac Stones is an alignment of thousands of stones that stretches nearly two miles in length in Carnac, France.

* The Rollright Stones, located in the English Midlands, are long rumored to be the remains of an enchanted king and his men.

* The Callanish Stones of the Isle of Lewis are slender megaliths arrayed in the form of a large Celtic cross.

STONEHENGE

The ancient monument of Stonehenge is inarguably the best-known prehistoric monument on earth. Located on the Salisbury Plain in the geographic center of England, the site is more than 4,000 years old and may have been erected on the remains of an even earlier circle constructed from timber. On the plains, there is evidence that a large settlement once surrounded the site.

The origin and purpose of Stonehenge have puzzled historians and archaeologists for centuries. In medieval times, its conception was attributed to the Saxons, the druids, Merlin, and even to the devil himself, who was said to have built it from stones spirited from Ireland. In the centuries following, it was assumed to be a Roman temple and, later, a druid observatory.

Time and patient excavations have shown all of these ideas to be false, although the romantic notion of druids conducting solemn solstice rituals at the monument has been impossible to shake. Beyond a shadow of doubt, the monument predates the druid orders by thousands of years; nonetheless, Stonehenge is still home to annual rituals conducted by druid revival groups.

Perhaps because people were so accustomed to its presence, Stonehenge wasn't regarded as very remarkable by most people until relatively recently. In fact, in 1915, a lawyer named Cecil Chubb purchased the monument as a gift for his wife for less than $10,000. History records her reaction as less than enthusiastic, and he eventually donated the site to the British government for use as a public park.

NOT A HENGE

Despite its name, Stonehenge is not a true henge. A genuine henge consists of a circular or oblong ditch, surrounded by a raised earthen mound or ridge. Stonehenge is technically not a true henge at all because the position of its mound and ditch are reversed.

When compared to other prehistoric stone circles and monuments, Stonehenge is unique in both structure and layout. Its stone trilithons, the unique groupings of three that make up the remaining ring of the monument, are not found in any other monuments. There is archaeological evidence that Stonehenge may have begun as a ring of timber, which was later replaced with stone. There is also evidence that the monument was rebuilt several times over its long existence.

STANDING STONES: MENHIRS

The word *menhir* is from the Welsh meaning "long stone." It is a pretty exact description of the monuments, which occur most often as solitary standing stones. Often carefully shaped, they sometimes appear in groups or as part of stone circles. They are often decorated with a variety of symbolism and imagery. Menhirs are primarily an artifact of the Neolithic period.

Though their purpose is unknown, it is assumed they served some religious function. Theories about the purpose of menhir range from territorial markers to memorial monuments—at one time, it was even suggested they were sacrificial altars. Roman observers noted that when the stones were erected, sacrifices would be placed in the holes they were set in and that the stones were regularly anointed and hung with garlands of branches and flowers.

There are some hints that they served a religious or magical purpose, as they are tied to various supernatural occurrences in mythological stories. Whatever their purpose, Christians found them loathsome pagan idols and toppled them by the thousands. All the same, literally thousands of the enigmatic stones remain standing. The Carnac site in Brittany, for example, contains more than 3,000 individual stones arranged in clusters. Brittany is also home to the largest standing menhir, which reaches an astonishing height of 30 feet.

The standing stones have many connections with fertility rites, and even in the present day they are believed to promote conception and prevent complications of childbirth.

ECHOES OF AVALON: GLASTONBURY

Perhaps the most revered of Britain's sacred sites is Glastonbury, the site of a former great abbey that many believe to be the ancient entrance to Avalon home of Gwyn ap Nudd, lord of the Otherworld. Among the many legends surrounding Glastonbury, it is rumored to be the location of the entrance to Otherworld, the site of ancient Neolithic chalkworks, the grave of king Arthur and Guinevere, the home of St. Patrick, and even a depository of the Holy Grail! Glastonbury and its towering hill are mysterious, even magical places.

The most recognizable feature of Glastonbury is the tor, a conical, terraced hill that rises from the surrounding plain. The plains that surround the tor were once a flood plain, and because of this, the ancient Celtic name for the area was Ynys Witrin, the "Isle of Glass."

There is much speculation about the tor's seven terraces. Because of their unusual shape and number (seven), there is some debate whether they are natural or manmade and, if the latter, what their purpose might have been. When viewed from above, the terraces create a winding, labyrinthine path, which may have served some ancient ritual purpose.

Archaeological explorations of the area have found evidence of continuous occupation of the site, from Neolithic settlements to Roman fortifications until finally it was home to Christian monasteries and a medieval church, which was destroyed in a thirteenth-century earthquake. All that remains of the abbey is St. Michael's Tower at the top of the tor. Ancient groves of apple trees give Glastonbury another connection to the Otherworld, and it features in several mythological tales as the location of the entrance to Avalon.

AVALON AND ARTHUR

Glastonbury is heavily connected with the legend of King Arthur. Early in the Arthurian cycle, Glastonbury was identified as Ynys Affalon, or Annwn, where the mythical Arthur is mentioned for the very first time, in the account of the quest for the Cauldron of the Chief of Annwn. In the Arthurian romances of the twelfth century, Arthur returns to Avalon mortally wounded, to remain there for eternity.

Besides being connected with Avalon, Arthur's final resting place, Glastonbury is close to the ruins of Cadbury Castle, a hill fort closely associated with the historical Arthur. The fortification dates to the correct period, and nearby place-names can be linguistically connected to the name *Camelot*. (*Cadbury* in the Saxon language is "battle fort"; the castle lies near the River Cam.) The connection was first made in writing by antiquarian John Leland in 1532, recording a local legend of some age. Evidence is mostly circumstantial, but it is clear from the archaeological evidence—including quantities of Roman gold and evidence of a great feasting hall—that the fortress belonged to a chieftain of no little importance.

THE FAIRY RAID

One Glastonbury legend links Arthur with the tradition of the fairy raid or wild hunt. Once every seven years, at sundown on Midsummer's Eve, Arthur and his party would ride out from underneath the Glastonbury hills, making a raucous circuit of the neighborhood before returning underground.

Local legends of Arthur and his court abound, but whether they spring from a germ of historical truth or are simply self-perpetuating is unknown. A number of legends linking Arthur with Glastonbury appeared in written form beginning in the twelfth century, when a Welsh story identified the tor as the location of the fortress of Melwas, a rival king who kidnapped Arthur's wife Guinevere. Soon afterward, Geoffrey of Monmouth identified Glastonbury as the location of Avalon.

JOSEPH OF ARIMATHEA

Even older than the legend of Arthur is the widespread belief that Glastonbury was where Christianity was first established in the British Isles. The emissary was no less a figure than Joseph of Arimathea, the wealthy apostle of Christ, who was said to have traveled there after the crucifixion. This idea was first put to paper in the ninth century by Archbishop Rabanus Maurus, in his biography of Mary Magdalene. In this work, Maurus claimed that Joseph traveled to Britain along with Mary Magdalene, Lazarus, and other members of Christ's inner circle. In later, more fanciful versions, Joseph arrives accompanied by a youthful Jesus, who receives training from the druids of the island.

The claims about Joseph could be dismissed out of hand as so much fantasy, were it not for one curious fact. Church father Tertullian, writing around C.E. 200, marvels at the spread of Christianity in pagan lands, even as it has yet to take hold in Rome:

> . . . all the limits of the Spains, and the diverse nations of the Gauls, and the haunts of the Britons—inaccessible to the Romans, but subjugated to Christ.

Why he believes this to be the case is unknown, but his observation probably reflects a widespread belief. The sentiment was echoed about a century later by Church historian Eusebius, who accepted as fact that Jesus' apostles had visited the "Britannic isles."

Through Joseph, the Holy Grail was said to have traveled to England, providing a connection between the chalice and the legendary King Arthur that has excited many so imaginations. The Joseph idea was first put to paper in the twelfth-century Arthurian tale "Joseph d'Arimathe," by French poet Robert de Boron. In de Boron's story, Joseph uses the chalice of the Last Supper to catch the blood of Christ as he hangs on the cross. Joseph then carries the cup with him to Avalon, to keep it safe until it comes to be discovered by Arthur and his knights. This is the first story that connects the Grail explicitly with Christianity.

Another legend that connects Joseph with Glastonbury is the sacred thorn, an otherwise ordinary hawthorn tree that grew outside the abbey.

It was reportedly remarkable in that unlike other hawthorns, it flowered twice a year—first in the spring, and again at Christmastime. The tree became entwined with Joseph in the sixteenth century, when the legend first began to circulate that the tree originated from the staff of the saint. Supposedly, when Joseph came to the end of his journey, he struck his walking staff into the earth, where it blossomed. It became traditional to make gifts of cuttings from the thorn to monarchs and other VIPs. That tradition continued until the seventeenth century, when the tree was burned as a pagan superstition by Oliver Cromwell's troops. The tree was eventually replanted from one of its own cuttings, but the new tree died in 1991. The original thorn was propagated with many cuttings, however; its offspring, given as gifts, can be seen throughout Britain and as far away as Canada.

THE FLOWERING OF THE THORN

The holy thorn was so well regarded that its opinion was sought after the then-unpopular Gregorian calendar was adopted. It was reported that visitors flocked to the tree on the date of the "new" Christmas, but that the tree preferred the "old" date, refusing to bloom until then.

THE CHALICE WELL

Today, Glastonbury is extremely well trodden by spiritual pilgrims of all stripes. Without a doubt, the biggest draw is not the tor itself but the sacred Chalice Well that lies at its foot. The spring that fills the well is believed to have been in continuous flow for nearly 2,000 years, and it has likely been regarded as a holy site for at least that long. The water of the well is heavily pigmented with iron, giving it the appearance of blood. Because of this reddish hue in the water, it is sometimes called the "red spring" or even the "blood spring." The well is tied into the legend of Joseph, where it is suggested as the hiding place of the Grail, which continually refreshed the water with the blood of Christ.

TARA: SEAT OF THE HIGH KINGS OF IRELAND

The ancient site of Tara (Teamhair na Rí, "Hill of the King"), is one of the most ancient sacred sites in Ireland. Tara is located in Meath, the symbolic center of Ireland. Tara is home to numerous monuments, including the Mound of the Hostages, a Neolithic-era passage tomb; various earthworks; and the standing stone Lia Fáil, the "Stone of Destiny," which according to legend was one of the four treasures brought to Ireland by the Tuatha Dé Danann.

Tara is the legendary seat of Irish kings. It is where the high kings of Ireland would be chosen and where they would celebrate their coronations. The Hill of Tara is surrounded by an Iron Age ringed fortification known as the Fort of Kings or the Royal Enclosure. Within this circular boundary are two interior rings, a smaller ring fort and a circular earthwork, which have the appearance of breasts when viewed from above.

It was here that the Feis Teamrach ("mating of Tara") was held, a great assembly of lawmakers, scholars, and priests. This assembly, also known as the Parliament or Feast of Tara, was, according to legend, instituted over 3,000 years ago by King Ollamh Fodhla, the namesake of Ulster.

In the manner of ancient tribal assemblies, the Feis Teamrach met every three years (or seven, depending on the account) at the feast of Samhain to discuss matters of history, decide laws, and record history.

The ritual owes its name to the ancient kingmaking rite of sacred marriage, the symbolic mating of the Morrígan and the Dagda before the battle of Magh Tuireadh. It is very likely that the ancient assembly evolved from a sexual ritual designed to reinforce the high king's symbolic marriage with the land, represented by the goddess Sovereignty.

SPRINGS AND HEALING WELLS

Water was held especially sacred to the Celts, a symbol of life and nurture and a source of wisdom, intuition, and magic. Water was the vehicle for rebirth and reincarnation and the domain of the gods of healing. Lakes, streams, rivers, and wells were all considered entrances to the Otherworld, and they were frequently used as depositories of sacrificial offerings to the gods.

Every body of water had its attendant gods and goddesses, nymphs, and spirits. Water was often assigned to a particular deity based on its aspect: bubbling streams and brooks may have belonged to the goddess Coventina or other nymphs. Rivers were often under the provenance of a local goddess. Hot springs were usually associated with solar deities, but they often had attendant goddesses as well, as they were viewed as a marriage of sorts between the solar deity and the goddess of the spring.

Water also figured in the Celtic cult of the head. Severed heads were among the many offerings left at the bottoms of lakes and ponds, and scarcely a well from ancient times does not contain a severed head or three. The heads seem to have been intended to give the waters a healing benefit. In some cases, they may have served an oracular purpose, as attested by the abundance of folk tales involving severed heads that prophesy from magical wells. It is also possible that a healing benefit was sought, as drinking from the skulls of one's ancestors was widely thought to be a curative.

Many of the deities of the Otherworld were originally associated with bodies of water, and water was one of the most popular places to leave offerings for them. Much evidence suggests that natural springs, waterfalls, and even many lakes were the domain of the gods of healing; these were very popular with pilgrims, who left many offerings at these sacred sites. During the period of Roman occupation, these offerings expanded to include "curse tablets," tiny strips of engraved lead containing entreaties to the gods to exact all manner of vengeance on enemies, thieves, straying lovers, or indifferent objects of affection.

AQUAE SULIS: THE SPRINGS AT BATH

The three hot springs of Bath, England, were considered magical by the Celtic Britons, who dedicated the largest to the water goddess Sulis. When the Romans invaded Britain in C.E. 43, they recognized the site as sacred. They identified Sulis with the Roman goddess Minerva, and she was thereafter referred to as Sulis-Minerva. They built a great complex bathhouse around the site, with many elaborate temples and buildings. Both the Celts and the Roman occupiers revered the baths for their healing qualities, and the site became a tourist mecca.

DRESSING THE WELLS

A possible remnant of the veneration of well goddesses is the practice of well dressing, a tradition of rural England that was first recorded in the fourteenth century and continued in one form or another until the present day. The modern ritual begins with the creation of a wooden frame that is covered with a soft clay, into which is incised a design, usually with a religious theme. The design is then filled and colored with flowers, foliage, and berries, after which the frame is erected over the well.

Well dressing is connected to May Day practices and is similar to the Roman festival of the Fontinalia, in which the guardian-nymphs of wells were honored with garlands of flowers. The well-dressing ritual seems to have similar pagan origins. Curiously, many of the towns associated with the rite are home to hot springs or other water features.

CLOUGHTIE WELLS

Cloughtie (or Clootie) wells are named for the strips of rag ("cloots") hung on nearby trees as votive offerings left by petitioners in need of healing. The rags are dipped in the well, often in conjunction with prayers, incantations, and ritual circumambulation. Sometimes, they are touched to an afflicted body part or made from clothing worn by the afflicted. They are then hung from the tree in hopes that as the rag disintegrates, so will the illness.

One such well is the Knockanare Well, whose history betrays its pagan origins. The well, located on the grounds of Blackwater Castle in County Cork, figures in a story of Fionn mac Cumhaill, wherein the hero was cured after receiving a mortal wound. The site until recent times contained a stone Sheela-na-gig, a female "grotesque" carving.

BRIGHID'S WELL

Numerous wells throughout Ireland are associated with St. Brighid, but the main one is, of course, the well located at Kildare Abbey. Like other sacred wells, Brighid's well features a cloughtie tree and is popular with pilgrims seeking healing or an answer to a prayer. The small chapel adjacent to the well is strikingly similar to descriptions of ancient sacred wells. The narrow chamber is crowded with statuary and literally crammed with offerings—prayers, photos, rosary beads and religious objects, prayers, and other objects.

CHALKWORKS

One of the most mysterious features of the ancient landscape is the enormous hill figures—massive drawings literally carved into the landscape, created by hewing away turf and earth to expose bright chalk below. Only a handful of such figures survive intact, all in the English countryside:

* The Cerne Abbas Giant is also known as the "Rude Man" for his remarkable genitalia. The giant is bald and carries a large club, leading to speculation that he represents the god Ogmios or even the Roman Hercules.
* The "Long Man" of Wilmington may represent a warrior or a god. This enigmatic standing figure appears to hold two spears.
* The Uffington Horse is one of a great number of horse-figures, most of which have been lost. The image appears on coins unearthed in local archaeological explorations and may reflect the image of a goddess.

The purpose of the hill figures is unknown although they have obvious religious import. They may have been intended to promote fertility, mark festivals, or serve as a votive offering.

CHAPTER FIFTEEN

King Arthur and the Celts

Beyond doubt, the best-known and most enduring of the legendary Celtic heroes is Arthur, the semi-mythological High King of Britain who serves a dual purpose as both a quasi-Christ figure and a pagan god-hero. The legends of Arthur constitute a sort of Celtic mystery religion (similar to the mystery religions of ancient Greece in which true knowledge of the god was restricted to the initiates) with symbolism that transcends pagan and Christian mythology.

THE ORIGINS OF ARTHUR

The legend of Arthur emerged at a time when Christianity had the most tenuous hold in Celtic lands. During the period in which Arthur's real-life existence was said to have taken place, Britain was a rough place. The Romans had largely given up and left the country at the mercy of squabbling warlords and Saxon invaders. The new religion of Christianity had limited influence outside of its monasteries, and the Church of Rome struggled to keep the local churches in line and away from then-powerful pagan influences. In a very real sense, the character of Arthur perfectly represents this period, a melding of Christian and Celtic spirituality that most beautifully preserves the ancient heroic ideal and merges it with the idealistic hopes of the new faith.

THE NAME *ARTHUR*

There is much speculation about the origin of the Arthurian legend. The name *Arthur* may be Gallic in origin, from *artios viros,* "bear man," or it may be of Roman origin. (In Welsh, the word for *bear* would be "Art" or "Arth.") One theory that seeks to explain Arthurian symbolism claims that Arthur is a personification of the constellation Ursa Major, The Bear, whose Latinized Brythonic name was *Arturus.* Curiously, the folk-name for the constellation was "Arthur's Plow." This symbolism may have been understood by later Arthurian chroniclers, and underscored by symbolism such as the Round Table, which may have originally been intended to symbolize the zodiac.

Historical records of the sixth century mention the heroic battle victories of an unnamed chieftain; these battles, chiefly the battle of Mount Badon, were soon afterward attributed to Arthur. In the ninth century, Welsh monasteries recorded a number of battle victories, and the deaths of Arthur and Mordred, and compile lists of his heroic company, but they give little else in the way of details of his life or identity. In any case, it is generally assumed that Arthur was a chieftain or even a sort of mercenary soldier employed by British kings. Later Welsh legends identified Arthur as a cousin of the hero Culhwch, and it is through these tales that Arthur began to evolve as a mythological hero.

ARTHUR AND CULHWCH

One of the earliest mentions of Arthur is related in the Welsh *The Mabinogion*, in the story of the hero Culhwch. The name Culhwch means "son of pig," due to the hero's birth in a pigsty. Culhwch seems to have some relation to an ancient Gallic boar-god. This is worth mentioning because there is evidence from this period of another Gallic god, an anthropomorphic bear called Artios. Perhaps the story of Culhwch and Arthur is derived from a long-lost Gallic myth.

WELSH ORIGINS OF ARTHUR: CULHWCH AND OLWEN

Culhwch is the penultimate Welsh god-hero, who is best known from romance "Culhwch and Olwen." Culhwch's legends are filled with ancient Celtic religious imagery and certainly date from a much earlier era. Culhwch's story contains many parallels to the tales of Cuchulainn and other divine heroes. Many of the companions of Culhwch, such as the river-deity Cei or the one-armed Beddwyr, reappear in the Arthurian corpus as companions of the Round Table.

Culhwch is clearly a prototype of the mythological Arthur, and Arthur makes an appearance in the tales of Culhwch as a cousin or companion, alongside many other characters who later emerge as central figures in the Arthurian tales. Culhwch himself may be related to an ancient Welsh god and is closely associated with boar symbolism; Arthur as the bear seems to round out the woodland gods hypothesis.

GEOFFREY OF MONMOUTH

By the twelfth century, a scattering of folk legends had blossomed into a full-fledged mythology, and the familiar legend known today was the work of a twelfth-century monk named Geoffrey of Monmouth, who stitched various narratives together into his fanciful history of British kings, *Historia Regum Britanniae*. Geoffrey's work popularized the myth of Arthur and introduced the character of Merlin. Although Geoffrey always claimed his source was an ancient manuscript, that text was never recovered or mentioned again.

ARTHUR AS TRICKSTER

Before Geoffrey of Monmouth, Arthur was perceived as a warrior but not a terribly romantic hero. In many tales he is portrayed as a hothead, even a murderer, and is the victim of trickery on a number of occasions. Arthur is himself placed into the trickster role himself in a number of folk legends and is even sometimes identified as the leader of the raucous and violent Wild Hunt.

Geoffrey's tale begins with an entirely mythological British king of Roman lineage, a son of the Roman Constantine called Uther Pendragon. Uther takes as his mistress Ygraine, with whom he has become smitten.

However, she is the spouse of his enemy, Gorlois of Cornwall. Uther obtains Ygraine's affections through deceit, with the aid of the wizard Merlin, who agrees to aid Uther's deception on the condition that he be given any resulting child to foster. Uther agrees, and Merlin disguises him as Ygraine's husband, sneaking him into Ygraine's chambers. When Ygraine's true husband is killed in battle that night by Uther's own men, he does not reveal his deception, and she agrees to marry him, not realizing they have already met.

The son produced from their union is Arthur, who is sent for fostering under the watchful eye of the wizard Merlin. Uther dies, seemingly without an heir, while Arthur is still young, which plunges the nascent kingdom into chaos. The remaining chieftains squabble for control until the teenaged Arthur emerges as the heir. Later versions of the story introduced the legendary sword in the stone, and either due to fate or Merlin's tinkering, it is only Arthur who can remove the fateful sword. The act convinces the chieftains that Arthur's claim to the throne is genuine, and he is proclaimed king. The holdouts rebel, but they are quickly put in their place on the field of battle.

SWORDS AND KINGS

Arthur's sword clearly relates to the ancient ritual of kingmaking. The name *Excalibur* is linguistically linked (through its Latin name, Caliburn) to Caladcholg, the mythological sword of light possessed by Fergus, the ancient high king of Ulster. The stone is reminiscent of the Stone of Lia Fáil, which chose Irish kings by screaming aloud when touched by a worthy candidate.

KNIGHTS OF THE ROUND TABLE

Arthur continues in a series of military victories, putting down one rebellion after another until the kingdom is restored. Like any self-respecting hero, Arthur then seeks out the affections of the most beautiful woman in the kingdom and marries her. He builds a fabulous castle in the mythological Camelot and assembles a council for himself out of the wisest, bravest, and cleverest knights of the kingdom, who become the legendary Knights of the Round Table.

As the tale unfolds, however, it returns to its roots in the Celtic myth cycles, becoming a tale of tragedy, betrayal, and ruin. In earlier versions of the legend, Arthur embarks on a series of conquests, and while he is away, his scheming nephew (who is later portrayed as his secret son) takes Guinevere as a mistress and attempts a coup of Arthur's kingdom. In the later, more familiar version of the story, it is Lancelot, Arthur's trusted lieutenant and the most heroic of his knights who becomes his betrayer, after the two return from their fruitless quest for the Holy Grail. The king is forced to face the reality that his best friend and his queen are lovers, and reluctantly agrees to put them both to death. The lovers flee together, but guilt overtakes them, and Guinevere enters a convent. Arthur is mortally wounded in battle with his own son, and the Golden Age comes to a crumbling ruin.

GUINEVERE

Guinevere, or Gwenhwyfar, is the tragic, faithless, sometimes traitorous wife of Arthur. She is renowned as a great beauty, and Arthur loves her upon first glimpse. He marries her despite many warnings from Merlin that she will bring him to ruin. She is unable to conceive him an heir, but despite this, Arthur loves her and refuses to put her aside. In the end, she betrays him in an act that brings Arthur to ruin and death.

Guinevere's origins are mysterious. Her name is undeniably Celtic, most likely meaning "white ghost" or "white fairy." Her fairness and even the root of her name makes her similar to Olwen, the wife of Culhwch, whose name means "white track," or even to Blodeuedd, the faithless wife of Lleu.

THE ORIGIN OF MERLIN

Although the character of Merlin first appears in Geoffrey of Monmouth's fanciful medieval history, he appears to be a composite character based on two separate historical characters: Myrddn, a magician/prophet mentioned in earlier poetic tales, and Ambrosius Aurelianus, a fifth-century Romano-British war leader. Myrddn, who might be considered the earliest incarnation of Merlin, was not a wizard but a Welsh warrior-bard who received the gift of prophecy as a result of madness caused by the grief of losing his loved ones on the battlefield. Myrddn is described as living among the forest creatures until he obtains the gift of prophecy. (This early origin tale is echoed in later tales of Merlin, where he is said to have lived his final days as a wild madman in the forest.) Myrddn is himself a very curious character, perhaps a druid. One telling story of Myrddn claims that he prophesied his own triple death by beating, drowning, and impalement—a fate not unlike that of certain sacrificial victims. Geoffrey calls his composite creation Merlin Ambrosius.

To further muddy the waters, Ambrosius Aurelianus is one of the leading candidates for the role of the historical Arthur. Little is known of the biography of Aurelianus except that he was Roman by lineage and the survivor of a great onslaught by the Saxons. He organized the remainder of the Britons and achieved a number of victories against the invaders.

It is unclear why Geoffrey identifies Merlin and Aurelianus, except that both Myrddn and Aurelianus figure in stories about Vortigern, another early ruler.

CHILD OF THE DEVIL?

In later versions of Merlin's biography, it was claimed that his mother was a nun in a convent who was seduced by the devil himself, in order to beget an antichrist. The pious nun repented and foiled the plan by having the child baptized immediately upon his birth.

MERLIN THE PROPHET

Merlin, according to Geoffrey, was born the son of a mortal woman and an incubus, to whom his supernatural powers are attributed. Merlin makes his debut as a prophet when, as a young man, he is kidnapped by the warlord Vortigern. Vortigern had been attempting to build a tower fortress, which tumbled down repeatedly until he is advised by his magicians that it will not stand unless the foundations are sprinkled with the blood of a man who has no human father.

The young Merlin is the obvious choice, but he escapes a gruesome fate by revealing the true cause of the tower's collapse. He reveals to Vortigern that a pair of dragons are doing battle in a lake under its foundations. These dragons are later revealed to be symbolic of the continual battles between the Britons and the Saxons, which only Arthur is able to calm.

Merlin is not simply an accessory to Arthur but a legend unto himself, appearing in numerous tales of his own. Tales of Merlin's parentage are many and varied—some, such as the medieval telling that Merlin was the son of a nun's congress with a demon, are quite ridiculous. Invariably, however, it is understood of Merlin's parentage that he has no human father. It is the wise Merlin who engineers Arthur's birth, bringing Britain a savior.

THE FALL OF MERLIN

Merlin's downfall, like Arthur's, is due to a woman. Unlike Arthur's tale, Merlin's seems more typically medieval, the great man brought down by the scheming wiles of the evil sorceress to whom he has entrusted his deepest secrets. While Morgan and Guinevere appear to be diluted goddesses, Merlin's scheming lover Nimue embodies every medieval superstition about the evil nature of women. Nimue is described as a beautiful but cruel girl who entreats the elder Merlin to teach her his magic; the magician, quite besotted, agrees against his better judgment to do so. Nimue turns out to be quite ungrateful for Merlin's lessons. At the first opportunity, she uses her newfound skills to destroy him, binding him for eternity in a tower of glass or in the interior of an oak—both clearly symbols of the pagan Otherworld.

OTHER WOMEN IN ARTHUR'S LIFE

One of the strangest additions to the Arthurian legend was Arthur's sister, the fairy woman Morgan. Morgan sleeps with Arthur and bears him an unacknowledged son, who proves to be his undoing. Morgan's name and demeanor recall the ancient goddess of sovereignty and war, the Morrigán—and indeed, the story of Arthur and Morgan echo many of the tales of the encounters of ancient kings with the goddess of sovereignty. Although in the Arthurian stories Morgan is cast as a villain, it is Arthur's dismissive behavior toward Morgan and his son that lead to his downfall. Celtic mythology is filled with tales of heroes who were defeated and killed because they angered or otherwise failed to heed the goddess of the earth.

RAVENS AND THE GODDESS

Another curious legend dating to around the sixteenth century provides more connections between Arthur and the goddess. It was said that Arthur and his company were transformed into ravens upon their deaths, and that the sight of a raven by a knight or soldier was an omen of his impending death.

It is also telling that the death of Arthur is due to a challenge from his sister's son, a retelling of the archetypal story of the elder king contending with the younger for the affections of the goddess of the land. It is originally Mordred, Morgan's son, who was said to have stolen Guinevere away from Arthur, and only later is Mordred's parentage associated with Arthur's incestuous affair.

Curiously, although Morgan is portrayed as the greatest villain of the Arthurian stories, there is much that hints at her divine roots. Morgan not only mothers Arthur's son, but it is she who heals him of a symbolic wound to the groin and who provides him with magical protection in the form of an enchanted scabbard that protects him from harm. When Arthur fails her, Morgan removes her protection from Arthur to make way for her son to defeat him. It is also telling that although she is the architect of Arthur's death, she is present at his last journey as she accompanies him to the isle of Avalon, the realm of the dead. It is clear that no matter how muddy the details become, Morgan is intended to represent the goddess Sovereignty.

THE GODDESS AND THE HAG

In many Celtic tales, the goddess Sovereignty is represented by an ancient hag who guards the well of wisdom (or dispenses the magical mead that initiates the king). Only the wise or brave man sees through the hag's guise and is given kingship over the land. The hag's guise may represent the difficulties of sacred responsibility, or it may hold an even deeper meaning.

The sovereignty symbolism in the Arthurian cycle is repeated in other aspects of the Arthurian legend. In the story of Gawain and the Loathly Lady, Gawain, Arthur's purest and most chivalrous knight, makes an agreement to marry a hideous hag, a clear representation of the ancient goddess, in return for granting some request or favor. Despite his bride's ugliness, the knight decides to do his duty by her, and she is transformed into a beautiful maiden. It is probably not coincidental that Gawain is the only knight in these tales to achieve the elusive grail, which perhaps owes to its connections the ancient practices of pagan Britain.

Gawain's bride clearly echoes ancient Celtic notions about the goddess. For example, both the Welsh goddess Cerridwen and the Irish Cailleach have the appearance of withered hags, but each possesses a font of wisdom and riches for those who look beyond appearances.

THE LADY OF THE LAKE

Another mysterious character who can be interpreted as fulfilling the role of the goddess Sovereignty is the enigmatic Lady of the Lake, who makes several appearances in key parts of Arthur's life. The Lady is clearly an Otherworld denizen. Although her residence is given as Avalon, she is clearly a water goddess, and most interactions with the Lady take place in her lake, which may be identified with the waters surrounding Glastonbury.

The Lady of the Lake is credited as the foster mother of Lancelot, but she is better known as Arthur's mysterious benefactor. When Arthur's sword of kingship is destroyed in battle, it is the Lady who famously gives him the Otherworld sword Excalibur, which he takes great pains to return to her when he knows he is about to die. The Lady makes a further appearance when Arthur receives his last fatal wound, and she accompanies him to Avalon. Strangely, the Lady of the Lake is later confused with Morgan le Fay, whose name connotes a water fairy.

THE CUP OF CHRIST

The best-known tales of Arthur—those of the quest for the Holy Grail—are much later. The origin and meaning of the tales have been debated and speculated upon in countless books. Like Arthur himself, they represent a curious merger of Celtic pagan legends and Christian symbolism. The cup that Arthur and his knights seek out is ostensibly the cup of Christ, present at the last supper, the emblem of the transformative Eucharist.

ARTHUR AND THE CAULDRON OF ANNWN

Arthur's earliest quest is mentioned only briefly in early Celtic tales. In the enigmatic Welsh poem "The Spoils of Annwn," Arthur is one of the seven heroes who return from the fruitless underworld quest for the cauldron of Annwn. The cauldron reappears in some versions of the story of Culhwch and Olwen, as one of the thirteen treasures collected for Olwen's dowry.

THE QUEST FOR THE GRAIL

The grail quest is actually a later addition to Arthurian tales although it is unquestionably drawn from the earliest stories of Arthur and other Celtic heroes and their search for the cauldron of illumination. The exact nature of the grail is also disputed, seen variously as an emblem of conversion, the realization of love, the neglected goddess of the land, or even the marriage bed of Christ. No matter how Christian the tale, however, it is clear the story has its roots in ancient Celtic quests for the cauldron of the gods. Both the cup and the cauldron are symbols of divine grace, emblems of rebirth and spiritual illumination.

While the tale of the Holy Grail is Christian on the surface, it is deeply pagan underneath. One of the earliest tales of the Holy Grail is the unfinished twelfth-century grail romance of Chrétien of Troyes, "Perceval, the Story of the Grail," wherein the grail is the mysterious magical object through which the injury of the mysterious Fisher King can be healed. The injury of the king's groin is an obvious phallic symbol of the vitality of the land, symbolism with clear roots in the ancient connections of the king and the land, the living goddess through which the king's authority was derived. An important symbol of the goddess Sovereignty was a wine goblet, offered to the would-be king on the occasion of his betrothal to the goddess. Curiously, Arthur himself receives a similar wound in many stories.

By the time the grail is associated with Arthur and his knights, its symbolism has been transferred. It is now the cup of the Last Supper of Christ and his apostles, which, according to legend, was filled with Christ's blood at his crucifixion. The transition of the symbol from an emblem of the goddess to an emblem of Christ can be seen as an almost perfect analogy of the uneasy spiritual transition of the Celtic people— Christian on the surface, with a pagan heart and sensibility underneath.

THE GODDESS AND THE GRAIL

Many Arthurian researchers have tackled the multilayered Arthurian symbolism and concluded that in many cases, the story preserves the anxiety of a culture transitioning from a very dual system to a monotheistic outlook. The qualities once borne by the goddess now reside in the mother of Christ and many female saints, but the deeper symbolism of the goddess is represented by the grail.

Some see a clear parallel between the wounds of the Fisher King (and, later, in Arthur's injuries) and the fate awaiting a Celtic king who did not fulfill his marriage obligation to the goddess. Celtic kingship was wholly tied to the fertility of the land and the prosperity of its people. A king who was not righteous and fair, who did not accept the full responsibility of leadership, would see the land suffer barrenness and drought. Indeed, infertility is a persistent theme in Arthur's story. Although Arthur is a heroic and wise ruler, he is cursed. His wife can bear no heir, and the kingdom he has built is destined to fall to ruin at his death. Even more strangely, it is Arthur's son by his sister, whom he refuses to acknowledge, who becomes the instrument of his ruin.

MORDRED AND THE DEATH OF ARTHUR

There are a number of versions of the story of Mordred's birth and his role in the death of Arthur. The best known is that Mordred was the product of an incestuous union between Arthur and his sister Morgan (sometimes, Morgause) and fostered as the true son of Morgan's husband, Lot of Orkney.

His conception is sometimes described as an accidental act, sometimes as the product of a rape brought on by Arthur's lust for his beautiful sister. In any case, Arthur did not recognize Mordred as his son, even when his marriage to Guinevere failed to produce an heir.

Mordred is born at Beltaine, a birthday he holds in common with Arthur, and also with Culhwch, Lleu, and Mabon. This connection of Arthur and Arthur's son with the divine son archetype, like much Arthurian symbolism, is likely not accidental.

In Geoffrey's tale, Mordred is introduced as a confidant and friend of Arthur, whom Arthur makes regent while he travels abroad to make war on Rome. During Arthur's absence, Mordred betrays Arthur by having him declared dead, then marrying Guinevere and declaring himself king. Arthur returns immediately upon learning the news, and in the ensuing battle, Mordred is killed and Arthur fatally wounded. In Welsh versions of the tale, Guinevere willingly betrays Arthur, a theme repeated in later versions with the character of Lancelot.

ORIGINS OF THE GREEN KNIGHT

The origins of the enigmatic Green Knight aren't clear, but some see in him an obvious parallel to the Green Man, a medieval archetype of nature, who in turn may be descended from Celtic woodland deities like Cernunnos and Fionn.

In the Middle Ages, Mordred came to be treated with a bit more sympathy. He is cast as a conflicted character who betrays the father who refuses to acknowledge him as his heir because of the embarrassing circumstances surrounding his birth. As in every tale of the tragic Celtic hero, it is Arthur's own failures that bring about his destruction.

THE GREEN KNIGHT

Another element of the Arthurian tales that has certain pagan origins is the Green Knight, a character who appears in a number of Arthurian romances and poems. He is a bizarre character, almost invariably described as a knight with green skin, eyes, and hair, dressed all in green clothes and armor.

Sometimes the Green Knight is a malevolent figure, and sometimes he is a neutral character. The Green Knight, like the hag, appears in a testing context. He is most often matched with Sir Gawain, who is portrayed as Arthur's greatest knight, a paragon of chivalry.

The Green Knight invariably stands between the hero and the object of a quest, and the tale usually involves some sort of test of the hero's character. In most versions of the tale, Arthur's court is in the midst of celebration, and the Green Knight appears as a sudden challenger. He asks that any member of the court step forward and strike a blow against him, and in one year's time he will return the blow. Gawain steps forward, and he slices off the giant's head in one heaving blow. The giant, however, is not killed. He calmly picks up his head, sets it back on his shoulders, and reminds Gawain that he must meet him in the "green chapel" in one year to exact his half of the bargain. Gawain, being utterly honorable, agrees. At the end of the year, he sets off to find the knight at the green chapel.

Gawain's journeys vary, but he almost always undergoes some form of temptation, usually in the form of a seductive maiden. His tests successfully passed, he proceeds to his certain doom—but when he again meets the fearsome knight and lays his head before him, the giant delivers only the most glancing of blows. The Green Knight in these stories seems most likely to represent the hero's lower nature, and the temptations that plague even the most resolute. Having faced his challenges with courage and honor, he now finds the monster much less formidable.

CHAPTER SIXTEEN

The Turn of the Year

The Celtic calendar is frequently referred to as a wheel, and the ancients likened it to a fiery wheel, a clear allusion to the sun. Sometimes this wheel was linked to the harp of the Dagda, likening the recurring seasons as a repeating story. Whereas spring and summer were the domain of innocence, youth, love, and virility, the dark half of the year was given to mysteries, wisdom, aging, and death.

SAMHAIN:
THE LOWERING OF THE VEIL

Samhain, from the more ancient Irish form *Samhuinn*, was the most widely celebrated of the ancient Celtic festivals. It was a celebration of the harvest, of the closing of the year, and the beginning of the new year. Agriculturally, it was the time when the last fruits of the harvest were collected and stored, and the livestock were culled and quartered for the winter ahead.

The dark time of the year had many magical and mythical associations as well. Samhain was also the time when the gates of the Otherworld were thrown open, allowing the spirits of the ancestors and the Sídhe-folk to mingle with the living. It was at this time that the fabled Wild Hunt, a procession of animals, fairies, and spirits, was most often said to occur.

THE HISTORY OF SAMHAIN

The Gauls marked the year into just two halves, the dark or winter half being Sam or Samonios, the light half Gam or its Latinized form, Gamonios. Like other ancient cultures, the Celts marked the beginning of a day at sunset; likewise, the year was counted as beginning in its dark half.

Caesar remarked on the practice in his writings on the Gallic Wars:

> All the Gauls assert that they are descended from the god Dis, and say that this tradition has been handed down by the druids. For that reason they compute the divisions of every season, not by the number of days, but of nights; they keep birthdays and the beginnings of months and years in such an order that the day follows the night.

Samonios, the dark half of the year, was reckoned first in the Celtic calendar. The festival marking the beginning of Samonios was Samhuinn

(Samhain), a three-day feast celebrated on the new moon closest to the autumnal equinox. As Beltane marked the beginning of the summer season, Samhain marked its end. In fact, the word *Samhain* most likely means "summer's end" and is the current Gaelic name for the month of November. In the first-century Celtic Coligny calendar, a similar three-day festival ushered in the new year in the late autumn.

THE MANY NAMES OF SAMHAIN

The festival now commonly referred to as Samhain has had numerous names. In Wales, it was known as Calan Gaeaf, "winter's eve." In Ireland, it was Oiche Shamra, "Samhain night," sometimes "pooka night." In Manx, it is Sauin.

The Samhain festival marked the transition between two very different seasons. The growth season was at an end, with the majority of crops long harvested. The time for festivals and tribal gatherings was coming to an end, and warfare and trade would be largely suspended until warmer weather returned. This was a last opportunity for merrymaking and celebration before a long winter confinement.

Samhain was celebrated at the cusp of the seasons, marking the end of the light and the beginning of the dark of the year. In mythical terms, the youthful aspect of the goddess Sovereignty gave way to the withered hag of winter, and the fruits and flowers of the warm season were replaced with the barren cold of winter. It was marked at Tara with a great feast, the Feis Teamrach, or "Mating of Tara," at which the high king was symbolically mated with the goddess of sovereignty, a celebration that marked the Samhain-night coupling of the Morrigán and the Dagda on the eve of the battle of Magh Tuireadh.

Indeed, the Samhain was a favorite time for tribal assemblies, during which all of a tuath would gather together for feasting, games, and amusements and also to settle debts and disputes. In ancient times, great offerings would have been made at lakes, shafts, and the entrances to the Sídhe-mounds, as the denizens of the Otherworld would be particularly receptive. Horse races and other feats of strength were not uncommon at this time, a tradition going back to the earliest days of the Celtic peoples.

FALSE LEGENDS

A common urban legend claims that the Samhain celebration was in honor of a ghastly god of death by the same name. Although a few minor Celtic gods have similar names, none has any connection to the Samhain festivals.

Samhain was considered a time of great change; it was also a time of great transparency between the world of man and the Otherworld. Samhain was a traditional time for divination and prophecy, an auspicious time for sacrifice. The transformation of the world brought about other transformations, and it was at this time one could enter the Otherworld. Celtic myth tales involving Otherworld magic often take place during Samhain, and now is when Otherworld denizens make benevolent journeys or even warfare against the living. Samhain was the preferred day for beginning an adventure or setting out on a quest, especially a divine one. Many important events in Celtic mythology take place or begin at the time of Samhain. For example, it is at Samhain that Aenghus seeks to recognize his lover Caer in her swan form.

SACRED BONFIRES

Samhain was celebrated all over Ireland and Great Britain with the lighting of sacred bonfires. As in similar rituals in the north, the Samhain fires were the first fires of the season. In a ritual that would repeat at Beltaine, all other fires would be extinguished and ritually relit from the sacred bonfires. The bonfires themselves were inaugurated by the druids, the first according to some accounts being lit on the hilltop of the druid Tlachtga, where it would be easily visible from Tara.

The bonfires were not the only fire rituals associated with Samhain. A popular ritual called "lating the witches" involved a solemn candlelit procession, the purpose of which was the discovery of dark magic. If a candle flickered or died out during the procession, it meant that the person carrying it was a certain victim of witches, and special precautions would be taken to protect him or her.

Other precautions would be taken as well. As the Tuatha Dé Danann were well known to roam the countryside, it was customary to leave gifts of milk and bread for them, not just on Samhain but on the other festival days as well. This customary offering was sometimes referred to as the fairy tax, honoring the ancient agreement between the Milesian Celts and the denizens of the Otherworld.

SAMHAIN AND HALLOWE'EN (ALL HALLOWS)

Even after the demise of the pagan Celtic culture, Samhain remained a popular holiday, and in early Ireland, it was the most important of the four great festivals. There is a common theory that floats about that the institution of Hallowe'en by the Catholic Church was intentionally

begun as an answer to the reluctance of the people to give up pagan rev-
elries or the remembrance of the dead.

The truth is actually much less clear-cut. The various churches in the
first centuries instituted celebrations of their saints and martyrs, which
varied according to location, but were celebrated mostly in the spring.
By the year 800, German and English churches were commemorating
the saints on the first of November, and by 835, most of the rest had followed suit at the urging of Pope Gregory IV. Before this time, however,
the Celtic observance was held in the springtime, near the Easter feast.

Also, although there was a definite connection with death and passages, there isn't a lot of evidence that Samhain was held to honor the
dead. Most such claims come much too late to be of any use, and the
idea is never mentioned in the surviving mythological tales. It is a fair
assumption, however, that in this traditional time of tribal gathering,
some commemoration would have been made on behalf of the ancestors. It is known that it was sometimes customary to light torches at the
entrances of the ancient tombs, to make clearer the passage from the
Otherworld.

CHRISTIAN PRACTICES RISE

From the earliest days of the Church, it was customary to observe a
day in memorial to the saints; later, this expanded to include all of the
dead. The saints of the church were celebrated on November 1 with a
solemn mass and singing.

As it was already customary to honor one's ancestors during the
Samhain period, it was only natural that the Church's own observances
followed suit. It became customary to visit cemeteries on this day, to
sweep and clean the graves, and echoing the older custom, lights were lit
outside of homes and in cemeteries. Water and other provisions would
be left out, and the doors left unlocked. The ancient tombs were not

neglected, either; the old custom of walking in deasil (clockwise) procession three times about the ancient monuments carried well into medieval times.

The November celebrations were eventually worn away as the popularity of the All Saints festival increased. Within a few hundred years, the commemoration of the dead also moved from an earlier date to coincide with the November observation, so that eventually, the two would be held back-to-back. In any case, the Christian observations were quite unlike their pagan predecessor, and by the medieval period, the feasts became solemn reminders of mortality and the grisly fates awaiting the sinner.

In medieval times, as during other feast days, it became customary to spend Samhain night going door to door collecting food and other offerings for the poor, often in exchange for prayers said for the homeowner.

However, the Samhain ritual often involved a costumed masquerade, some say in imitation of the fairy procession. If a homeowner gave generously to these masked visitors, the visitors would make a solemn procession around the kitchen fire—a tradition that clearly echoes the ancient Samhain rituals. Were the hosts less than generous, they would be cursed in a similar manner.

SAMHAIN TODAY

Neopagans, especially Wiccans, have embraced Samhain as their most sacred holiday, an adoption based on Samhain's importance as a celebration of endings and beginnings. The modern pagan take of Samhain is more of a composite holiday, often mingling traditions of the ancient Celts with later European practices. Samhain is generally viewed by modern pagans as a time for reflection and meditation and a time to commune with the spirits of dead loved ones, honor one's ancestors, and prepare for prosperity or good fortune in the coming year.

A typical Wiccan or neopagan celebration of Samhain may include memorials for the departed, visits to cemeteries, and rituals to honor ancestors. Traditional harvest goods such as pumpkins, apples, and mead are often featured.

FEAST FOR THE ANCESTORS: THE DUMB SUPPER

A later custom that bears mentioning is the medieval practice of the "dumb supper," still celebrated in many rural areas in Europe and popular as well with modern neopagans. In a typical dumb supper (the word *dumb* having its ancient meaning of "silent"), a banquet is prepared, with places set at the table for both the living and the dead. Prayers are recited, and candles or other sources of light are passed around the table and around each participant. The places set for the ancestors and loved ones are filled with their favorite foods, and the meal progresses in silent communion with the dead.

THE CORN SPIRIT

An autumn tradition that almost certainly carries over from ancient pagan practices is the creation of the so-called corn dolly. While today's corn dolly is a simple harvest craft, it was once imbued with deep spiritual significance. In Celtic territories and elsewhere in Europe, it was customary to leave a small portion of grain unharvested, in the belief that removing all of the stalks would leave the spirit of the grain homeless and unable to return. The reserved grain would be shaped into the form of a man or woman or other symbolic shape and was often treated to lavish ceremonial processions and feedings. The bundle was sometimes dressed in clothing, and would be reverently displayed—sometimes on a pole, or kept in a cradle or bed.

The resulting "doll" represented the essence of the grain, the god of vegetation who would be "born" at the beginning of winter, and ritually sacrificed in the spring by burning or plowing under before the sowing of new crops. There is some speculation that the corn dolly tradition replaced an earlier blood sacrifice.

TRADITIONAL "CORN"

The word *corn* in this case refers to its oldest use, as a generic term for grain. Today *corn* is used almost exclusively to refer to the Native American maize plant, a grain unheard of in Europe until brought back by New World explorers.

The earliest reference to this tradition can be found in accounts of St. Eligius (or Eloi) of Flanders, who castigates his countrymen for following local druid customs, among them the creation of the *vetula*, or old woman of the corn.

In Christian times, corn dollies evolved into a rural household practice, featuring elaborate symbolic figures crafted from straw left over from the harvest. These were usually placed over doorways or in barns as good luck charms; they were typically burnt at Christmastime; possibly in mimicry of the old mistletoe traditions. Even today, it is not unusual to see elaborately braided corn dollies given pride of place in winter decorations, and there are literally hundreds of specialized designs that vary from region to region.

GUY FAWKES

Vestiges of the sacrificial vegetation god may survive today in the British celebrations of Guy Fawkes Day. Fawkes was a seventeenth-century Catholic revolutionary implicated in the infamous November 5 Gunpowder Plot, in which he attempted to blow up the Houses of Parliament and end Protestant rule in England. Fawkes was caught in the act and swiftly executed. Within a hundred years, an effigy of Fawkes had become a proxy for the ancient corn effigy. The harvest deity was replaced with a figure of the infamous traitor, which would be paraded from house to house by children who would beg coins or sweets in return. Afterward, the effigy would be burned in a great bonfire.

BELTAINE:
THE EXALTATION OF THE SUN

The spring festival of Beltaine or Beltane ("bright" or "shining") was probably celebrated in honor of Belenos ("shining"), an ancient Gaulish sun god. Belenos was widely worshipped, from Gaul to Austria and as far as Italy. The Romans identified him with their own solar deity, calling him Belenos Apollo. Belenos was strongly associated with water, especially hot springs, and his shrines and sanctuaries were dedicated to health and healing.

BELTAINE, NOT BAAL

The Christians were somewhat horrified by the Beltaine, which they erroneously associated with the demon Baal. This unfortunate association led to all sorts of speculation about human sacrifices and other dark rituals.

Although there is little mention of Belenos in Irish myth, the festival that bore his name remained an important part of the Celtic religious calendar. Beltane was celebrated by the druids beginning on the eve before. After every household fire was extinguished, gigantic bonfires, called needfires, were built on the hillsides overlooking the community. The fires were kindled ritualistically, using nine sacred woods.

According to the glossarist Cormac, it was during Beltaine that the druids blessed and purified the community's livestock, driving them between the great fires. Afterward, villagers would themselves leap through the flames, and at the end, the embers from the sacred fire were carried home to relight the household fires. It was these bonfires that were reportedly the largest bone of contention between the Christian establishment of Ireland and the remnant druids.

The story of Patrick and Lóegaire, credited as the last pagan king of Ireland, records such a conflict. The dispute comes at Beltaine, with the preparations for the sacred fires at Tara. According to custom, all fires in the vicinity of the sacred hill of Tara were extinguished, until such time as they could be relit from the sacred bonfire. The prohibition against fires within view of the hill carried the force of law and could be punishable by death. Patrick, knowing of the sacred tradition and fully aware of the possible consequences, traveled to Tara and deliberately lit a bonfire on the plain, which was easily visible from the hill.

One version of the tale claims that Lóegaire moved to arrest Patrick, but found his arguments in favor of Christianity to be so eloquent that he was granted the freedom to preach as he wished. A later, somewhat snarkier version of the story has the king's druid advisers dying miserable deaths while attempting to harm the saint, ending in the happy conversion of the king.

St. Patrick is implicated in the origin of a curious medieval ritual in the church. Beginning on Maundy Thursday (the Thursday before

Easter Sunday) and continuing for two days thereafter, it became customary to extinguish all of the lights of the church. A small fire would be struck from a flint and blessed. This would be used to light a candle held in the end of a special staff. This was the Arundina Serpentina, a staff capped with a bronze serpent or dragon, from which all of the church candles would be relit. There seems to be an obvious relation between this practice and the Beltane fire ritual.

IMBOLC

Imbolc means "in milk," and refers to the lactation of livestock in preparation for the birth of new babies in the spring. Imbolc is celebrated on February 2, in the midst of one of the coldest months of winter. All the same, it is a celebration of the coming of the light and the promise of new life to come. The "darkest part" is over, and the weather will only become brighter and warmer. Although it may not seem so, winter is ended and spring has begun.

GROUNDHOG DAY

The western tradition of Groundhog Day is an echo of Imbolc rituals past, likely brought to the New World by immigrants from Ireland and England.

Imbolc was sacred to the goddess Brighid, mother goddess of the Celts. Brighid was goddess of fire, thresholds, and transformation, and so mother and protector of crops, pregnancy, and sexuality. Brighid was the patron of the arts, especially poetry and metalworking. The festival of Imbolc was a festival of lights, celebrated as an encouragement of the sun to ensure fertility in the coming season. Brighid was the daughter of the Dagda, "the Good God." She was wife to the giant Bres, and mother of sons Ruadan ("red-haired") and Ogma, the god of eloquence.

As with the other great festivals, Imbolc was a time to rekindle sacred fires, especially those of the hearth and the forge. The Church was as eager to embrace this as it was the other ancient festivals, and the day was christened "Candlemas," where it was literally a mass in honor of the lights of the church. The old wax and partially burned candles would be removed from the church, and new candles would be blessed and set in place. Overall, it was a good time of year to be a candle maker.

BRIGHID

As discussed, it's entirely possible that the great goddess Brighid, through her absorption into the Irish church, became St. Brigid of Kildare, by legend a powerful abbess whose miracles not so coincidentally coincide with the powers of the goddess whose name she bears. St. Brigid was extraordinarily important to the Irish; she was counted in Irish legend as the foster mother of Christ and is seldom left out of any Irish prayer. She has a special affinity for fire, and is often invoked in prayer as a charm against house fires. The saint's miracles likewise correspond with the powers of the goddess—she is the patron saint of poets, blacksmiths, newborns, and herdsmen. St. Brigid's feast day is celebrated, not surprisingly, on February 1, the feast of Candlemas, where the bride's doll and the fire wheels are still constructed in her honor.

As said earlier, a traditional custom of Imbolc was the creation of corn dollies, effigies created with leftover grain saved from the previous year's harvest. The dolls represented the resurrection of the crops, as well as the return of the goddess from winter sleep. After her procession, she would be placed in a representative marriage bed to encourage the return of her mate, the sun god. This custom continued well after the mantle had been passed from pagan goddess to saint.

BRIGHID'S THREE ROLES

Brighid fulfils a special role among the Celts, being the only goddess who was a mother, a daughter, and a spouse to the gods, fulfilling all of the roles of the divine female. Both the goddess and the saint were said to have two sisters also named Brighid, making them both triple goddesses of sorts.

Other customs of the feast of Brighid included the fashioning of sun wheels, or bride's crosses of straw, which were hung over thresholds. These were considered especially protective against fire and lightning. Grains from the sheaves used to fashion Brighid's dolls and crosses were blessed and saved; these would be added to next year's seed, with an invocation to Brighid to protect the crops.

Because Brighid was believed to roam the countryside on her night, it was also customary to leave cakes and a bit of ale outside the gates for her. A linen cloth might also be left draped over a hedge, in imitation of the saint's cloak; this she would bless as she passed by, and the cloth would be protection against all manner of disease, especially in livestock.

LUGHNASADH: THE FEAST OF LUGH

The Feast of Lughnasadh falls on the cross-quarter day between the summer solstice and the autumn equinox. The festival was, according to legend, instituted by the god Lugh on the occasion of his foster mother Tailtiu's death, as a funeral-feast. It is clear, however, that the feast originated as a commemoration of Lugh's slaying of the giant Balor, and the prising of agricultural secrets from the dark god Bres. This victory over the Fomorians marked the beginning of the rule of the Tuatha Dé Danann.

In the calendrical pageant of the gods, Lughnasadh commemorates this victory over darkness and celebrates the fruit of that victory, the first fruits of the harvest. It can be looked at as the victory of Lugh, the gentler solar aspect, over Balor, his harsher aspect. The feast of Lugh is held at the hottest time of the year, when the battle against the harshness of the sun was often very real.

Tailtiu seems to have been an ancient agricultural goddess, about whom little is known except for the harvest festival held in her honor. In Lugh's story, she is the Fir Bolg princess who fosters him. During the period of starvation that marked the captivity of the Tuatha Dé Danann by the Fomorians, she performs heroically, clearing a massive plain for planting so that the people will not starve. She dies as a result of her exertions, and the grieving god institutes a funeral feast in her honor. The month of August in Ireland has long been associated with sorrow and mourning—this may reflect a tradition of mourning for the "sacrifice" of the grain.

Tailtiu is connected with a number of ancient agricultural goddesses, in particular Macha, who dies in childbirth. These goddesses may have been symbolic of the crop, which "dies" while giving up its yield.

Lugh was called "many skilled," and his feast was a pageant of skill as well, from feats of athleticism and competitive games to displays of handicrafts and metalwork. Lughnasadh represented the last period of rest before the major work of the agricultural year began. It was a time for trade between tribes, for sport and friendly competition, and for reciting songs of praise for the heroic deeds of the heroes and the fallen warriors of the tribes. The crops were ripened, and there were trades and goods to be purchased with the new bounty. Lughnasadh was also a popular time for new couples to enact temporary partnerships called "Tailtian marriages." These trial marriages were solemnized at the festival and typically lasted until the next year.

These traditions in particular remained strong through Christian times. Predictably, the church discovered yet another festival to commemorate, which just happened to fall at this time—the Lammas festival. Lammas also celebrated the harvest, and it was celebrated in much the same way, with games and contests and open-air markets. The name Lammas is believed by some to be derived from "loaf-mass," but this explanation is not universally accepted.

CHAPTER SEVENTEEN

Celtic Christianity

There are no clear boundaries between Celtic paganism and the beginning of Christianity in Ireland. The process of transition from pagan to Christian was a gradual one, and many elements of the pagan religion were absorbed, making Celtic Christianity quite different from that practiced in the rest of Europe, which had long been under Roman rule. The Celtic monasteries established in Ireland were not considered very different from the schools of druidry, and for a long time the people looked on these monks as more or less a new class of druids.

THE COMING OF CHRISTIANITY

Christianity was introduced to Ireland around C.E. 440, only a few decades after the Romans began recalling their troops from Britain. The faith was brought by a bishop named Patrick, who established his domain at the ancient fortress of Emain Macha (Armagh), a city reputedly founded by the ancient Celtic Queen Macha.

CELTIC TONSURES

The ubiquitous tonsure haircut of the Catholic monk, in which the hair is cut to leave a portion of the head bald, with a fringe around or in the back, is a custom that originated in druidry. It was later adopted by early monastic groups in Ireland. To the druids, baldness was a sign of wisdom, and the haircut symbolized the adoption of the path of wisdom.

Christianity in Ireland followed a different path of development than in most other European countries. Where European Christianity followed powerful bishops who had immense power over local governments, Christianity came to Ireland at a time when Roman military control over Europe was fading, making for a unique set of circumstances for the newborn Irish church.

Irish Christianity flowered in the form of independent monasteries, which operated in many respects outside the authority of the Roman Church. These monasteries absorbed not only pagan clerics, but pagan customs, superstitions, and even gods. Because of the autonomy enjoyed by these early churches, they were able to incorporate many elements of the local religion into their doctrines.

With its isolation from both church and government, the Celtic Church avoided many of the eruptions, conflicts, and doctrinal wars that plagued Rome, and the result was a church heavily concerned with the mystical, spiritual side. To the Celtic Church, God was not a distant concept, but a continual presence, manifest in the wholeness of nature. It was not uncommon for the Irish monk to seek the life of a forest hermit, finding God imminent in his natural surroundings.

The similarity between Irish pagan symbolism and Christian symbolism is striking. Along with a tripartite god, the newcomers brought with them a god who was sacrificed and reborn, and the practice of baptism by immersion in water, for the purpose of attaining eternal life—both concepts already well understood by the druids and their devotees.

THE SYMBOLISM OF THE SHAMROCK

It has long been taught that St. Patrick, when explaining his religion to the pagan Irish, picked up a three-lobed shamrock and used it to expound on the nature of the trinity. The story is unlikely, but it probably has a grain of truth in it, as the compatibility of druid symbolism would have made many aspects of Christianity easier to assimilate.

Because of the relative ease with which the two faiths mingled, Celtic Christianity also absorbed elements of pagan belief. Celtic gods were slowly transformed into Celtic saints, and in turn, Celtic saints took on the characteristics of the Celtic gods—tales of Ireland's first Christians are as fanciful and filled with magic as the tales of the Tuatha Dé Danann. Early Irish images of Jesus on the cross show not the sorrowful Latin corpus Christi but a resplendent, smiling god with wide-open eyes who looks not the least bit concerned about his crucifixion, and if not for the presence of the cross, might be mistaken for the visage of Lugh.

PATRICK: PATRON OF IRELAND

Tales of the Irish saints are filled with as much fantastic embellishment as those of the ancient Celtic gods. They are attributed miraculous powers that rival those of the ancient druids, and their biographies detail all sorts of fantastic adventures, from flying to battling dragons. The reality of their lives is more difficult to pin down.

Accounts of the life of Patrick are no exception, filled with fanciful details and miraculous feats. Patrick's biographies are muddled, complicated by the fact that written records were not introduced to Ireland until well after the introduction of Christianity. Further complicating matters, no connection can be made between Patrick and any of Ireland's early churches, although the general consensus is that he was active in Ireland at the end of the fifth century c.e.

The earliest record of the life of Patrick is contained in two letters that are generally recognized as his own. One of these is a letter condemning Roman raiders who have carried off some of his congregants, but the more important document is his *confessio*, or confession, which contains a brief account of his early life along with his defense against barbs from unknown accusers. While St. Patrick's confession is filled with self-deprecation, it is also filled with boasts about the many people he has converted and baptized. He seems especially proud to have converted a number of wealthy members of the nobility.

THE CONFESSION

Patrick relates in his confession that he was born to a wealthy Roman family in Britain, the son of a deacon, although he claims he himself was not a Christian. He enjoyed a life of privilege until, at the age of sixteen, he was kidnapped along with many of his countrymen by Irish raiders. He was taken to Ireland, where he lived the next six years under the servitude of Milchu, a chieftain and a druid priest, working as a shepherd and suffering from cold and deprivation.

By Patrick's account, Milchu was a cruel and intolerant master, and Patrick grew to hate the druid religion. The young slave sought solace through daily prayer, and he tells that after six years of fervent supplication, a voice appeared and commanded him to seek "his ship," as his captivity was at an end. Patrick fled his master and sought out the nearest port, where he found a waiting ship. He credited God for his deliverance from slavery, and when he returned to his family, he made the decision to devote his life to God.

Patrick traveled to France and entered the religious life, eventually becoming ordained. He spent twenty years rising through the ranks of the church, until, some twenty years after leaving Ireland, he was consecrated a bishop. Patrick then made the decision to return to the place of his captivity, and to Christianize pagan Ireland. His family implored him not to leave, but a vision convinced him that he had to return. He writes:

> And after a few years I was again in Britain with my parents, and they welcomed me as a son, and asked me, in faith, that after the great tribulations I had endured I should not go anywhere else away from them. And, of course, there, in a vision of the night, I saw a man whose name was Victoricus coming as it from Ireland with innumerable letters, and he gave me one of them, and I read the beginning of the letter: "The Voice of the Irish," and as I was reading the beginning of the letter I seemed at that moment to hear the voice of those who

were beside the forest of Foclut which is near the western sea, and they were crying as if with one voice: "We beg you, holy youth, that you shall come and shall walk again among us." And I was stung intensely in my heart so that I could read no more, and thus I awoke. Thanks be to God, because after so many ears the Lord bestowed on them according to their cry.

Patrick records in his confession his many successes in baptizing thousands, ordaining priests, and convincing many women to become nuns. Patrick remained in Ireland until he died, a few years before the end of the fifth century.

PATRICK OF LEGEND

Later tales of St. Patrick have none of the humility of Patrick's own writing. They rival the tales of the druids in their fantastic accounts of wizard's battles, although Patrick accomplishes his miracles through prayer rather than magic. Many stories of Patrick's exploits involve triumphs over the druids. In a version of the story of Lóegaire, his druid councilors stand against Patrick in his attempt to light an Easter fire, an opposition to pagan custom. Patrick prays for the death of the pagan priests, and the ground opens up to swallow them. There are numerous variations on this theme—Patrick prays, and God smites the pagans.

PATRICK'S DRUIDIC SPELLS

Not all of Patrick's magic came about by prayer. Irish tradition claims that Patrick possessed many of the same spells credited to the druids, including the ability to make himself invisible, through the use of the *faeth fiada* ("cry of the wild beasts").

PATRICK AND THE SNAKES

One of the most famous tales of St. Patrick is his driving of the serpents from Ireland. This certainly mythical tale purports to explain the lack of snakes in Ireland, but it also carries overtones of Christian/pagan conflict. If the snakes are viewed as the emblems of the druids (who revered the serpent as one of their holy symbols), the tale takes on another level of meaning, namely, that the serpents are not animals, but the pagan way of life.

This interpretation is borne out by many other references to battles with dragons or serpents undertaken by the saints, which invariably occur on sites formerly sacred to the druids. This is not to say such battles necessarily took place at all. Instead, these stories may use poetic license to deal with the embarrassing reality of many a church sited on former pagan holy grounds, which may have mattered much more as the centuries passed.

Oddly, the tale of the snakes echoes the ancient story of the Fomorians, described as sea serpents, who are driven into the sea by the Tuatha Dé Danann.

ST. BRIGID: MARY OF THE GAELS

There is much speculation over the life of Ireland's second patron saint, so-called Brigid of Kildare. Brigid is the name of both a saint and a great Celtic goddess. The ancient Celtic Brighid was the daughter of the Dagda and the patroness of poetry and seership. Brighid was especially revered by the filidh as their special goddess. Brighid was one of the triple goddesses, with two sister aspects, also called Brighid, goddesses of healing and of the forge. Additionally, the legendary Brighid was guardian over livestock, and her feast day was celebrated on the first of February, which marked the first day of spring and the lactation of the ewes.

Whether or not the Christian St. Brigid existed is a mystery lost to time. It is, however, indisputable that the saint took on many of the attributes of the Brighid who had gone before, and many of the legends of the goddess became legends of the saint.

LIFE OF BRIGID

According to Irish tradition, Brigid was born in Faughart, in Northern Ireland. She was the daughter of a powerful druid, Dubthach, a king of Leinster, and his Pictish slave, Brocca, reputedly one of St. Patrick's converts. The young Brigid was reportedly entranced by the preaching of St. Patrick, and she opted to enter religious life as a nun over much opposition from her father. She became a nun and quickly progressed to a position of leadership, eventually founding a combination monastery/convent at Cill-Dara (Kildare), over which she presided as abbess. Brigid wielded considerable power in the Irish Church, and her abbey became renowned throughout Europe.

BRIGID THE ABBESS

One of the curious legends of St. Brigid concerns her consecration as abbess, which was carried out by another well-known Irish saint, St. Mel. The story tells that Mel inadvertently read the rite to ordain a bishop, an irrevocable act that is meant to explain the great authority held by the abbess, who was said to have had the power to appoint bishops in Ireland.

Alongside the abbey, Brigid was said to have founded a thriving community of artisans. Most notable of these were the scriptorium, which produced illuminated manuscripts, including the beautifully decorated Book of Kildare, and a legendary forge, which specialized in fine metalwork.

MIRACLES OF PLENTY

A great many of Brigid's miracles have to do with milk and the fertility of cows, an echo of the great goddess for whom she is named. Among the miracles attributed to Brigid were turning water into milk or beer. She was also credited with many miracles of increase—creating large quantities of beer with a little malt, or causing a single cow to produce the milk of ten. On one occasion, she was said to have touched an altar post at communion and caused it to burst into flower. Another legend of Brigid concerns her acting as midwife to the Virgin Mary to deliver the infant Jesus, an impossible act that earns her the moniker "Mary of the Gaels."

ORIGINS OF HER NAME

The name Brigid is derived from the Gaelic *breo-saigit*, or "fire-arrow." Both the goddess and the saint are heavily associated with fire and the forge. On Brigid's death, an eternal flame was kindled in her honor, which burned continuously for hundreds of years. It is widely believed that this flame may have been a preexisting sanctuary of the goddess Brighid.

Brigid reportedly died in 525 at the age of seventy and was entombed near the altar of her church. She inspired widespread devotion, and her feast day was not so coincidentally fixed at February 1, the feast day of the goddess. Her emblem as a saint is the flame, and she is often depicted in the act of milking. Brigid is the patron saint of brewers, blacksmiths, poets, midwives, and newborns.

Today, there are dozens of churches dedicated to Brigid throughout Europe, and hundreds of place-names in Ireland reflect her influence. Variations on the name Brigid (Bridget, Bride, Bree) remain some of the most popular for Irish girls. Brigid's sacred flame was extinguished during the reformation, but it was rekindled at Kildare in 1993 and is tended there by the sisters of Solas Bhríde.

COLUMBA: CHRIST IS MY DRUID

The life of Columcille, popularly known as St. Columba ("the dove"), is one of the most interesting. Columba was a contemporary of Patrick's although his journey began under very different circumstances. Columba was born as Creimthne ("fox") into an Irish royal family, the Nialls, which put him in line for the throne. He was the nephew of one king, and the uncle of another. As a child, Columcille reportedly studied under both a priest and a druid, learning writing from the former and poetry from the latter. As an adult, Columcille is described as a tall, imposing man with a booming voice and many talents—he is an accomplished navigator, poet, and scholar. Even though he could have chosen a career in politics, Columba became a Christian and forsook his privileged life, opting to become a simple monk. He was ordained in Glasnevin, on the eastern coast.

A line from a poem attributed to Columba reads:

> I do not hold to the voice of birds, or any luck on the earthly world,
> or chance or a son or a woman. Christ the Son of God is my druid;

Christ the Son of Mary, the great Abbot; the Father the Son and the Holy Spirit. My estates are with the King of Kings; my order is at Cenacles and Moen.

Columba's love of learning was legendary. One story tells of an episode early in his career which was to set his destiny. It appears Columba desired a psalter, or prayer book, but the only one he had access to was the single precious copy owned by Finnian, abbot of the local church, which could not be removed. Columba undertook to copy the psalter, and sealed himself inside the church with the precious book, copying it painstakingly by hand. Unfortunately, he was discovered in the act, and the abbot demanded his copy, claiming it was too precious to allow outside the confines of the church. Columba refused to surrender his book, and the matter was referred to the king, Diarmaid, who decided in favor of Finnian.

THE MONASTERY AT IONA

The dispute carried over when Columba offered sanctuary to the son of the king of Connacht, who had killed the son of Diarmaid's steward in the course of a dispute. The shelter of the church was supposed to be sacrosanct, but Diarmaid had the boy dragged from Columba's sheltering arms and slaughtered. Columba, outraged at this great injustice, sought help from his powerful family. He returned at the head of an army, which deposed the king in a long and bloody conflict, resulting in tremendous bloodshed.

The result of the battle was condemnation of Columba by his closest friends and his peers in the church. Accounts differ whether Columba's next action was of his own accord, out of sorrow for what he had caused, or ordered by the church. Filled with remorse, Columba exiled himself to the land of the Picts, on a mission to convert as many of the Scottish pagans as possible. With twelve companions, he traveled to the tiny isle of Iona, off the west coast of Scotland, which was at that time a wilderness.

Columba and his companions set to work immediately. He chose a high spot on the western side of the island and commenced work on a monastery. Despite its remote location, Columba's monastery grew and thrived, eventually becoming one of the largest and most active seminaries in Britain. One of the most important activities of Columba's monastery was the creation and preservation of books and scripture. The best-known achievement of Columba's order was the creation of the fabulously decorated Book of Kells, arguably the most famous work of art ever produced in Ireland.

THE MIRACLES OF COLUMBA

To Columba, too, are ascribed many miracles. Columba's talent, fitting for a member of the filidh, was prophecy. Columba made many prophecies regarding the future of Ireland, the reign of kings, and the victors of battles. On one occasion, he predicted his own impending death.

One of the strangest episodes in Columba's biography concerns the poets of Ireland, the druid filidh. It seems the poets, while exceedingly popular among the people, were not much appreciated by the lords and kings they satirized; the poet class was threatened with banishment. Columba, himself raised a filidh and still a poet, interceded on their behalf. Columba pleaded the bards' case to the chieftains, asking the king to consider who would keep their histories if they did away with them. This is not Columba's only friendly encounter with druidry, and accounts of his encounters with druid priests indicate that they held him in some esteem.

Columba went on to found dozens (some say hundreds) of churches and monasteries throughout Scotland. He lived to the age of seventy-seven, a fantastic age in a time when one was considered fortunate to live beyond forty.

A favorite story tells that the aged Columba was out walking one afternoon when he grew weary and sat down by the roadside to rest. As he sat there, the old white horse who carried milk for the monastery came to him and laid his head upon the saint's breast, to give farewell to the master he knew was dying.

THE CROSS OF LIFE

The unique symbol of Celtic Christianity is the so-called Celtic cross, also known as the Cross of Iona, after the belief that Columba erected one at his monastery on the island. The connection with Columba, who represents the union of pagan and Christian spirituality in Ireland, is apt. The Celtic cross is said to be derived from the ancient Roman monogram of Christ, made from the combination of the Greek letters chi and rho, but this seems unlikely. The form of the cross, with its scooped-out arms and enclosing circle, is derived from an ancient form dating thousands of years before Christianity, an ancient symbol of the sun. The placement of the crosses at crossroads and marketplaces also echoes ancient custom, and some suppose this was done in conscious imitation of pagan monuments.

THE SOLAR CALENDAR

The ancient Celtic solar calendar consisted of two solstices, two equinoxes, and four cross-quarter days marking the seasons. The four solar festivals, marked on a round representing the path of the year, form a solar cross, the basis of the Celtic cross.

As a spiritual symbol, the Ionic cross represents the coming together of earth and heaven—the crossroad of life and death joined with the eternal circle of heaven. From the pagan viewpoint, it can be seen as the joining of male and female symbolism. The four arms can also be seen to represent the zodiacal calendar important to early Christians—four cardinal directions, and the four fixed signs of the zodiac as represented by the evangelists Matthew (and his emblem, the angel), Mark (the lion), Luke (the ox), and John (the eagle), with Christ represented by the center solar disk.

CELTIC CHRISTIAN ART

The founding monastic communities of Ireland and Scotland, free of the political and religious strife of the mainland, developed into hubs of intellectual and artistic activity, which reached a peak in the sixth to eighth centuries. The ability of the monastic communities to draw membership from a variety of backgrounds led to a harmonious blending of artistic styles known as the Celtic Insular period. Some of the most fantastic art produced by the Celtic religious groups includes fine metalwork, intricate stone carving, and vivid illuminated manuscripts.

Fine metalworking of the period encompasses shrines and reliquaries, liturgical implements such as chalices and patens, ornamental covers for books, and personal ornamentation. Some of the finest examples include these works:

+ The Ardagh chalice is a fantastic liturgical chalice of gold, silver, and bronze that was created using numerous techniques, including casting, engraving, filigree, and enameling.

+ The Monymusk reliquary, which was made to house the bones of Columcille, is covered in copper and silver and decorated with leaping beasts and intricate knotwork.

+ The so-called Tara Brooch, a decorative clasp of gold, silver, copper, and glass, is decorated with enamel, filigree, and gilt. At just under seven inches long, the brooch contains more than twenty tiny dragons in its decorations.

ILLUMINATED BEAUTY

The great illuminated manuscripts produced during this period are some of the finest ever created in Europe. The designs woven into and around the text of these brilliant illuminated books draw from both classical and ancient Celtic art, and the texts are rich with intricate spirals and interlaced knots, loops, and whorls, as well as detailed portraits of angels, saints, and biblical figures alongside images drawn from nature. Typically, every free space not taken up by text is filled in with geometric designs, curling vines, mythological creatures, intertwined people and animals, and ornamented letters. Some of the finer examples of the art are the seventh-century Book of Durrow and the Lindisfarne Gospels.

These books were so elaborate, detailed, and magical in appearance that Christians of later periods believed them to have curative powers. A twelfth-century commentator remarked after viewing one such book:

> If you take the trouble to look very closely, and penetrate with your eyes to the secrets of the artistry, you will notice such intricacies, so delicate and subtle, so close together and well-knitted, so involved and bound together, and so fresh still in their colorings that you will not hesitate to declare that all these things must have been the result of the work, not of men, but angels.

The most precious and beautiful of all the Celtic illuminated books is the gospel manuscript attributed to the monks of St. Columba, the Book of Kells. The book contains the elaborately hand-copied text of the four gospels—Matthew, Mark, Luke, and John. Each gospel is preceded by richly colored illustrated portraits of each evangelist. The book also abounds with Christian symbolism, including crosses, monograms of Christ, and images of the four tetramorphs representing the eponymous authors of the gospels.

THE VIKING INVASIONS

Sadly, the small renaissance of Celtic art came to an abrupt end with the arrival of Viking raiders in the late eighth century. Precious artworks were stolen, manuscripts destroyed, and reliquaries emptied of their remains. The Viking onslaught began with raids on monasteries in Lindisfarne and Dublin, and a new era of foreign invasions began.

ANAM CARA: THE SOUL FRIEND

A custom unique to Celtic Christianity is the tradition of the anam cara. *Anam cara* is Gaelic for "soul friend," referring to a tradition that arose in the convents and monasteries of Ireland and Scotland. The anam cara was a lifelong platonic friend and spiritual guide who acted as a counselor and confessor and usually read the last rites of the deceased. As time went on, the idea became popular with the laity, who would have such a relationship with a member of the clergy.

The anam cara became indispensable to Celtic Christians; the anam cara was not simply a friend, but a soulmate who was one's connection to God. A ninth-century story of St. Brighid of Kildare, recounted in the *Martyrology of Oengus*, illustrates the importance of the soul friend:

> A young cleric of the community of Ferns, a foster son of Brighid's, used to come to her with wishes. He was with her in the refectory, to partake of food. Once after coming to communion she struck a clapper. "Well, young cleric there," said Brighid, "hast thou a soulfriend?" "I have," replied the young cleric. "Let us sing his requiem," said Brighid, "for he has died. I saw when half thy portion had gone, that thy quota was put into thy trunk, and thou without any head on thee, for thy soulfriend died, and anyone without a soulfriend is a body without a head; and eat no more till thou gettest a soulfriend."

This story shows that the spirit-companion is so vital, one is considered imperiled without one. The anam cara's function wasn't just as a close friend, but as someone entrusted with the well-being of one's soul. The anam cara was vital to a healthy soul.

Nobody is quite certain where the concept of the soul friend originated. There is some speculation that the practice developed from traditions of the monasteries of the Eastern Church, where monks typically paired up to support one another's spiritual progress. Still others suggest the concept is a carryover from earlier pagan tradition, an adaptation of druid mentorship to fit the Christian demand for confession. Though this idea would have been unfamiliar to the Celts, it would have naturally been likened to the druid traditions of spiritual mentorship.

Index

Aenghus, 43–44, 148, 157, 169, 173, 175, 218
Alder, sacredness of, 159
Alphabet, ogham, 161–65
Amergin, 19, 61, 101, 104–8
Amergin mac Eccit, 108
Anam cara (soul friend), 246–47
Andraste, 34, 89
Animals. *See* Sacred beasts; *specific animals*
Annwn, 12, 141–42, 210. *See also* Avalon
Apples of Avalon, 159–60
Aquae Sulis, 195
Archangel Michael, Lugos and, 45
Arthur, King, 199–214
  Avalon and, 189–90
  burial of, 142
  cauldron of Annwn and, 210
  death of, Mordred and, 12, 36, 200, 208, 212–13
  Geoffrey of Monmouth and, 36, 142, 202–5
  Glastonbury and, 142, 188–93
  Green Knight and, 213, 214
  Guinevere (Gwenhwyfar) and, 142, 190, 204–5, 207, 208, 213
  Holy Grail and, 210–12
  Joseph of Arimathea and, 190–92
  Knights of the Round Table and, 204
  Merlin and, 124, 179, 186, 202, 203, 205–7
  origins of, 200–202
  other women in life of, 207–10. *See also* Morgan le Fay
  sword (Excalibur) of, 73, 142, 203, 210
  as trickster, 202
  Twrch Trwyth and, 116–18
  Wild Hunt ("fairy raid") and, 149, 190
Ash tree, sacredness of, 155
Athirne, 108
Avalon
  Annwn as, 12, 141–42, 210
  apples of, 159–60
  Arthur and, 12
  Glastonbury and, 188–93

Balor, 71–72, 75–76, 158, 229
Banshees, 137
Baptism, rebirth and, 77, 233
Bard-craft and smith-craft, 108
Bards (wisdom keepers), 85, 88, 97, 98–104, 108, 109
Bath, springs at, 195
Belenos, 45, 224–25
Beltaine, 45, 224–26
Birch, sacredness of, 158
Birds (messengers of gods), 173–76
Bith, 16–17
Blood and war, gods of, 48–50
Boars, 90, 117, 170, 171–73, 201
Book of Invasions, 16–20, 67, 73, 79, 157, 162
Boudicca, 34, 89
Bounty, cauldron of, 76–77
Bran, 26–27, 58–61, 77–78, 159, 174

Branwen, daughter of Lir, 58–61
Breasil, 144
Brendan of Clonfert, St., voyage of, 121–24, 146
Bres, 70–71, 72, 229
Brighid, 38–40. *See also* Brigid, St.
　arts and, 38
　children of, 15–16. *See also* Nuada; Ogham
　cities built by, 15
　Dagda and, 14–16, 39, 227. *See also* Dagda
　feast of, 227–28
　forms, domains and roles of, 38, 39, 67, 228
　Imbolc and, 226–28
　temple/abbey in Kildare, 39–40, 155
　three faces of, 103
　well of, 196
Brigid, St., 39–40, 131, 227, 237–40, 246–47
Brownies, 129–30
Bull(s), 23–24, 49, 69, 177–78

Caesar, Julius, 10, 46, 48–49, 82–83, 84, 91, 162, 216
Cailleach, 37, 39
Cairpre, 70
Calendar, Celtic, 215–30
　Beltaine, 45, 224–26
　Hallowe'en (All Hallows), 219–21
　Imbolc, 226–28
　Lughnasadh (feast of Lugh), 229–30
　Samhain, 141, 175, 216–24
　solar calendar, 243–44

Cambrensis, Giraldus (Gerald of Wales), 40
Caradoc, 59, 61
Cattle Raid of Cooley (Táin bó Cuilainge), 23–24, 34, 171, 178. *See also* Bull(s)
"Cauldron of Poesy," 109–10
Cauldron(s)
　of Annwn, 141, 189, 210
　of Bounty (Plenty), 76–77
　druid rituals and, 52
　of illumination, 211
　importance of, 76
　of Rebirth, 59, 77
　three, giving poets inspiration, 103
Celtic mythology, overview and sources of, 13–14
Celts
　artistic and spiritual orientation of, 12
　Celtic society and, 11
　defined, 9
　origins and background, 9–10
　women's place in society, 11
Cerddorion, 109
Cernunnos, 24, 50–53, 150, 167, 178, 179
Cerridwen, 25, 38, 100–101, 209
Chalice Well, 192–93
Chalkworks, 197
Christianity, 231–47. *See also* Brigid, St.; Columba, St.; Patrick, St.
　anam cara (soul friend), 246–47
　animals in, 179
　Annwn and, 141
　Celtic art, 244–46
　Celtic cross, 243
　coming of, 232–34

Druids and, 94–95
fairies and, 125, 126, 127, 130,
134, 136, 137, 138
heroes, 114
Holy Grail and, 210–12
mistletoe and, 161
prediction of St. Patrick and, 95.
See also Patrick, St.
rise of, 220–21
shamrock symbolism and, 233
trinity doctrine and, 102
Wild Hunt ("fairy raid") and,
149–50, 190
Church of the oak, 39, 155
Cloughtie (Clootie) wells, 196
Clurichauns, 129
Columba, St., 240–43
Connor, 21–22
Corn spirit, 222–23
Coventina, 30, 194
Cross, Celtic, 243
Cuchulainn, 21, 22–23, 24, 32–33,
34–35, 49, 89, 171, 175, 177, 178
Culhwch and Olwen, 30, 56, 115–18,
171, 201–2, 210

Dagda
appetite for food and women,
42–43
Brighid and, 14–16, 39, 227. *See
also* Brighid
cauldrons of, 59, 76–78
children of, 15–16. *See also* Nuada;
Ogham
harp of, 103–4
leading Tuatha Dë Danann
underground, 106
magical accoutrements of, 42

Nuada and, 16, 69–71
origin/birth of, 15
as "the Good God"/other names
for, 42
Danu, 15, 19, 31, 66
Deer, red, 26–27
Derg Corra ("man in the tree"), 49, 53
Destiny, stone of (Lia Fáil), 78–79,
203
Devil, Cernunnos and, 51
Diarmaid, 30, 171–73, 241
Diocletian, 89–90
Diodorus Siculus, 82–83
Dôn, 31, 57, 66
Dragons and serpents, 122, 178–79,
226, 237. *See also* Snakes
Druids, 81–95
bards (wisdom keepers), 85, 88, 97,
98–104, 108, 109
becoming a druid, 83
Christians and, 94–95
class of, 85–86
decline of, 93–95
female, 89–90
filidh (seers and poets), 85, 87–88,
97, 98–99, 109, 111, 242
geas (magical proscription) of, 24,
86, 118–19, 172, 173
legal system, judges of, 86
origins and background, 82, 84
place in Celtic society, 81
power of, 85–86
predicting St. Patrick, 95
roles and functions, 83, 87
Roman/Greek perspective on,
82–83
sacrifices by, 90–93
specialties of, 87

Druids–continued
   theology of, 83–84
   training of, 84–85
Dullachan (headless horseman),
   134–35
Dumb supper, 222

Efnissyen, 58, 60–61
Elm, sacredness of, 158
Epona, 32–33, 67, 176–77
Esus, 46, 49–50, 92, 158, 178
Eye of Balor, 71

Fairies and fey folk, 125–38. *See also*
   Sídhe, people of
   avoiding and repelling, 126
   brownies, 129–30
   categories of, 126, 127–30
   changelings, 127
   Christianity and, 125, 126, 127,
      130, 134, 136, 137, 138
   the clurichauns, 129
   leprechauns, 128–29
   the lurikeen, 129
   people of the Sídhe and, 69, 128
   pixies, 130
   singular phantoms, 138
   trows and sea trows, 131–32
   water spirits, 132–36
   Wild Hunt ("fairy raid"), 149–50,
      190
   wraiths and seductresses, 136–38
Fawkes, Guy, 223–24
Fenian/Fionn Cycle, 14, 24–27. *See
   also* Fionn and Fianna
Fenius, 162
Fianna, about. *See also* Fionn and
   Fianna

Filidh (seers and poets), 85, 87–88,
   97, 98–99, 109, 111, 242
Finntan, 17, 18, 168
Fionn and Fianna (Fionn mac
   Cumhaill, or Finn MacCool),
   24–27, 52, 53, 69, 144–45, 157–58,
   167, 172–73, 196
Fir Bolg ("bag men"), 18, 19, 68, 70,
   229
Fomorians, 17, 18, 19, 35, 42, 70,
   71–72, 229
Forest gods, 50–53

Geas (magical proscription), 24, 86,
   118–19, 172, 173
Geoffrey of Monmouth, 36, 142,
   202–5
Giants. *See* Balor; Bran; Bres;
   Efnissyen; Fomorians; Green Knight;
   Yspaddadden
Glastonbury, 142, 188–93, 209
Gods and goddesses. *See also specific
   gods and goddesses*
   about: overview of gods, 41;
      overview of mother goddesses, 29
   forest gods, 50–53
   gods of blood and war, 48–50
   gods of light and art, 44–47
   horse-mothers, 31–33
   in threes, 30, 67–68
   of Tuatha Dé Danann, 66–68
Gráinne, 30, 172
Green Knight, 213, 214
Green Man (Derg Corra, "man in the
   tree"), 49, 53
Guinevere (Gwenhwyfar), 142, 190,
   204–5, 207, 208, 213

Guy Fawkes Day, 223–24
Gwion Bach, 25, 100–101. *See also* Taliesin

Hag, goddess and, 209
Hallows, four, 72–80
Harp, Celtic, 103–4
Hawthorn, sacredness of, 155–56
Hazel, sacredness of, 157–58
Headless horseman, 134–35
Healing wells and springs, 194–96
Herne the Hunter, 150
Heroes, 113–24. *See also* Culhwch and Olwen
    about: overview of, 113
    Christian and cult/tales of, 114
    fantastic voyages, 118–24
Holy Grail, 210–12
Horse-mothers, 31–33
Horses and horsemanship, 176–77
Hounds, 23, 26–27, 100, 116–17, 172, 177
Human sacrifice, 91–93
Hy-Breasil/-Brasil, 144

Illuminated manuscripts, 245–46
Imbolc, 226–28
Invincible Spear. *See* Spear of Lugh
Iona, monastery at, 241–43
Ireland
    destruction of, 60–61
    five parts of, 17
    founding of, 104–8
Iron, fear of, 66
Isle of Apples, 12, 142. *See also* Annwn; Avalon
Ivy and mistletoe, 160–61

Jacob, Stone of Destiny and, 79
Jesus, 43, 50, 79, 191, 233–34, 239
Joseph of Arimathea, 79, 190–92

Kelpie, 132–33
Kildare, Ireland, 39–40, 122, 155. *See also* Brighid; Brigid, St.
King stones, 80
Knights of the Round Table, 204
Korrigan, 138

Lady of the Lake, 209–30
La Tène culture, 10
Leprechauns, 128–29
Lia Fáil (Stone of Destiny), 78–79, 193, 203
Light and art, gods of, 44–47
Loathly lady, 37, 209
Love, god of. *See* Aenghus
Lugh, 22, 30, 45–47, 71–72, 159, 174
Lughnasadh (feast of Lugh), 229–30
Lurikeen, 129

The Mabinogion, 55–63
    about: overview of, 55–56
    Branwen, daughter of Lir, 58–61
    Celtic mythology and, 14
    legend of Pwyll, 57
    Math, son of Mathonwy, 62–63
    tales of Manawydan, 62
Mabon ap Modron, 43, 116
Macha, 22, 32–33, 229, 232
Mac Riagla and Snedgus, voyage of, 124
Mael Duin, 118–20, 121–22
Mag Mell, 143–44

Magh Tuireadh, battles of, 35, 68, 70, 71–72

Manannan mac Lir ("Manannan, son of sea"), 54, 67, 143–44, 180

Manawydan, 62

"Man in the tree" (Derg Corra), 49, 53

Math, son of Mathonwy, 62–63

Mathowlch, 58–61

Medb, Queen, 23–24

Menhirs (standing stones), 187–88

Merlin, 124, 179, 186, 202, 203, 205–7

Merrows (mermaids), 136

Metamorphosis, magic of, 168–70

Míl, 19, 68, 105, 106

Milesians, 19–20, 68, 104–8, 143, 219

Miracles of Brigid, 239

Miracles of Columba, 242

Mistletoe and ivy, 160–61

Monuments, stone, 10

Mordred, 12, 36, 200, 208, 212–13

Morgan le Fay, 35–36, 142, 207–8, 210, 212

Morrigán, the, 22, 33–36, 67, 68, 138, 142, 159, 194

Mother goddesses, overview of, 29. See also Brighid; Cailleach; Gods and goddesses; Horse-mothers; Morrigán, the

Mythological Cycle, 14

Nemed, 18, 152

Newgrange, 44, 183–84

Niamh, Oisin and, 144–46

Nine, hazel and, 157

Noah, son of, 16–17

Nuada, 15, 16, 69–72, 73, 74–75

Oak, church of the, 39, 155

Oak, sacredness of, 154–55

Ogham, 15, 48, 157

Ogham alphabet, 161–65

Oghma (Ogmios), 15, 16, 44, 47–48, 67, 163, 197

Oisin and Niamh, 144–46

Olwen, 115–16, 171, 201–2, 205

Osiris, Nuada and, 74

Otherworld, 139–50. See also Sídhe-mounds
    about: overview of, 12, 139–40
    as Annwn, 12, 141–42, 210
    beyond the visible, 140
    entrances to, 140
    oak doorway to, 154
    Oisin and Niamh, 144–46
    portals to, 182–84
    St. Patrick's purgatory/journey to purgatory, 146–49. See also Patrick, St.
    Wild Hunt ("fairy raid"), 149–50

Owain, 35, 137, 147–48, 174

Palms, wisdom of, 111–12

Patrick, St.
    about: overview of life, 234–35
    Brigid and, 238
    confession of, 235–36
    druid spells of, 236
    home of, 188
    legend of, 236
    Lóegaire and, 225
    medieval ritual associated with, 225–26
    Oisin and, 145
    patron saint of Ireland, 234–37
    prophecy about, 17, 95

purgatory of, 146–49
rituals banned by, 102
shamrock symbolism and, 233
snakes and, 237
Phantoms, singular, 138
Pixies, 130
Plenty, cauldron of, 76–77
Pliny the Elder, 82, 160, 178–79
Poets. *See* Filidh (seers and poets)
Pooka, 133–34
Powers, three enchanting, 103
Purgatory, of St. Patrick, 146–49
Pwyll, 57, 62

Ravens, 58, 174, 208. *See also* Bran
Rebirth, cauldron of, 59, 77–78
Reincarnation, 12, 84–85, 168, 174, 194

Sacred beasts, 167–79
    about: overview of, 167
    birds (messengers of gods), 173–76
    in Celtic Christianity, 179
    domestic animals, 176–78
    dragons and serpents, 178–79
    metamorphosis magic, 168–70
    woodland creatures, 170–73
Sacred places, 181–97. *See also*
    Glastonbury; Tara; *other specific places*
    about: overview of, 181
    chalkworks, 197
    portals to the Otherworld, 182–84
    springs and healing wells, 194–96
    stone circles and alignments, 185–88
Sacrifices, druid, 90–93
Samhain, 141, 175, 216–24
Sea trows, 131–32

Seductresses and wraiths, 136–37
Seers. *See* Filidh (seers and poets)
Selkies (seal people), 135–36
Serpents. *See* Dragons and serpents;
    Snakes
Shining brow. *See* Taliesin
Sídhe, people of, 69, 128
Sídhe-mounds, 143–44, 184, 218
Silver hand, Nuada of. *See* Nuada
Smith-craft and bard-craft, 108
Snakes, 51, 148, 237
Snedgus and Mac Riagla, voyage of, 124
Solstice rituals, 183–84, 186, 229
Song of Taliesin, 101–2
Songs of Amergin, 105–8
Spear of Lugh, 75–76
Springs and healing wells, 194–96
Stone circles and alignments, 185–88
Stonehenge, 185, 186–87
Stone monuments, 10
Stone of Destiny (Lia Fáil), 78–79, 193, 203
Storytellers, 97–111. *See also* Amergin;
    Bards (wisdom keepers)
    about: overview of, 97
    Celtic harp and, 103–4
    filidh (seers and poets), 85, 87–88, 97, 98–99, 109, 111, 242
    mystical threes and, 102–3
    Taliesin (shining brow), 25, 38, 99–102, 108, 109, 168
    wisdom of the palms, 111–12
Strabo, 82–83, 153
Swans, 44, 169, 174–76, 218
Sword, of Arthur (Excalibur), 73, 142, 203, 210
Sword of Light, 73–75, 203

Tacitus, 89, 90
Táin bó Cuilainge. *See* Cattle Raid of Cooley
Taliesin (shining brow), 25, 38, 99–102, 108, 109, 168
Tara, 78–79, 193–94, 217, 219, 225
Taranis, 46, 48–49, 176
Teutates, 46, 50, 92, 177
Thorn tree, sacredness of, 155–56
Threes
    gods in, three mothers and, 30–31
    mystical, 102–3
    trinity doctrine and, 102
Tir na Nog, 73, 121, 143, 146
Tombs, passage, 183
Travelers, patron saint of, 121
Tree, man in (Derg Corra), 49, 53
Tree of life, 151–65
    about: overview of, 151
    apples of Avalon, 159–60
    mistletoe, ivy and, 160–61
    nine sacred woods, 153–59. *See also specific woods*
    ogham alphabet, 161–65
    world tree and tree worship, 152–53
Trickster god. *See* Manannan mac Lir
Trows and sea trows, 131–32
Tuan, 18
Tuatha Dé Danann, 65–80. *See also specific gods and goddesses*
    about: overview of, 10, 19, 65
    artistic abilities, 10
    defined, 66
    four hallows of, 72–80
    gods of, 66–67
    Nemed and, 18
    old gods to fairy-folk, 66–69

    Sídhe-mounds and, 184
    triple goddesses, 67–68
Twrch Trwyth, 116–18

Ulster Cycle, overview of, 14, 21–22

Veleda, 90
Viking invasions, 246
Voyages, fantastic, 118–24

War and blood, gods of, 48–50
Washer-woman, 137
Water spirits, 132–36
Well, of Brighid, 196
Wells (healing) and springs, 194–96
Wild Hunt ("fairy raid"), 149–50, 190
Willow, sacredness of, 158
Wisdom keepers. *See* Bards
Wisdom of the palms, 111–12
Women
    in Arthur's life, 207–10. *See also* Guinevere (Gwenhwyfar); Morgan le Fay
    in Celtic society, 11
    druids, 89–90
Woodland creatures, 170–73
Woods, sacred, 153–59
Wraiths and seductresses, 136–38

Yeats, William Butler, 9
Yews, sacredness of, 156–57
Yspaddadden, 115–16, 118